THE NORTH POLE CHALLENGE

By: Kevin George

PROLOGUE
ORIGINS OF OLD MAN WINTER

For countless centuries, Old Man Winter ruled his cold kingdom. His massive ice castle was located in the most distant reaches of the South Pole, far away from where humankind had ever dared to journey. Luckily, he was spared an existence of complete loneliness by his group of tiny servants, who were not affected by the frigid conditions. These servants provided Old Man Winter plenty of joy from their mischievous and comical antics, but they also served a more practical purpose. They had an amazing ability to build Old Man Winter whatever he wanted in a matter of seconds, no matter how large or complicated. A special few servants had a gift to create something even more valuable – magical dust. But the secret of making that dust was unknown even to Old Man Winter.

As Lord of the South Pole, Old Man Winter's sole duty was to control the weather on Earth, a task he was able to perform because of his most prized possession: a mystical snowglobe. He stored the snowglobe in a small cauldron in his bedroom, away from the prying eyes of his servants. It wasn't that Old Man Winter had trouble trusting his loyal servants but he had to be extra careful. A change in the snowglobe's possession would change control over the South Pole and thus the world's weather, a power that could be tempting to even his most trusted allies. To further ensure the snowglobe's safety, he filled the cauldron with a special freezing liquid. The dangerous liquid would freeze the limb of anyone foolish enough to try removing the unbreakable snowglobe.

Every year, Old Man Winter followed the same weather pattern: cold and snow in the winter, warmth and sun in the summer. He was very careful to maintain balance in the world. But he still kept his South Pole kingdom in a constant state of winter – his favorite season. Spoiled by his effort to provide six months of warmth, many humans dreaded winter. People across the globe constantly complained about the cold weather and failed to appreciate the beauty of snow and ice, not to mention the necessity of winter in the circle of life. Old Man Winter had the power to plunge the world into a new Ice Age, but he was far too merciful and loving to do this. Instead, he hoped to change humankind's negative opinion of winter through positive means.

"I need to figure out a way to make people excited about the colder months," Old Man Winter told his two most trusted servants.

"A celebration, a time of happiness and being with loved ones," one of the tiny servants suggested.

"And don't forget presents for the children," the other servant added. "Toys will make their hearts glow and have them counting down the days to winter."

Old Man Winter was not one to imagine such an idea on a small scale. He envisioned a magical place where toys could be built and then delivered on his winter holiday. But he and his advisors quickly realized that the South Pole was too small to house their ambitious plans. They considered building just beyond the South

Pole border but human explorers had ventured farther south with every passing year. It was important to keep their holiday village safely away from human eyes, as this would make the winter holiday more magical. Therefore, Old Man Winter decided that only one other place would be suitable for his village: the North Pole.

With his great understanding and appreciation for balance, Old Man Winter knew that the North Pole was the perfect selection. Just like the South Pole, a part of the North Pole was also inaccessible to humankind. Since his servants had no problem enduring the extreme cold – and since an amazing use of their magical dust allowed them to travel long distances in the blink of an eye – his two advisors quickly scouted the North Pole location and deemed it ideal for their plans.

Although Old Man Winter had gone countless centuries without his winter holiday, he was too excited to put it off another moment. He gathered together his remaining servants and told them of his grand plans. Though many were nervous about leaving their lifelong home, Old Man Winter's energy was contagious. As one group, they traveled to a location just outside the North Pole's border. But as the two main advisors led the group toward the North Pole border, Old Man Winter experienced a sensation he'd never felt before: weakness. Being the most powerful entity in the world, he was shocked and confused to feel his legs grow heavy and his breathing labored. Coldness flowed within him that had nothing to do with the blustering snow or sub-zero temperatures.

Upon noticing his absence, one of the advisors soon reappeared from the North Pole and found his master unable to continue forward. When Old Man Winter explained what was happening to him, his advisor questioned whether they should proceed with their plans. Knowing that there would never be a better place to build, Old Man Winter didn't hesitate to make his decision. He gave up the chance to witness construction of his holiday village and returned to the South Pole.

Once home, his strength returned to full force. Old Man Winter immediately headed to the cauldron in his bedroom. He reached his hand inside the cauldron and the freezing liquid instantly parted for him, allowing access to the snowglobe. While possession of this sacred object provided Old Man Winter his power, the snowglobe also answered any question asked by its master.

"Why can't I enter the North Pole?" Old Man Winter asked.

He shook the snowglobe. Inside, the real snowflakes floated gently before disappearing into a cloudy haze. The answer came as it always did, through a voice that only Old Man Winter could hear in his mind.

"You already know the answer to that question," the globe responded.

"Balance."

"That is correct, my Lord," the snowglobe said. "If you enter the North Pole, then you would disturb Earth's balance and risk plunging the planet into eternal winter. You have dedicated your existence to maintaining balance in the world. You've always done this from the South Pole for a simple reason: *this* is where you belong."

"Should I have the holiday village built here instead?"

"With all due respect, my Lord, you ask questions despite already knowing the answers," the snowglobe said. "The village is destined for the North Pole. You made the correct decision allowing your servants to begin construction there. And the answer to your *next* question is no, none of your servants will accept the task of running the North Pole. Unfortunately, they are too comfortable being followers, not leaders. However, there *is* a way of finding someone suitable to fulfill your vision."

Old Man Winter stared into the snowglobe as the cloudy haze faded away. The image of a baby appeared.

"A child?" he asked.

"*Your* child, My Lord. Created of winter, dust and you."

Old Man Winter watched as the snowglobe instructed him what to do before promptly fading back to its simple snowy interior. He carefully placed the globe back inside the frosty cauldron. For the first time that he could remember, he was unsure about a decision. The prospect of raising a child to carry out his holiday vision was not an easy one to make. But with his ice castle empty of servants for the first time, Old Man Winter realized that having a son would not *just* give the world a reason to celebrate winter. It would also provide *him* a family he never expected.

Old Man Winter marched out of his ice castle, dreaming about the son he would create. The child would be kind and loving to all the children of the world, a son who would treasure the task of leading the winter holiday. Raising a child to follow his plans would postpone the start of his holiday for many years, but that would allow more time to expand the village far beyond Old Man Winter's original expectations.

He scooped up a large mound of snow and carried it inside, laying it carefully on the castle floor. Old Man Winter reached into his pocket and removed a small pouch of magical dust. He sprinkled dust over the snow mound that he cradled with his other arm. A bright blue light erupted from the snow and nearly blinded Old Man Winter, who had to turn away. When he turned back, he saw a handsome baby boy, who was more striking than any child he'd ever seen. With glowing pale skin, ice-blue eyes and a full head of white-blond hair, the baby was the future of the North Pole.

In the corners of Old Man Winter's eyes, tiny ice crystals began to form.

"From now on, I will be known *not* as Old Man Winter but *Father* Winter," he told his son, who did not cry. The boy simply stared at his father through piercing blue eyes. "And you, my son, I shall call Jack."

CHAPTER ONE

Dodgeball Dodged

The two team captains stood in front of the class, studying the other kids with more focus than any test. Finally, the first captain pointed to someone in the front.

"I'll take Rob."

Rob was big and burly beyond his twelve years of age and could throw the hardest. The second team captain took an equal amount of time before making the next-best selection.

"Cory."

The next biggest kid jumped off the gymnasium floor and joined his new team. The biggest and best athletes were chosen first, followed by the smaller scrappier kids, then the bookworms, the band geeks and finally, the students most overweight. The selection process went this way every day in class. The gym teacher – he of the high-shorts, long-socks, whistle-toting variety – never noticed the cruelty of the process, especially for the one student picked last *every* time. In fact, the two teams began to head toward their ends of the gym, leaving one student sitting all by himself.

"Hold on just a minute," the gym teacher said. "You still got one… *person* left."

The second team captain looked at the last kid and rolled his eyes, sighing loudly before he made his last choice – not that he had much *choice* in the matter.

"Okay, let's go, Flea."

Flea scurried toward his team, nearly tripping over his own two feet along the way. He received dirty looks from everyone on his squad – from the most athletic jock to the fattest nerd.

"Just make sure you stay out of the way," the team captain told Flea.

Not only did Flea have the dubious distinction of being the smallest kid – boy *or* girl – in the entire class, he also looked much different from the other students. His features could be described by no other term but pointy: *pointy* nose, *pointy* chin, *pointy* ears. Even his right ear – the top of which was split halfway down the middle – had *two* sharp points. As if his tiny size and strange looks weren't bad enough, Flea had a dandruff problem that was impossible to miss. His real name was weird but the students and teachers called him by the nickname he'd had for as long as he could remember.

Flea was in his fourth month at this particular school. He finally reached the point where he was being ignored rather than teased. But the daily game of dodgeball seemed to bring out the worst in everyone.

The whistle blew and the gym teacher released a sack of bright-red dodgeballs in the center of the gymnasium. Although Flea had been picked last –clearly for good reason – he refused to fade into the back of the gym and wait to be picked off like all the other athletic outcasts. A small part of him hoped that by trying hard, he could earn the respect of his fellow students. An even *bigger* part of him hoped that he could get lucky and eliminate one of the better athletes.

Once the fastest kids on both teams retrieved the dodgeballs, the game officially began. Deemed a weak, insubstantial target, Flea was overlooked at first and picked up a stray ball missed by the others. Unfortunately, the targets he *wished* he could hit were on the far side of the gym, so Flea picked out a rail-thin girl nearby. Although he felt guilty for going after a weak link, he needed to prove to his teammates that he could be *somewhat* useful. Using a running head start, he wound up and threw the ball as hard as he could.

In a perfect world, the dodgeball would have found its intended target. Better yet, the other team's captain would have drifted directly into the ball's path and been the first person eliminated. But the thin girl easily stepped aside as Flea's dodgeball lazily fluttered by her like a butterfly. Any shot of dodgeball glory – or even respectability – had instantly evaporated. He quickly retreated to the back of the gym, where he joined the other sorry saps who had no business playing this game with the real athletes. As he watched his teammates picked off one by one, Flea somehow managed to dance and duck away from several balls. But his time was quickly running short. There were fewer and fewer targets remaining on his team and the biggest athletes on the other side were licking their lips at the chance to peg the new, 'weird-looking' kid.

"Excuse me, may I interrupt for a moment?" a voice called out near the gym's doors. The gym teacher blew his whistle seconds before the best athletes could unload on Flea.

"Can I help you with something, Mr. ... what was your name again?" the gym teacher asked.

"Mr. *Strick*," said the man with the bright red hard hat. "We've only met about a *dozen* times in the faculty room during the last four months."

"Yeah, yeah, Mr. Stick, what do you need?"

"Actually, it's *Strick* and I need to borrow one of your students for a while," the other teacher said. "I'm working on a very important project and there's only one student who can help me."

"We're kind of in the middle of a game here," the gym teacher said, "but I *guess* you can take whoever you want, as long as he – *or* she – wants to go."

Mr. Strick turned to Flea, who ran toward the gym doors before even being asked. The tiny boy passed the dodgeball-armed athletes, who sneered at him like a pack of hungry wolves unexpectedly denied their dinner. Flea knew he couldn't avoid dodgeball forever, but he was more than happy to put it off for the time.

"Thanks for saving me back there, you showed up just in time. I still have welts all over my body from yesterday's game," Flea said. He looked up at the teacher's head. "Do you wear that hard hat *everywhere* you go?"

Mr. Strick smiled and rapped himself in the bright red hard hat several times, causing a shower of sawdust to rain down on Flea.

"You never know when one of these can come in handy," Mr. Strick said. "You might think of wearing one the next time you're playing dodgeball."

Flea laughed though he did not find Mr. Strick's joke particularly funny. Still, Flea felt better every time he was with his favorite teacher. Since he'd started at this school, Mr. Strick was the only person – student *or* teacher – with whom Flea had felt any sort of connection. That was probably because they were both so weird. Mr. Strick didn't seem to care that Flea was different from everyone else so Flea didn't mind either.

As usual, the two headed toward the only room in school – or *anywhere* for that matter – where Flea felt confident, where he truly felt at home. The school's shop classroom consisted of nothing more than a dozen oversized dusty tables, a large rack of tools that looked ancient and three table saws that were cordoned off by a few pieces of yellow-and-black caution-tape. Still, Flea felt excitement running through his veins whenever he stepped inside this room and saw the large stacks of lumber against the wall. This was the first school he'd ever attended that had a shop program in its curriculum and it hadn't taken long for Flea to take a liking to the class. Ever since he was a little kid, Flea had enjoyed playing with toy building blocks – one of the few toys he'd had growing up – but he *never* would have expected to be so skillful when it came to the real thing. Flea's amazing ability had delighted Mr. Strick the first day of shop class. The teacher had called him a 'natural.' Flea had never been called a natural at *anything*.

But as the initial shock of Flea's talent wore off, the relationship between the teacher and student became business-like. Mr. Strick pointed to a table that held a large stack of lumber, a few cans of spray paint, some small nails and two tools: a hammer and a simple handsaw.

"Don't tell me," Flea said disappointedly. "More birdhouses."

"I know, I know, birdhouses are boring to you now," Mr. Strick said. "But hopefully *these* ones will be a bit more challenging."

Mr. Strick handed him three sets of detailed blueprints. Somehow, Flea understood exactly what he was looking at though he'd never seen a blueprint in his life. While Flea might have been amazed by this a few months earlier, he was no longer surprised by any of his instinctive shop class skills.

"Well, at least the birdhouses are getting a bit more interesting," Flea said as he pointed out several new additions to the design. "Functioning garage door, multiple levels, birdfeed dispensers inside *and* out. I see these are much larger, too, and need to be painted several different colors."

"Like I said, more challenging. *And* there are three of them that I need finished today," Mr. Strick said. "Think you're up for it?"

Flea looked at the clock and saw that his gym class was scheduled to end in about thirty minutes. He glanced down at the detailed blueprints and smiled, knowing it would take a highly advanced shop student an entire semester to finish only one of these birdhouses.

"No problem." Flea cracked his knuckles and picked up the saw and first piece of wood. "Here we go."

Over the next half-hour, Flea worked at a frenetic pace never before witnessed by *any* shop teacher. The tools were like an extension of Flea's hands, working in such fluid unison that he didn't waste a single movement. Sawdust flew and nails were hammered and paint was sprayed, all without Flea needing to stop a single time to check the specifics of the blueprints. Flea didn't understand how this came so naturally to him but he didn't question his good fortune since he'd caught so few breaks in life. With a final spray of paint, Flea finished the third and final birdhouse with five minutes to spare. Once done, Flea finally had the chance to step back and check out his work as a whole.

"Wow, your plans really turned out great," Flea said, admiring the three houses – each of which was taller than him. When he turned to see Mr. Strick's reaction, though, Flea was surprised to see that the teacher appeared sad, at least until he saw Flea looking at him. Strick smiled but Flea sensed there was a problem. "Is something wrong? Did I do something wrong?"

Flea checked the blueprints but already knew he'd followed the plans to every tiny detail.

"No, they're absolutely perfect," Mr. Strick said, eliciting a prideful smile from Flea. "Your talent is quite extraordinary. But the paint needs time to dry so we better get you back to gym class before the period ends."

Flea took a final look at his work before Mr. Strick shut off the lights and led him into the hallway. Flea asked when he would get a 'real challenge' but before Strick had the chance to answer, a large balding man interrupted them. He had a thin mustache, long bushy sideburns and a face that always burned bright red.

"Mr. Strick, I need to talk to you," the man said sternly.

"I'm sorry, Principal Baldy, but I have to bring Flea back to class," Mr. Strick said.

"What did you call me?" the principal asked, his face turning a darker shade of red. The man forced his way between Flea and Mr. Strick as though the small boy wasn't even there. It wasn't the first time that Flea had been totally ignored.

"Principal *Crawley*," Mr. Strick said coolly, apparently unaffected by the large man's growing anger. Flea thought he noticed the shop teacher's lips curl in the slightest of mischievous smiles. "I'm sorry, have I been pronouncing it incorrectly the entire time I've known you?"

Mr. Strick seemed to be prodding an angry bear and Flea had to bite his tongue to stop from laughing. Principal Crawley, however, did not find anything humorous about him.

"Maybe you could explain something to me, *Mr. Strick*," the principal started.

"I'm sure I could explain *many* things to you, sir."

"Why has the budget for shop class gone through the roof this year? Our last shop teacher didn't require nearly as much money," Crawley said.

"I don't know what to tell you, sir," Mr. Strick said. "I suppose I just have more…advanced students. Flea here is one of the finest –"

"I don't care if you're building *Noah's Ark* in there. If you even want to *think* about coming back to teach a second year here, then you need to clean up your budget," Principal Crawley yelled, his face so bright that it looked like his head was on the verge of popping. "And while you're at it, clean up your classroom, too. I went in there earlier and it was a mess. Sawdust covered everything."

Mr. Crawley stormed off down the hallway, undoubtedly to find his next victim.

"That guy sure isn't very nice, he never has been," Mr. Strick said as he and Flea headed back to the gym.

"You better be careful around him, I don't want you to get fired."

Mr. Strick shrugged his shoulders. "I wouldn't worry if I was you, *I'm* certainly not concerned about Mr. *Baldy*." Flea laughed again, though he still didn't find the joke funny. "Besides, my future is growing brighter by the minute. I doubt I'll be at this school much longer anyway."

"I know what you mean," Flea said. He tried to sound agreeable but hated the thought of being at this school without Mr.

Strick's shop class. "I never seem to stay at a school for more than a year or two."

"Do you like moving around so much?" Mr. Strick asked.

Flea rarely spoke about himself or his personal life and immediately regretted bringing it up.

"It's okay, I guess. At least I've gotten to see a bunch of different parts of the country, mostly north of here," Flea said.

"So this crazy weather must not be as strange to you as it is to the rest of us in North Carolina," the teacher said.

"No, not really," Flea said. Mr. Strick did not push him for any further details but for some reason, Flea had the urge to share one final thought. "I will say, though, that I wish I had a place to think of as home."

Flea blushed from revealing so much, especially to someone who was practically a stranger. But Mr. Strick merely nodded in understanding. Still, Flea was relieved when they'd reached the gym doors – and even *more* relieved to hear the gym teacher blow the whistle to end the day's dodgeball massacre.

"Are you going to need help with any more projects today?" Flea asked hopefully.

"I'm not sure, I'll have to check on that later," Strick said, though he never mentioned *where* exactly his projects came from. "But if I do, I'll be sure to find you."

The shop teacher turned away as Flea entered the gym. He joined the rest of the boys heading into the locker room and hoped to blend in. But big, burly Rob purposely bumped into Flea and the other bullies gathered around to make a promise.

"You might have escaped from us today, but you won't always be so lucky," Rob said. The others nodded in agreement.

Flea figured that the next game of dodgeball would be particularly brutal now that he had a bullseye on his back. He could only hope that Mr. Strick would have more work for him tomorrow, though Flea knew he couldn't dodge gym class forever.

Little did Flea know that the bullies weren't planning to wait until the next day before attacking.

CHAPTER TWO

Snowball Massacre

Once the bell rang to end the day, hundreds of kids poured out of school and into a world of whiteness. It was snowing yet again and Flea could plainly see that his fellow classmates despised the cold weather. Many were bundled up in snow boots, gloves, mittens, wool hats, scarves and any other article of clothing made to protect from the winter weather. Flea had heard that this weather was quite rare for North Carolina. According to his teachers, this area usually received a mere inch or two of snow all winter. But that amount of snow had covered the ground during this school day alone. The snow had started falling ever since the end of September and had gotten worse over the last few months.

Flea looked around and noticed steam coming out of everyone's mouth but he wasn't nearly as bothered by the cold air. He wore only a winter coat as protection against the weather, although he didn't feel like he needed it. Maybe it was because he lived farther north his whole life – where this weather was normal for the middle of December – that he was numb to the cold. In fact, Flea couldn't *ever* remember feeling cold the way others did. He watched his classmates rush into school busses parked just outside. Because Flea's apartment complex was only a few blocks away, no bus transportation was available to him.

I guess it's a good thing this weather doesn't bother me, he thought. The other students that lived in his apartment complex ran all the way home to avoid the harsh weather but Flea took his time walking. He enjoyed being outside and wished he could be out more often. As he crossed the faculty parking lot, he suddenly heard a loud *honking* and saw a brand-new pickup truck approaching. The driver waved and it took Flea a moment to recognize the familiar red hard-hat worn by Mr. Strick. His teacher used to drive a smaller truck that was much older and dilapidated. Flea waved back just as a gust of wind blew off the tarp that had been covering the back of the truck. Flea could now see the truck's contents as it drove away: birdhouses, dozens of them. Farthest back were the three he had just built today and Flea was certain that the rest were all of his past 'projects.' It suddenly dawned on him what Mr. Strick was doing with all of the birdhouses he'd built over the last few months. The brand-new truck was evidence of Strick's recent salary increase.

Flea angrily picked up a snowball, ready to hurl it at his teacher's truck, but Mr. Strick already disappeared around the corner.

No wonder the shop budget has gotten so high this year.

Flea had little time to stew about that, though. He turned down the next street and immediately noticed two freshly built snow forts, one on each side of the road. Beyond the forts was a snowman and as Flea got closer, he could have sworn the snowman's green eyes followed his every movement. He didn't know what was weirder: that the snowman had green eyes or that those eyes could move. Before he could figure it out, another sudden movement caught his attention.

"I told you that you wouldn't be lucky the next time we saw you."

Big, burly Rob stood up from behind one of the forts while Cory stepped around the other. Joining them was both dodgeball captains as well as several other boys from gym class, nearly a dozen in all. They lined the street, blocking Flea's path, each holding snowballs.

"Now!" Rob yelled as every boy prepared to throw.

Flea had to put up with a lot of grief over the years but he tried to stay as good-natured as possible. But being ambushed by so many bullies made him angrier than ever before. He put his hands up and his head down and braced for the impact of a dozen snowballs *whizzing* toward him.

Not a single snowball hit him.

At first, Flea wondered if the bullies simply had bad aim or didn't know how to roll a proper snowball. But two sounds made him realize that there was something more than poor accuracy. First was the *splash* of falling water, which now pooled around his feet. The second was a surprised – and simultaneous – intake of breath from every boy standing in front of him. Flea wasn't sure what had happened but he recognized the look of fear on the faces of several boys.

Still, not *all* of them were frightened.

"You won't get lucky *three* times in one day," Rob called out. He and Cory each grabbed another handful of snow.

When they threw the snowballs this time, Flea's curiosity outweighed his fear. He kept his hands raised but did not look away, even as the snow zoomed directly toward his face. Just inches before hitting him, both snowballs turned to water and splashed harmlessly on the ground. Most of the kids turned and ran away, but Rob and Cory began to slowly approach Flea. Cory yelled that Flea was a 'freak' while Rob appeared ready to pummel him with fists since snowballs hadn't gotten the job done.

Flea was just as surprised as the others and considered turning to run away. But he knew the bullies would easily catch him. He did the only other thing that he could think. He bent over and picked up his own handful of snow, which instantly formed a perfectly round shape in his hand.

Rob and Cory nearly doubled over in amusement.

"Is that *actually* supposed to scare us?" Rob asked between fits of laughter. "We've seen you play dodgeball, you throw like a girl."

"No, he doesn't," Cory added. "He throws *worse* than a girl."

Flea knew that their insults weren't far from the truth but he refused to give in without fighting. He took aim at Rob's big laughing face and hurled the snowball with as much power as his tiny body could muster. The fact that the snowball hit Rob directly in the chest would have been amazing enough, but the bully was thrown ten feet backward. Rob grunted loudly just as he crashed through the first of the two forts. Everyone – including Flea – stared in shock, but Cory quickly recovered and charged at Flea. Without thinking, Flea scooped another handful of snow and launched this one at the other bully. Cory was also struck in the chest and soared backward into the other snow fort. Neither bully could do anything but lay on the ground and squirm while the rest of their so-called 'friends' turned and ran away.

Flea stood there and stared in shock at what he'd done. But now that he had the group of bullies on the defensive for once, he could not just let the rest of them escape totally unpunished. He quickly grabbed another snowball and launched it halfway down the street. It struck the nearest fleeing bully directly on the rear-end and sent him headfirst into a nearby pile of snow. Flea grabbed even more snow and began his chase, launching the snowy projectiles at the meanest kids while letting a few of the more innocent ones go unscathed. For once Flea actually had fun playing with other kids – despite the fact that they seemed fearful for their lives.

By the time he reached his apartment complex, Flea had a smile from ear to ear. There was little doubt that the bullies would regroup and come after him one day – *probably tomorrow,* Flea thought – but he was going to enjoy his victory today. Unfortunately, Flea's feeling of happiness was quickly replaced with increasing weakness as he approached his apartment. His feet began to feel like they were encased in cement and the light feeling of giddiness he'd just had turned into light-headedness. Flea didn't know what was wrong with him nor did he have much time to figure it out before collapsing to the snowy ground mere feet from his front door…

CHAPTER THREE
Full Moon Maid

When Flea finally woke up, the first thing he saw through squinted eyes was a large, round black woman standing over his bed. His vision was still slightly impaired and for a moment, he thought he saw sparkly flashes raining down on him.

I must've hit my head if I'm still seeing stars, Flea thought.

The woman appeared very concerned until she noticed that Flea's eyes had opened. Any worry she might have had instantly transformed into anger, the usual expression she wore.

"It's a good thing I came outside when I heard all that ruckus. You almost gave me a heart attack when I saw you lying on the ground. Just what the heck were you doing out there?" she demanded.

Flea sat up in bed a bit too quickly and had to take a moment to catch his breath before answering.

"I'm sorry, Miss Mabel, I got in a snowball fight with some of the other kids from school," Flea explained. "I must have gotten light-headed and passed out."

Miss Mabel still looked mad regardless of the explanation, but that was nothing new. Miss Mabel *always* seemed mad at Flea. She was Flea's foster mother and the closest thing to a family he ever had. She'd raised him as long as Flea could remember and did a pretty good job considering the unpredictable circumstances of their life together. But there were a few odd things about her that Flea started noticing more and more as he got older. Miss Mabel rarely went out in public with Flea and always warned him to behave and stay out of trouble, to keep his head down and try not to draw any unnecessary attention to himself – and to her.

She took this opportunity to reinforce those warnings yet again.

"What did I tell you about playing in the snow? You're a sickly boy, you shouldn't be playing in this freezing weather. Do you realize what could have happened if you passed out in front of someone else's door? That could've led to a lot of questions that we don't need," Miss Mabel yelled. Flea's foster mother was on a roll and Flea learned long ago that he should *never* interrupt her. "And what if you caught pneumonia? Do you *know* how serious that could've been?"

Flea could not remember being sick a single day in his life nor did the cold weather faze him in the least. But rather than reason with Miss Mabel, he decided to prove that he was fine by jumping out of bed. He felt dizzy for a moment but quickly regained his balance.

"Miss Mabel, you should have seen what happened out there!" Flea said excitedly. He proceeded to explain the day's events, from his narrow escape in gym class to the snowball ambush to his amazing abilities to stop the snowballs and throw them back with such force. Miss Mabel watched him with concern and did not look nearly as impressed as Flea had hoped. "It was incredible, Miss

Mabel, a dozen bullies all running away from *me*. Can you believe that?"

"No, I *can't* believe it, I'm sure you are over-exaggerating how *awesome* you were. Next time, you should be smarter and just run away. Or you can let them hit you so they'll leave you alone after that," Miss Mabel said.

Flea couldn't hide his disappointment with Miss Mabel's attitude, especially since he'd overcome the odds in such a dramatic – and unexpected – manner.

"But I'm tired of being picked on all the time, no matter where I go. Why wouldn't you want me to stand up for myself?"

"Because what happens if you hurt one of those boys? What happens if you had hit them in the face with a snowball?" Miss Mabel asked.

"It was only snow, I'm sure they would've been fine," Flea said quietly, not so convinced by his own words. He pictured Rob and Cory flying backwards, crashing into the snow forts after being hit in their chests. Had Flea's snowballs struck them in the face, he wasn't so sure they would have been fine.

"Imagine if the parents of those boys came around here asking questions," Miss Mabel said with serious concern. "You *know* that's exactly the kind of attention we need to avoid. You never know who could be out there watching, looking for us."

"You're right, I'm sorry," Flea said simply so Miss Mabel wouldn't become angrier. "Next time, I'll just take my punishment without fighting back…or maybe I'll even take the longer route home."

Miss Mabel walked to Flea's bedroom window and pushed aside the heavy curtains enough to glance outside. The snow fell heavier than before.

"Don't worry about those bullies, you won't have to deal with them much longer," she said. Miss Mabel carefully closed the curtains so nobody could see inside. Paranoia of being watched was yet another of Miss Mabel's quirky traits that made Flea's life difficult. She started to walk out of Flea's room but decided to drop a bombshell on him. "I think it's time to consider moving again."

"What? Why?" Flea asked as he immediately thought about leaving Mr. Strick and woodshop class. "We've only been here four months, the school year isn't even half over."

Flea shouldn't have been surprised by this news. If there was one thing Miss Mabel liked more than lecturing him it was moving, which she chose to do as casually as deciding what to eat for dinner. The two had moved on a yearly basis – sometimes more than once a year – for as long as Flea could remember. There had been a few schools Flea liked over the years but this was by far the most heartbreaking 'moving' announcement yet.

"Look at this weather, it's snowing as hard here as did in Maryland and New Jersey and Ohio before that. I moved us to North Carolina because I thought we'd be *escaping* this, not moving directly in the middle of constant snowstorms again," she said. "It's like we're cursed, like the snow is following us wherever we go."

Miss Mabel made no secret of her hatred of snow. She often spoke of the winter weather as if it was her mortal enemy, as if the snow fell for the specific purpose of spiting her. She headed out of Flea's room so he quickly followed her.

"When exactly do you plan on leaving?" Flea asked, hoping that she was bluffing as a way to punish him for the snowball fight.

"I don't know for sure, I just decided that it was time to leave," Miss Mabel said. "I'll have to give it some more thought tomorrow since I have work tonight. I hope you haven't forgotten."

Miss Mabel peeked out of the living room window as the sun finally set. The snow still fell but there was a break in the clouds allowing Flea to spot the large moon. With all of today's excitement, Flea *had* in fact forgotten that tonight was Miss Mabel's one monthly work night. Had he realized there was a full moon tonight, he surely would have remembered.

"Doing some more *cleaning* tonight?" Flea asked. "You better hope that you'll be able to find another job as a cleaning woman when we move again, especially one with such good hours."

"Don't you worry about my job, boy," Miss Mabel said. "I'm sure I'll be able to find work wherever we go. And don't you get all sassy on me now."

Flea was becoming too smart to keep being fooled about her job, though he still knew better than to ask too many questions. Still, it was too coincidental that she found the same job with the same schedule no matter where they ended up. Flea didn't exactly have an over-active imagination when it came to a lot of things, but the fact that she left during the full moon every month sometimes made him suspect Miss Mabel was a werewolf. Flea was too old to believe in such fairy tales but there was no other possible explanation. Miss Mabel always looked different the day after she worked, too. There was always a youthful glow to her that Flea couldn't understand.

Before Miss Mabel reached the front door, Flea sneezed and saw several small speckles flutter past his face. His dandruff problem was growing out of control and even Miss Mabel noticed. She marched over to Flea and brushed her hand across his shoulder.

"I told you I need that specialty shampoo to help control my...problem," Flea said, his face turning crimson.

"There's a shampoo to get rid of *sawdust?*" Miss Mabel asked. "Care to explain how *that* got in your hair?"

After arriving at this school months earlier, Miss Mabel had been so angry about Flea being put in shop class that she called the school and demanded he attend another class that wasn't so 'dangerous.' The fact that she broke her rule of silence and called the school – the first time she'd contacted *any* of Flea's schools – proved just how serious she'd been. So after only a few days, Flea was transferred to cooking class. Luckily, Mr. Strick had already seen Flea's talents and was impressed enough to take him out of other classes on a daily basis, a secret that Flea kept from his foster mother.

Until now.

"Mr. Strick – the shop teacher – needed my help to finish a special project," Flea said. "Don't worry, I was very careful. I didn't use any of the dangerous tools."

"Mr. Strick, huh?" Miss Mabel asked angrily. "Now I know who to complain about when I call the school tomorrow."

"No, please, it wasn't his fault," Flea said. "There's no need to get him in trouble if we're just going to leave anyway."

"We'll discuss this later, I don't want to be late," Miss Mabel said, opening the door as the cold wind blew into their small apartment. Nearby, Flea heard a *banging* sound as the wind caused something to fall to their living room floor. "Make sure you stay inside, don't open the door for any reason."

Miss Mabel slammed the door behind her and Flea opened the curtains to see her trudge off through the deep snow. He ran his hand through his hair and saw the rest of the dust flutter to the floor. Once Miss Mabel was safely gone, Flea participated in his own monthly ritual: he headed straight for the cookie jar and poured himself a tall glass of milk. He brought his food back to the living room where he opened the curtains and stared out at the beautiful snowy world. With Christmas about a week away, he saw plenty of houses along his street that were heavily decorated. Multi-colored lights and white lights, large lawn ornaments of Santa Claus and his reindeer, huge decorated Christmas trees shining brightly through living room windows, all the things that Flea loved about the holiday time but never experienced himself. Miss Mabel allowed nothing but a tiny plastic tree on their coffee table, though it constantly tipped over. He picked it up off the floor and straightened a few of the bent branches. He thought he noticed a red light blinking in one of the branches but it stopped when he looked closer. Flea quickly turned back to the chocolate-chip cookies and outside Christmas displays.

Once his stomach was loaded with milk and cookies and the lights no longer held his attention, Flea grew bored. He had a long night ahead of him and with nothing else to pass the time he decided to start on his homework. However, he couldn't find his backpack in his room or anywhere else in the small apartment. Flea headed to the window again and tried to see the section of walkway where he'd passed out earlier. The only thing he could think was that the bag had fallen off his shoulders when he fell to the ground and Miss Mabel missed it when she came outside to pick him up. Unfortunately, the lighting wasn't so good now and there was no telling how much more snow had accumulated on the ground. Flea couldn't see anything but white snow and knew that he would have to go out there if he hoped to find his backpack.

"I have to go outside, it's for school," Flea said aloud, as if Miss Mabel was still here. "I can't tell my teachers that I didn't do my work because I got into a snowball fight and left my books outside."

Flea knew that Miss Mabel's paranoia was just part of her craziness but when he opened the door, he still hesitated to walk out. The outside world was dark and cold, the wind *whined* eerily. In the back of his mind, Miss Mabel's warning replayed over and over. But Flea refused to be frightened of the world like his foster mother was.

He finally stepped out and walked along the icy walkway, which had been partially cleared of snow but not of the slick iciness. As Flea suspected, he found his backpack covered in snow and ice. He began to dig it out, but barely scooped a few handfuls of snow when chills ran up and down his spine.

But this wasn't caused by the cold.

Flea had the feeling that he was being watched. Sure enough, he spotted yet another green-eyed snowman nearby that seemed to be staring straight at him. Flea couldn't remember having seen this snowman through the window. Despite the fact that he knew a snowman couldn't really 'look' at him, he was still scared. He planned to dig through the snow and ice even faster but when he looked back down at the ground, he found a large watery hole in the middle of the snow where his hands were. Flea didn't hang around long enough to figure out how the snow melted so quickly. He grabbed his backpack and rushed back into the apartment, locking the door behind him. Flea stole a final glance out the window before shutting the curtains. His heart pounded for several minutes while he stared at the front door, afraid that the snowman might bust in at any moment.

"I've been around Miss Mabel for too long," Flea said with a chuckle once his heart rate steadied. He knew the idea of a snowman coming after him was insane but he still left the curtains closed... just in case. Flea did his homework and watched TV for a few hours (nothing good was on since they didn't have cable) before finally going to bed. It took him a little while longer to fall asleep but he finally dozed off and slept through the night, not waking until he heard the front door open early the next morning. He peeked his head out long enough to see Miss Mabel, who looked exhausted and yet glowing at the same time.

"Did you have an eventful evening?" she asked softly.

"Nope, I just did my homework and watched TV before going to bed. I promise I didn't stay up past my bedtime," Flea said, omitting the part about his excursion outside.

"Good boy, I'm going to bed now so make sure you aren't late for school," she said before disappearing into her bedroom.

Flea got ready for school and headed for the front door. Before he left, he spotted a trail of dust near the door and shook his head. Flea hoped that Miss Mabel had calmed down about the whole 'woodshop class' incident and he certainly didn't want her to spot the sawdust later and get mad all over again. He hurried to the kitchen and grabbed the broom, using it to sweep the dust outside before he rushed off to school.

CHAPTER FOUR
DVD of CTV

"Time for dodgeball!" the gym teacher yelled after blowing his whistle. The students gathered around and sat on the gym floor. Like usual, Flea stayed near the back of the group. But today, none of the other boys sat within twenty feet of him. "Okay, it's time to choose teams. I think today's captains will be…" The teacher slowly looked over the group until he pointed to two boys – the same two who happened to be massaging their chests. "…Rob and Cory."

The two boys glanced at each other before jumping to their feet. Rob and Cory nearly stumbled over the others as they raced to the front. Cory was obviously faster but Rob grabbed him around the waist and dragged him to the floor, thus reaching the front first.

"That's not fair!" Cory yelled. He pushed Rob and the two nearly came to blows.

The gym teacher blew his whistle and separated them. "Whoa! Let's save that fighting for the start of the game."

"I get first pick, I was up here first!" Rob called out loudly. Cory obviously didn't agree. He yelled his objections while still trying to get past the gym teacher and at Rob.

"Jeez, what's the big deal?" the teacher asked. "There are *plenty* of good players to choose from – and plenty of bad ones, too." The gym teacher laughed at his own joke though none of the jocks or bullies found him funny today. "The teams always end up being fair. Besides, *I* say who gets to pick first. Cory, go ahead."

Cory yelled 'yes' and pumped his fists while Rob looked like his soul had just been crushed. Flea had no idea why the two bullies had been fighting amongst themselves but then Cory pointed straight at him.

"I choose Flea," he said.

The rest of the students turned and stared at Flea. For the first time, they looked at him with admiration instead of hatred. Flea had to admit that it felt pretty good. The story of the snowball fight had apparently made its way around school, at least to everyone but the teacher.

"*Flea*? Is this some kind of joke?" the gym teacher asked laughing. When he realized that Cory's pick was serious, the smile disappeared from his face. "Get your butt up here, Flea!"

Flea nearly tripped several times while walking between the rest of the students, all of whom watched his every step.

"I'm sorry about everything that's happened in the past," Cory whispered once Flea stood next to him. "It's an honor to play on your team."

"Let's go, Rob, we don't have all day," snapped the gym teacher, who was in a bad mood since he didn't understand what was going on between Flea and the two captains. "Hurry up and make your pick."

Every time it was Rob's turn to choose, the other bullies and jocks shrunk away behind the other kids, praying that Rob wouldn't see them. Every time Rob said a name, the selected student groaned and marched slowly to the front. When it was Cory's turn, however, they all suddenly reappeared and raised their hands, waving frantically in the hopes of being chosen. The gym teacher shook his head in confusion. When it was time to start the game, the teams jogged to their respective sides. The teacher blew his whistle and released the large bag of dodgeballs.

Not a single person on the other team made any sort of move forward. Instead, there was a mass retreat, as Rob and his team moved as far away from the center as possible. If the other team could have squeezed under the bleachers, Flea was pretty sure they would have tried. Flea smiled and never felt more powerful. He slowly strolled to the center of the gym, where Cory handed him one of the dodgeballs.

"What's going on here?" the gym teacher called out to Rob's team. "If y'all are playing some kind of joke on me, I'll make sure we never play dodgeball again."

Cory and a few of Flea's other teammates let fly, as they took out several of the other team's players, who were more than happy to run off the court before Flea decided to throw. In fact, Rob *tried* to move himself in front of several thrown balls but missed every single one. It finally took the gym teacher yelling at the other team for Rob and a few others to retrieve some of the dodgeballs, all of which were on their side except for the one in Flea's hand. Now that he had everyone's attention, Flea was finally ready to show *everyone* – including his gym teacher – that he was a force to be reckoned with, that he was someone important, that he was no longer worthy of constant ridicule.

Flea took aim at Rob, got a running head start and threw the dodgeball exactly how he'd thrown the snowball the day before. All but one of the other team's players turned away in fear – the only nerdy kid left, who must've known that Flea had plenty of other targets to choose from. Unfortunately for Flea, his throwing aim was nowhere *near* as good as it was the day before and his dodgeball flew directly toward that one brave nerd. Flea's heart instantly sank as he imagined what the ball could do to that poor, unsuspecting kid, as he again remembered Miss Mabel's warnings about keeping a low profile. But within seconds of releasing the ball, he realized that not only had his accuracy returned to its old form but so had his throwing speed. The nerd clumsily put his hands up and caught Flea's dodgeball with the greatest of ease.

Though Flea was relieved that he hadn't hurt anyone, his shoulders slumped now that he had returned to being a nobody. His fall from grace had been speedy and spectacular, witnessed by all. Those players already eliminated – as well as Flea's own teammates – simultaneously gasped. Once Rob and the others realized they were still alive, they found the courage to remove their arms from their faces. When they saw the nerd holding the ball that Flea had thrown, it dawned on them what had happened. Rob's expression of fear and defeat instantly returned to its usual sneer. He didn't hesitate to charge, dodgeball in hand toward a surprised Flea.

The gym teacher's whistle blew seconds before Rob was about to throw. It was probably the first – and only – time that Flea ever appreciated the teacher.

"Flea, he caught your ball, you're out!" the gym teacher yelled.

Rob's sneer was animal-like. Flea wouldn't have been surprised if the bully ripped apart the dodgeball with his teeth. As Flea slowly walked to the side of the gym – the first person on his team eliminated – play resumed behind him. He could still feel dozens of sets of eyes on him, staring at him like the freak he truly was. Flea was confused as everyone else about what had happened to his ability. But mostly he was disappointed for having allowed himself to think that he could be special, that he could be more than just the 'weird' kid.

It didn't help hearing the gym teacher muttering under his breath. "And you were the first pick?"

Flea barely had the chance to take a seat when the gym doors opened and a familiar face suddenly appeared.

"Mr. … uh, what's your name again?" the gym teacher asked.

"Strick, his name is *Strick,*" Flea snapped.

"Yeah, Strick, whatever. Are you here to take your favorite student again?" the gym teacher asked. "He certainly doesn't need to be *here* anymore."

"If you don't mind," Mr. Strick said.

The gym teacher shrugged his shoulders and turned back to the game. Mr. Strick waved over Flea, who plodded toward the hallway, still brooding about what had happened. A dodgeball *whizzed* just inches above his head and when Flea looked back toward the game, he saw Rob smiling at him. By the time Flea exited the gym, he was in a terrible mood and there was only one person to take out his frustrations on.

"I saw what all of your special *projects* bought you," Flea said as soon as he reached Mr. Strick. "That's a nice new truck you have, I see you've made plenty of money from my special projects."

Mr. Strick was shocked into silence and Flea took this as an admission of guilt. Now that Flea was certain that his only ally in the world had been using him, he no longer cared that Miss Mabel planned to move them away from here. As far as Flea was concerned, a move couldn't come soon enough.

"Since you have nothing to say, I'll just be getting back to gym class now," Flea said, choking on his words. Right about now he would have gladly endured physical torture to escape the emotional kind.

"Go ahead and play dodgeball then if you don't want to watch this special DVD," Mr. Strick said. "But just realize that everything in life isn't always as it appears."

Flea stopped before opening the gym doors and looked back to see Mr. Strick – and his familiar red hard hat – walking off down the hallway. It was obvious that the shop teacher wasn't going to look back and the last thing Flea wanted to do today was make another enemy, especially if he had misunderstood the situation.

"Hey, wait up," Flea said. He rushed forward and caught up with his teacher. "What DVD are you talking about?"

Strick removed a DVD case from his tool belt and held it up. Flea noticed three big, bold letters on the front – CTV – but he had no idea what they meant.

"You've been working really hard for me all school year and I wanted to do something nice to show you my appreciation," Mr. Strick said. "But since you aren't interested…" He shrugged his shoulders and returned the DVD to the pouch in his tool belt.

Flea had trouble trusting people and suspected some sort of ploy. But deep down, Flea hoped that Strick deserved his trust. Besides, a loud *bang* against the gym doors behind him – undoubtedly caused by an errant dodgeball throw – reminded Flea that the bullies in gym class *would be* ready to attack the moment he showed back up. Flea followed Mr. Strick toward the shop classroom, though the teacher wouldn't give him any hints about the contents of the DVD.

"You'll just have to wait and see for yourself," Strick said.

With nothing left to discuss about the DVD, Flea couldn't help but mention the strangest part of his teacher's appearance.

"Why do you wear that weird hard hat all the time, even when you're not working?" Flea asked. A part of him was still angry with Mr. Strick and he finally had the courage to ask the question that had been on his mind for a long time.

"Let's just say I'm trying to make a fashion statement," Mr. Strick said. "Or maybe I'm starting the next trend in construction."

Strick chuckled to himself as they entered the empty shop classroom. He turned on the lights and Flea could immediately see that Mr. Strick hadn't followed Principal Crawley's orders: the room was still a dusty mess, even more than usual. *No wonder I had so much sawdust in my hair yesterday,* Flea thought to himself. He would have to brush himself off *before* going home, though the damage with Miss Mabel had already been done. An ancient TV and DVD player sat on a rolling cart in the middle of the classroom and Mr. Strick immediately turned them on and popped in the DVD.

"So you've never heard of CTV?" Strick asked before pushing the 'play' button.

Flea blushed and explained that he never had cable so he didn't know about most television channels.

"That's good, most TV rots the brain anyway," Mr. Strick said. "But I *do* like CTV. It's the Construction Channel so you can imagine my interest; you'd probably like it, too. Anyway, CTV has a popular new reality show called *The Great Build-Off.* I've been submitting your work the last few months and I just received this DVD in response from them. I thought you might like to watch it."

Flea instantly forgot his anger, which was replaced with a nervous excitement. Mr. Strick pushed the PLAY button and the show's intro began, which explained the rules of *The Great Build-Off.* Two construction teams were pitted against each other and given a stack of building materials, an hour-time limit and a secret theme on which they had to create the most impressive display. Flea thought the show sounded really cool and he looked forward to watching an episode, but when the opening credits came to an end, the show did not begin. Instead, the show's host stood on the empty set and spoke directly into the camera.

"Mr. Strick, thank you for your multiple submissions to *The Great Build-Off*. Your work has really been quite impressive," the host began. "I would also like to take this opportunity to congratulate you on being selected to participate on our show. We only select the best builders from across the country so you should be very proud of yourself and what you've built. The producers of our show will contact you shortly to provide more details. Again, congratulations and we look forward to seeing you on *The Great Build-Off*."

The host waved and the screen went black.

"Why was he congratulating *you* for *my* work?" Flea asked. He still felt used by Mr. Strick but now it was for a different reason.

"What's gotten in to you today? I've never seen you angry before, especially toward someone who's trying to help you get on TV," Mr. Strick said. "I only took credit for your work because the show has an age requirement; needless to say, I doubt they ever expected a junior high student would be skilled enough to deserve a spot on *The Great Build-Off*."

"So if I'm not old enough to get on the show, what's the point?"

"The *point* is that I can be a very persuasive person when I want to be," Mr. Strick said. "I guarantee you that once I bring you to the show's set and talk to the producers, they will let you compete. So, are you up for this? You always told me that you wanted more of a challenge."

Flea had to admit that the offer sounded intriguing, though the thought of being on TV in front of millions of viewers sent a wave of wild butterflies flapping in his stomach. Flea also had a new doubt – if he'd suddenly lost his ability to throw when a group of people was watching, could the same thing happen to his ability to build?

"What if I freeze? What if I suddenly forget how to use a hammer when I get there?" Flea asked. Mr. Strick nodded his head in understanding.

"You have every reason to be nervous. But I have complete faith that you'll not only do well, you'll mop the floor with the competition," Mr. Strick said. His voice did not contain an ounce of doubt. Flea felt better about himself even though he didn't totally share his teacher's confidence. "Besides, I'll be right there with you the entire time in case you need help…though *that's* never happened before."

"I'm in then," Flea said timidly.

"Great," Mr. Strick said, clapping his hands together. "We've been scheduled for their Holiday Special episode, which is being filmed tomorrow. I know it's a bit short notice but I have a really good feeling about you building with a Christmas theme. The show is shot during the school day so I'll need you to have your foster mother sign a permission slip allowing you to go."

Flea groaned, as the mention of a permission slip had the same effect on him as a dodgeball to the gut. *I knew this* had *to be too good to be true…* he thought.

"There's no way she'll sign that, I'm not even supposed to be in the shop room let alone some TV show on the Construction Channel," Flea said. He felt totally deflated, which was exactly how Mr. Strick now looked. Flea's only hope rested with something he remembered his teacher saying moments earlier. "Maybe you could try to talk to her since you can be so persuasive."

"*Me* talk to *Miss Mabel*?" Mr. Strick asked, obviously horrified by the suggestion. "I'm pretty sure we *both* know how bad of an idea that would be. I'm sorry Flea, but the only way Principal Baldy will let you go is if you can convince Miss Mabel to sign this form."

-     -   -   -   -   -   -   -   -   -

-     -   -   -

"Absolutely not!" Miss Mabel yelled.

Flea expected such a reaction. Still, he'd hoped his foster mother would at least listen to his argument about why he should go. But he barely had to mention Mr. Strick's name and the idea of being on television before she launched into her usual ranting and raving. Miss Mabel seemed like she could yell at Flea for several minutes straight without stopping to take a single breath. Of course she mentioned every point she'd ever pounded into Flea's mind – he was too fragile, construction was too dangerous, he needed to keep his head down, they needed to avoid unnecessary attention. But while Flea usually ended up nodding his head in order to stop her yelling, he was too disappointed now to accept what she had to say.

"This isn't fair," Flea shot back the moment Miss Mabel finally needed a breather. He felt himself turning red from a mixture of anger, fear and embarrassment. Miss Mabel looked surprised by his unexpected outburst. "I have a talent and I want to share it with the world. Mr. Strick said –"

"Mr. *Strick* isn't your mother!" Miss Mabel yelled back.

"Well neither are – " Flea started to say before stopping himself. The damage had been done however. He saw disappointment on Miss Mabel's face that he'd never seen before. Flea felt terrible. "I'm sorry, I just *really* want to do this. Please, Miss Mabel, this is important to me."

She sighed and her shoulders slumped. For several long seconds she stood there and stared at Flea, who felt so uncomfortable in the silence that he couldn't stop from fidgeting. Finally, Miss Mabel broke the silence and waved him toward her.

"You aren't going to stop until I take that form, will you?" she asked.

"No, I guess not," Flea answered.

"Then you better give it to me."

Flea smiled as he handed over the permission slip. He gave Miss Mabel a long hug but she was still so upset that she didn't hug back.

"Let me get you something to write with," Flea said once he let go of her. He headed toward his backpack but Miss Mabel stopped him.

"That won't be necessary."

Flea's stomach sunk. He knew what she was going to do before he heard the first *rip*. Flea felt like a balloon that had just been pricked with a pin. Miss Mabel ripped the form into pieces and dropped them to the floor. She walked to her bedroom and muttered to herself, though Flea could hear exactly what she said.

"I told *Mr. Strick* it was too dangerous but he *never* listens to me."

Flea hadn't known that Miss Mabel spoke to Mr. Strick before, but now he understood why the shop teacher had been so opposed to the idea of calling her. As Flea picked up the tiny pieces of paper, he couldn't help but feel that the best opportunity of his life had been ripped to shreds.

CHAPTER FIVE

Permission Required?

"Does he have his permission slip?" Principal Crawley asked.

As Flea approached the shop teacher and principal early the next morning, he could tell that the two had been bickering, like usual. They waited for Flea just outside the shop class but he was in no rush to deliver the bad news, especially since Crawley would undoubtedly be thrilled to thwart Mr. Strick's field trip.

"How would I know if he has it? He's just arriving now," Strick shot back.

"So, Flip, do you have the form?" the principal asked.

Although Flea's eyes met his teacher's for only a split second, it was more than enough time for Mr. Strick to understand. Before Flea had the chance to say 'no', Strick intervened.

"His name is *Flea* and we have to get something from the classroom," Mr. Strick said, throwing open the door to the shop class. A cloud of dust seemed to explode into the hallway. "Come on, Flea, we have to get ready to leave soon."

"What about the form? He can't go without – " Crawley started before he began to cough from the dust. "What did I tell you about cleaning up that room? This is a disgrace, I can't believe you would – "

Mr. Strick closed the door before the principal finished his complaint.

"We don't have much time before he comes in here," Mr. Strick said. "You couldn't convince Miss Mabel to let you go?"

"I tried, believe me I did. But once she decides something, there's no changing her mind," Flea said. He reached into his pocket and pulled out the dozens of tiny scraps that had once been the permission slip. A sympathetic smile crept across Mr. Strick's face. He had obviously learned a lot about Miss Mabel from the conversation he had with her months earlier.

"Do you still want to go?" Strick asked.

"But what about the permission slip?" Flea asked. "And if Miss Mabel ever found out, she would probably disown me."

"I'm sure she'd get over it," Mr. Strick said. "You need to make this decision based on what *you* want to do. Sometimes *you* need to decide what's best instead of listening to everyone else."

Flea nodded. The decision was an easy one for him when he considered his teacher's advice.

"Then yes, of course I want to go. But that still doesn't explain how we'll get past Crawley with my form all torn up."

Mr. Strick carefully took all the pieces from Flea and walked toward his desk. Outside the classroom, Principal Crawley knocked on the door and called out that he was going back to his office if they didn't come out soon.

"I don't think tape is going to fix that," Flea said.

But Mr. Strick proved that Flea wasn't the only one capable of making magic happen in this room. He remained by his desk for only a few seconds before turning back to Flea and handing him an intact form. As if that wasn't impressive enough, the signature at the bottom was even more amazing: *Miss Mabel*.

"How did you – "

Mr. Strick winked and led him back to the hallway, where Principal Crawley was fuming. Flea nervously handed the forged slip over, worried that the principal would see through their ruse or call Miss Mabel to verify. Crawley looked over the form very closely and slowly shook his head. Flea glanced at Strick to see that the shop teacher looked just as nervous as he felt.

"Flip, could you excuse us?" Mr. Strick asked. He opened the door to the shop room and motioned for Crawley to enter. "Could we please speak for a moment in private, sir?"

Crawley was clearly suspicious of Mr. Strick's sudden – and unusual – display of respect but he followed him into the room anyway.

"I don't know what you two are trying to pull here but I wasn't born yesterday," Crawley said just before the door closed.

For several minutes, Flea paced outside the door while the other students walked through the halls. Luckily, the shop classroom was in the back corner of the school where there wasn't much traffic so Flea didn't have the added worry of running into Rob or Cory or the other bullies. In reality, a simple bully problem would've been easier to deal with than the problem he was about to have with the principal. If Miss Mabel flipped out when she discovered that Flea had lied to her about working in the shop room, he didn't want to imagine what her reaction would be to forgery. He was just about to burst into the classroom and beg for the principal's forgiveness when the door opened. Mr. Strick walked out with a mischievous smile. Flea wondered if there was something odd about his teacher that he'd never before noticed.

"We're good to go," Mr. Strick said.

"Did you have to knock him out or tie him up?" Flea asked worriedly.

Mr. Strick laughed but didn't need to answer. Principal Crawley emerged from the room but he looked like a totally different man. His face was relaxed and pale white, no longer bright red or scrunched up in anger. He also wore a big smile, which showed a mouthful of teeth that looked oddly tiny against the backdrop of his oversized face. But the most significant difference about him was the red hard-hat he wore, just like the one Strick always had on. It was covered in as much sawdust as the rest of the shop room but Crawley did not seem to mind at all.

"Good luck on the show today, Flea, I'll be cheering you on," Principal Crawley said. With the forged permission slip in hand, the stern disciplinarian walked down the hallway, whistling Christmas tunes as he went along. Flea turned to look at Mr. Strick, who instantly read the confused look on Flea's face.

"There's no time to explain," Mr. Strick said tapping his watch. "We have to leave now if we're going to get there on time."

-    -   -   -   -   -   -   -   -   -   -

-    -   -   -

They arrived at the CTV studios nearly an hour later. The hectic pace around the set of *The Great Build-Off* was overwhelming to Flea, especially since the show's producers were very angry that Flea was a junior high student – one who looked even younger at that. The show's host – who had seemed so nice and friendly on the congratulatory DVD – also glared angrily in Flea's direction.

"So what does this mean?" the host asked the crowd of producers. "The episode is cancelled? Because I still plan on getting paid whether I have to work or not. I'll be in my trailer, come get me when you *geniuses* figure this all out."

The host stormed off but Mr. Strick told Flea not to worry.

"Is it time to be persuasive again?" Flea asked him.

His teacher winked and told Flea to stay put. Mr. Strick went to find the producers and after a couple minutes, they all came back smiling and laughing, as if there'd never been a single issue about Flea's age. One of the people on set led Flea and Mr. Strick to their positions in front of the camera. The host soon arrived, as well as a group of five strong, rugged-looking men who all wore similar flannel shirts. Behind them was the show's stage, a large room with a divider down the middle. Each side had identical tools and supplies, very well stocked with anything and everything a carpenter could ever need.

"Okay people, let's have a good show," the host told them. "Try not to do anything to make yourself – or more importantly, *me* – look stupid."

Flea looked out at the large studio audience and felt his insides churning like they were inside a washing machine. The thought of so many people watching him was utterly terrifying and his shoes suddenly felt like they were filled with iron. His mouth was dry and his head grew lighter with every passing second. The lights dimmed above the audience, the spotlight shined brightly on him and the others on stage and a red light began to blink repeatedly on the camera in front of them. The camera operator counted down from five before pointing to the host, who plastered a fake smile on his face. The show started but Flea barely heard a word of the host's explanation of the rules. It wasn't until the introduction of the show's contestants that Flea focused on what was happening.

"Our first team comes to us all the way from New York City, where they've helped to build some of our countries tallest skyscrapers. Ladies and gentlemen, please welcome the *Nail York Five*," the host said.

An applause sign blinked in front of the audience while the five-man team waved. When the clapping died down and the host turned to the other side, Flea's head began spinning quickly again and he felt on the verge of passing out. Thankfully, Mr. Strick placed a comforting – and steadying – hand on Flea's shoulder. This helped Flea just enough to stay conscious and standing on both feet.

"Our second team comes from a local junior high school. Please give a warm welcome to shop teacher Neal Strick and his student, Flea," the host said.

The applause sign lit up again but the clapping was more reserved this time. Flea could see the shocked expressions in the audience. He glanced over at the *Nail York Five* and saw confusion on a few of their faces, anger on the others. Flea wouldn't have blamed the five men if they thought some sort of practical joke was being played at their expense. As if the other team and the people in the audience didn't have enough reason to wonder what was going on, Mr. Strick's next move only added to their confusion. When the light clapping died down, he approached the host and borrowed the man's microphone.

"Actually, I'm only here because Flea needed a ride," Mr. Strick said. "He will be working by himself today."

The unexpected breach in the show's standard format momentarily threw off the host and he could do nothing but smile blankly into the camera. Flea looked over to the group of construction workers. Flea could hear the one angry man whispering to the others that they should leave, that this was a joke. His teammates calmed him down by saying that they would at least have the easiest win in the history of the show. The men had every reason to be overly confident but that only served to motivate Flea. After all, the main reason he'd come on this show was to prove to everyone – including himself – that he wasn't as weak and worthless as he might appear.

"Shouldn't we get ready to..." Mr. Strick whispered to the host.

"That's right," the host said, recovering from his stumble. "Ladies and gentleman, *let's get ready to build off...*"

The *Nail York Five* took their side of the stage and Mr. Strick led Flea to their section. Once they were in place, Flea could no longer see his opponents on the other side of the wall. With a wealth of supplies at his disposal, Flea only had to wait for one more piece of information before he could start.

"But before we begin, I must unveil this week's secret theme," the host said as he gestured to a large sign draped with a cover. "Since this is the holiday season and Christmas is only a few days away, we at *The Great Build-Off* thought this would be very appropriate. Today's theme is…" The host whipped off the cover and when the crowd saw the sign they erupted in cheers. For several long, anxious seconds, Flea wondered what it said until the host turned the sign around. "…the North Pole."

A loud horn blared, signaling the start of the competition. Flea looked up at the huge clock at the top of the stage and saw that it had started counting backward from the sixty-minute mark. For a moment, his mind went totally blank. He had no idea what to do and could already hear the sound of nails hammering into wood on the other side of the divider. But when Flea looked toward Mr. Strick, his teacher gave him a simple nod of the head. Something seemed to click in Flea's mind. He immediately walked over to the stack of wood and got to work.

"It looks like Flea has finally gotten an idea, let's hope those few minutes of wasted time don't come back to haunt him in the end," the host said.

Flea worked with as much speed and ease as if he'd been alone in shop class, working on just another birdhouse project. The enormity of his situation was the last thing on his mind as he simply focused on lumber, nails and tools. As usual, he barely had to think as he worked and had little idea of exactly what he was building, what the big picture of his overall project would look like. With his hands working as if they had a mind of their own, he allowed his ability to simply flow. His concentration was so intense that he heard nothing else happening around him – no sounds from the other side of the stage, no applause from the audience, no questions from the host that Mr. Strick took care of answering. Nor did Flea notice the constant commotion just off stage as the camera that was supposed to be filming his every action had trouble dealing with the blur of his quick movements. The camera frequently cut out, thus providing viewers at home with very little clear footage of what Flea was building.

The only person able to keep up with Flea was Mr. Strick, who acted as Flea's assistant when he wasn't busy answering questions from the amazed host. Strick explained that Flea was the finest student he'd ever had – and the nicest, most humble kid he'd ever met – and that his ability to build was nothing short of other-worldly. But the host had few follow-up questions as he and the rest of the crowd were seemingly in a trance watching Flea work. Strick returned to their half of the stage, somehow avoiding the whirlwind of Flea's motions while handing him the right tool or length of wood or can of paint at the exact moment he needed it. The *Nail York Five* also worked at a frenetic pace but very few people in the audience watched how the other team tackled their project.

Flea allowed his instincts to guide him in the building during the sixty minutes. He put his finishing touches on the last part of his project mere seconds before a loud horn blared to signal the end of the competition. With his construction complete, Flea's surroundings came back into focus. He saw hundreds of pairs of eyes – from those in the audience to the show's producers and cameramen to the host – all staring directly at him. Hundreds of mouths hung open. Someone in the production crew finally had the good sense to turn on the applause sign and the crowd snapped out of its trance by cheering wildly. This sudden explosion of noise alerted the show's host that it was his turn to talk.

"Wow, I think I can say that was the most action-packed hour in the history of *The Great Build-Off*," the host said. "Now it's time to unveil the creations that our two teams have built. Flea and Mr. Strick, will you please join me."

Teacher and student left their part of the stage and joined the host, who led them to the *Nail York Five's* side. The other team stood confidently in front of their creation, a five-foot tall building that was labeled "Santa's Workshop." Flea was very impressed with what the five men had accomplished in only one hour, but not *nearly* as impressed as the five men were in themselves. Their chests puffed out proudly as they stared at their building.

"So *Nail York Five*, please describe to the viewers exactly what you've built for us today," the host said.

Each man took a turn describing which section of "Santa's Workshop" that he was responsible for making. The first builder had been in charge of the overall design and fabrication of the building's exterior, which actually opened up to show the inside of "Santa's Workshop". Other features included blinking Christmas lights, a fully functioning conveyor belt that held tiny little presents, a chimney stack that actually blew smoke and a paint job that closely resembled a fresh snowfall. The men were very satisfied with what they'd made, but one person on the stage wasn't nearly as impressed.

"I'd say the conveyor belt seems about right but the rest doesn't look real to me," Mr. Strick whispered to Flea.

The host was still in such a state of shock that he had no further questions for the *Nail York Five* following the presentation of their functioning workshop. The five men assumed that the host's shock had been the direct result of what they'd built. The man who'd stared angrily at Flea before the competition took this opportunity to gloat about what he thought would be an easy victory for his team.

"You see that kid? Maybe with another twenty years of practice you'll be able to achieve this level of craftsmanship," he said.

The five men chuckled. After a moment everyone else joined in, including the audience, the host and even Mr. Strick. At first,

Flea didn't understand why they all laughed but Mr. Strick let him in on the joke.

"Don't worry, they aren't laughing at you, Flea," Strick whispered. "They're laughing at the man's mistimed arrogance."

Flea nodded but still didn't totally understand. The host led both teams to the door built into the wall divider, where he slowly turned the handle.

"*Nail York Five*, here is the project that you're up against," the host said and opened the door.

CHAPTER SIX
The Great Build-Off

The sound of Flea's excited heartbeat pounded in his ears but he still heard the simultaneous gasp from each *Nail York Five* member when they stepped into the other side of the stage. Four of the men silently stood in a state of shock, but the angriest – and cockiest – team member was quick to respond.

"I *knew* this was going to be some sort of joke," he snapped. "There's *no way* that two people could've done all of this in one hour."

"You're right," Mr. Strick said. "Two of us *didn't* do this, only *Flea* did. I already explained to you: I'm just here because he needed a ride."

"This is ridiculous, impossible," the man said and stormed off the stage.

"I assure you, Mr. Strick is telling the truth," the host told the remaining team members. "This talented young man didn't build just one aspect of the North Pole; he built the *entire* North Pole."

Now that Flea had a moment to stand back and look at what he'd built, he was pretty impressed with himself. If anything, he proved that his talents weren't merely limited to birdhouses. While the other team had constructed a single building, Flea had finished a half-dozen different buildings. Upon closer inspection, Flea found that his eye for detail was far superior to the other team's. His North Pole structures were of different size, shape and color but did not look brand new. Flea had constructed these buildings with a slight degree of 'wear and tear' to them. The buildings were spaced out on the floor in a very specific manner but instead of simply using white paints or bits of Styrofoam to represent snow, Flea had used the shavings from dozens of pieces of white wood to give the snow a more realistic and textured look.

While Flea stood back and enjoyed his version of the North Pole, the host joined the four other members of the *Nail York Five* in inspecting the individual buildings up close. With the exception of the one man who'd stormed off, the other four looked like excited little children, marveling at each of the things they saw. Each time one of them came across something new, he called over his other friends to point it out. After a few minutes of this – with the cameras still rolling – one of the men asked Flea a question.

"What building is this one supposed to be?"

He pointed to one of the larger buildings near the back of the stage. The main characteristic of that building was a large clock-face near the top, complete with little numbers as well as the hour- and minute-hands. The hands appeared to be pointed straight up at twelve o'clock but when Flea looked closer, he saw that the time was *slightly* before twelve.

"Yes, Flea, would you care to explain the inspiration for the design of your North Pole village?" the host asked, shoving the microphone in Flea's face.

The truth was that Flea had no idea. He had built everything purely on instinct and didn't know exactly what his buildings were.

Flea realized how crazy that sounded so he stared blankly into the camera instead of making a fool of himself. Sensing Flea's apprehension, Mr. Strick quickly stepped forward to field the questions.

"Well, that first building over there is the main toy factory," he explained. Strick proceeded to identify every other structure: the reindeer stables, the elf dormitory, the ice bank, Santa's private cabin, even some sort of toy school. As amazing as Flea had been while building these objects, Mr. Strick was equally amazing at providing a sensible explanation for everything on stage. The shop teacher was an incredible storyteller and Flea hung on his every word, just like the host and audience.

"What exactly is an ice bank used for?" the host asked.

Flea wondered the same thing. Although the ice bank was the smallest – and least detailed – building on stage, its central location in the North Pole village made it the most interesting for Flea. But Mr. Strick's storytelling ability had apparently reached its limit.

"I'd love to answer more of your questions but aren't we almost out of time?" Mr. Strick asked.

The host and producers looked down at their watches and were shocked by how quickly time had passed.

"Oh my, you're right!" the host said. "Normally we determine the winner by audience vote but it's safe to assume that today's vote would've been unanimous. Congratulations Flea, you are the winner of the North Pole holiday episode of *The Great Build-Off.*"

The crowd erupted in applause. Flea felt a warmth he'd never before experienced: the sensation of being a *true* winner. When the clapping died down, the host asked Flea if there were anything he would like to say. Flea knew what it felt like to be the loser in a competition so he wanted to congratulate the other team on a great effort. But before he could say a single word, Mr. Strick stepped between Flea and the microphone and gave his own closing comments.

"If you liked what Flea built on today's show, we invite you to visit our website – www.shopteachergoods.com – where you can purchase some of his other items for sale," Mr. Strick said. "You can also buy one of these stylish hardhats, which make great Christmas gifts for your loved ones. Hurry, supplies are limited."

Any satisfaction Flea had felt from winning instantly evaporated. Making matters worse was the fact that Mr. Strick refused to look Flea in the eye, as he *knew* he'd used his talented student. At that moment, Flea utterly regretted disobeying Miss Mabel, the only person who ever *truly* cared about him.

-    -   -   -   -   -   -   -   -   -

-    -   -   -

The ride back was mostly spent in silence. Mr. Strick asked a few questions in the hope of starting a dialogue, but Flea responded with one-word answers and continued to stare out the window. The snow still fell heavy yet the weather around Strick's truck somehow stayed clear enough so that driving wasn't dangerous. Flea felt hollow inside, as much from his guilt about defying Miss Mabel as discovering that Mr. Strick *had* in fact been using him. When they turned down Flea's street, he thought he spotted several green-eyed snowmen watching the truck. But Flea was too upset and nervous to care.

"Only one more school day until winter break," Mr. Strick said, making one final effort to open the lines of communication.

You can't persuade me to talk to you, Flea thought. He mumbled a quick 'yeah' in response, making it clear that he had nothing else to say. When Mr. Strick stopped in front of the apartment complex, Flea immediately reached for the handle. His teacher was quicker to push the lock button.

"I want to get out," Flea whispered.

"I know you're upset with me and might never want to talk to me again, I understand that," Mr. Strick said. "But I want you to know that I think you're the most naturally gifted builder I've ever seen and that's saying a *lot*. I also have something important I'd like to give to you."

Flea still refused to face his teacher and after a long moment, Strick unlocked the door. Flea quickly opened it and jumped out of the truck but stopped when he heard Strick sigh.

"What could you *possibly* have to give to me?" Flea asked, his voice shaking with growing anger. The snow now fell heavier and the wind suddenly kicked up its blustery pace. Mr. Strick held out his hand and opened his palm to reveal a simple gold ring.

"Go ahead, take it," he told Flea.

Flea had the strong urge to slap the ring from his teacher's hand and march off, but there was a sincerity in Mr. Strick's tone that he couldn't ignore. *He's a good liar, don't trust him*, Flea reminded himself but he took the ring anyway. Although the ring shined brightly in his hand, Flea had the sense that it was very old.

"A ring? That's really weird," he told Strick. "What is it and how could it possibly be that important?"

Although the wind shrilled loudly, both of them could still hear the single word being yelled at them in the distance.

"You!"

Flea didn't have to turn around to recognize the sound of Miss Mabel's angry voice. The better question was exactly how much information she knew. A glance at Mr. Strick's face showed his eyes wide and his lips turned down, so apparently he assumed the worst. When Strick spoke, he did so very quickly.

"Some strange guy at the television studio wanted me to give it to you as a thanks for your participation on the show. It looks pretty important so I'd make sure to be extra careful with it if I were you. Sorry I have to go, see you in school tomorrow."

Strick didn't even wait for Flea to close the door before stepping on the gas. The quick acceleration of the truck caused the door to slam shut. The tires fishtailed a bit in the snow-covered street but Strick kept control as he sped away. Obviously, he was more afraid of facing Miss Mabel than Flea was. When Flea turned around, he saw his foster mother moving quicker than he'd ever seen.

"You just *had* to go on that show, didn't you?" she yelled, breaking her own rule about never causing a scene in public. Flea's horrible day continued to get worse. For the life of him, he couldn't figure out how Miss Mabel found out about the show already. After all, they didn't have CTV *and* Flea had never seen her talk to the neighbors – or *anyone* for that matter.

"How did you find out?" Flea asked. If he was going to be in trouble, he might as well find out *how* he'd been caught.

"Uh uh, this isn't the time for *you* to be asking *me* questions," Miss Mabel yelled. She grabbed Flea by his ear – the split ear at that – and dragged him back into their apartment, yelling at him the entire time. "In one day, you've undone all the hard work I've done to make sure we stayed hidden."

"Well *what* exactly are we hiding *from*?" Flea yelled back once they were inside. He broke free from her vice-like grip on his ear.

"Don't you worry about that, that's *my* business," she said. Now that he could only hear the sound of her voice, Flea thought he recognized as much fear and concern from her as anger, though he knew Miss Mabel was unlikely to explain why. "Now that we're probably being watched, it's too dangerous to stay here much longer. Once the snowfall lets up, we'll head farther south to safety."

"But I don't want to leave," Flea argued weakly, unsure whether he really believed those words any longer. He expected Miss Mabel's usual reaction but she answered with an eerie calmness that was more worrisome to Flea than her screaming.

"We *are* leaving and you have no one to blame but yourself," she said. Miss Mabel headed toward her bedroom. "I'm going to start packing, I suggest you do the same."

CHAPTER SEVEN
Kidnapped!

One more day of school remained before winter break but Miss Mabel refused to let Flea go, which was just fine with him. The weather had gotten worse overnight – the snow falling heavier, the wind blowing harder – so Miss Mabel decided they wouldn't leave yet. Still, her paranoia had not eased the slightest bit. She didn't even accept Flea's offer to shovel the walkway, a task that he normally hated and avoided at all costs.

"It's our turn to do it, though. The neighbors shoveled yesterday," Flea said.

But Miss Mabel didn't care, arguing that the neighbors would have to shovel *every* day once they left. As she scurried about packing up their few belongings, she continued to mutter that the weather would break soon and it couldn't snow forever. However, one day of weather watching turned to two and two soon turned to three. Christmas Eve arrived and Flea had grown so bored with being stuck inside that he took every possible opportunity to peek out the curtains. Though the snow fell in sheets, Flea still thought he spotted several green-eyed snowmen staring in his direction, though he did not dare mention that to Miss Mabel.

"What did I tell you about keeping the curtains closed?" Miss Mabel yelled when she walked into the tiny living room. She hurried to shut them, overlapping the heavy fabric, ensuring that not a single beam of outside light invaded their apartment.

"Why are you so worried? There's nothing out there but snow," Flea said, conveniently leaving out the part about the strange snowmen.

"Snow is what I'm afraid of," Miss Mabel said. "Now finish packing what's on the table so we can escape when the snow stops." Flea looked at the coffee table, which held nothing but their sad little Christmas tree, its pathetic branches bent. As if reading Flea's mind, Miss Mabel added, "I'm sorry but we don't have time for Christmas this year."

"How will Santa know to come here if we don't have a tree set up?" Flea asked.

Miss Mabel snorted. "You don't have to worry about *that*."

Still, Miss Mabel didn't force the issue when Flea left the tree. After all, it was the last of their possessions left in the apartment that wasn't packed in one of the boxes piled near the front door.

When it became obvious that the snow wasn't going to stop, Miss Mabel sent Flea to bed early in case they had to wake up and leave in the middle of the night. But once inside his room, Flea could not even *think* about going to sleep just yet, not if this would be the last night spent in this apartment. Besides, Christmas Eve was always the toughest night of the year for him to drift off to sleep. He cracked the heavy curtains in his bedroom and stared out at the white, nighttime world.

Now that he'd had several days to think about what happened with Mr. Strick and *The Great Build-Off*, Flea had cooled down to the point that he no longer hated his shop teacher. He never would've been able to fully trust Strick again but he had already forgiven and wished he could tell him so. But since he and Miss Mabel would soon be leaving, Flea knew his final interaction with his favorite teacher was the moment Strick had given him the strange ring.

The ring, Flea thought, *I totally forgot about the ring.*

The last few days, he'd been so busy packing, bickering with Miss Mabel and being bored that he hadn't given his 'parting gift' a second thought. He reached into his pocket and found the shiny ring still there. Flea knew better than to turn his lights on and draw the ire of Miss Mabel so he studied the ring using the small amount of light that filtered through his window. The gold ring was very plain but there was something inexplicably elegant about it. Though it was too big for his tiny hands, Flea slipped it onto his finger.

Instantly, Flea yawned. The hours he'd spent sitting awake in his room finally caught up with him and his eyelids grew heavy. He lay down in bed and glanced at his digital alarm clock, its numbers switching to 11:59 – just one minute before it was officially Christmas. But Flea could not keep his eyes open any longer, not even when he felt the gold ring constrict tightly on his finger. Even with his eyes closed, Flea saw a golden glow from his hand and then a bright light in his room. He tried to fight impending unconsciousness but knew that was a losing battle.

"Are we sure about this?" a voice whispered nearby.

Although Flea only heard one voice, he sensed the presence of more than one person in the tight confines of his bedroom. Flea was frightened but still couldn't summon the energy to force open his eyelids. The last thing he thought before drifting off was whether these were the intruders that Miss Mabel had been worried about for so long...

\-   -   -   -   -   -   -   -   -   -   -

\-   -   -   -

As Flea's mind slowly began to awaken, he no longer heard any strange voices and wondered if he had simply dreamed it. He already passed out one time this week and worried that it had happened again. But he felt so comfortable lying in his bed at the moment that he forced the thought of being sick out of his mind. He considered drifting back to sleep when he heard someone shuffling in his room.

"Miss Mabel? Do we have to go now?" he asked groggily. Enough light permeated Flea's eyelids for him to know that it was bright inside his room. "Is it Christmas morning now?"

"Sorry, there's still a *lot* of time before Christmas," said the same strange voice Flea thought he'd heard earlier.

Flea's eyes snapped open and he sat up quickly, feeling momentarily dizzy from the sudden movement. He immediately realized that this wasn't his own bedroom. The walls were painted bright red and green and there was far too much natural light shining, something he rarely saw in any of the apartments he'd ever lived in. The bed he sat on was far bigger and softer than his own, though it was the only piece of furniture – *and* the only object for that matter – in the big, empty room. But while Flea had felt the presence of several people in his apartment bedroom, there was only one person here now. That person stood near a large window, through which Flea saw the snow still falling heavily.

"It's about time you woke up, I thought I was going to have to wait forever. I'm really busy here, you know, I don't have time for this."

When the mystery person stepped forward, Flea saw that the young man was short, not much more than an inch or two taller than Flea himself. He also took notice to the young man's strange outfit – a combination of all black clothing and a strange red Christmas hat that hung low over his ears. But the face below that hat was the most striking part about him. For years, Flea's classmates had referred to him as strange looking (with the meaner kids calling him 'just plain ugly') due to his unusually sharp features. But the guy standing in front of him had the exact same kind of features, with only slight differences. Upon closer inspection, it was tough for Flea to tell exactly how *young* this person really was, as he carried himself with an air of importance that suggested someone much older. Either way, the young man had obviously kidnapped Flea and appeared angry.

Flea jumped out of bed and instantly took a defensive position, even though he had no idea of how to fight.

"Where did you take me? What is this place?" he demanded to know, trying – unsuccessfully – to sound tough.

The young man sighed, clearly annoyed. "This is your new bedroom here at the elf dormitory. Now please save the rest of your questions for later, I don't really have time to answer them right now."

Flea's survival instincts kicked in and he looked for anything around the room that could possibly help him escape. Unfortunately, the snowfall filled the outside world with nothing but whiteness so he had no idea where he'd been taken. Flea's eyes were drawn to the other side of the room, where he noticed that the room's door had a simple knob, one without any kind of locks. Flea hoped that if he made a break for it, he could reach the outside world and use snowballs as weapons, much as he had against the bullies from gym class. Flea had to escape and either rescue Miss Mabel – who he hoped to find imprisoned somewhere nearby – or find a phone to call the police. But he didn't want to be hasty. He needed to find out more about his captors to gauge the level of danger he was facing.

One thing the young man had said stuck out in Flea's mind.

"Did you say the elf dormitory? Is that some kind of joke?" Flea asked. "You *obviously* saw my episode of *The Great Build-Off.*"

This realization made Flea feel even worse. As Miss Mabel had suspected, his participation in the TV show *had* placed them in this dangerous situation. And if his abductor wasn't the mysterious person that Miss Mabel feared, the only other possible culprit was the construction worker that Flea had angered on the show.

"The Great Build-Off?" the young man asked. "Are you speaking about *television*? Didn't you listen to what I said earlier? I'm way *too* busy to waste my time watching TV."

For some reason, Flea actually believed him. After all, the young man didn't sound angry as much as he did annoyed and rushed.

"Then how do you know about the elf dorm?"

"Because I *live* here," the young man said slowly, as if speaking to someone that didn't quite understand his language. The confusion on Flea's face must have been easy to read. "If you don't believe me, come over here and take a look out the window. I don't know how I can make this easier to understand."

The young man walked back over to the large window and gestured for Flea to join him. Though Flea was curious to see a better view of the outside world, the fact that the young man had his back turned to him was too good an opportunity to pass up. There was probably a good chance that guards would be stationed outside the door, but that was a risk Flea had to take.

CHAPTER EIGHT
Slidewells and Hopwells

He bolted as quickly as his feet would move, nearly stumbling as he reached the door and turned the unlocked handle. Flea was relieved to find that no more captors waited outside for him. Instead, a long red-and-white striped hallway extended as far as Flea could see on both sides.

"Hey, where are you going?" the young man called out.

Expecting to be attacked from behind at any moment, Flea had no time to figure out which way to go. He turned right and began to run before the young man could grab him. The red and white stripes stretched the entire length of the hallway, the colors only interrupted by dozens of unmarked doors along the way. Everything looked so similar that it was hard for Flea to tell how far he'd run. Since all of the doors he ran past looked exactly the same, finding the one that held Miss Mabel seemed an impossible task.

"Stop!" the young man yelled behind him.

Flea quickly tired from sprinting for so long. He felt like he was getting nowhere as he continued passing the same stripes and blank doors. But just when he thought the hallway might never end, he spotted a large glass window up ahead. He passed a labeled door and some sort of open chute but continued toward the glass. He was shocked to look down into the massive lobby of what appeared to be a very fancy hotel. Confused, Flea had no time to take in the details of the lobby since the young man was quickly catching up to him.

He looked into the chute and saw that it curved up instead of down so he moved on to the labeled door. Originally, Flea had assumed that this door led to some sort of stairwell. But instead of having a tiny picture of a staircase on the door, the picture was shaped more like a spiral and was labeled 'SLIDEWELL'. Flea had no idea what that meant but with his captor dangerously close to reaching him, Flea threw open the door and ran inside.

The door opened to a view of the lobby. At that moment, Flea regretted his intense fear of heights. He barely took a step forward when he slipped and crashed down on his behind, quickly picking up speed on the slick surface of a large slide that spiraled down at a dangerously steep angle. Round and round he went, moving faster and faster. Flea might have enjoyed such a fast slide under different circumstances.

Trying to look out at the lobby, Flea barely avoided the first ice bar that jutted dangerously over the slide. He quickly lay flat, slamming his head hard against the slide in the process. He immediately felt dizzy and the spiraling slide didn't help. From that point on, Flea kept his body flat and slid beneath numerous jutting bars, passing them with greater frequency as his speed increased.

"Keep your head down!" the young man's voice echoed from above.

Flea wanted to look up to see if his captor was getting closer but he knew better, barely missing yet another ice bar. The young man obviously knew how to deal with this 'slidewell.' With a feeling of sickness growing in Flea's stomach, he knew he had to get out of the spiral slide as soon as possible. He raised his arms and grabbed the next ice bar, propelling himself off the slide and into the next hallway.

He slid down the bar and landed on his feet but was so dizzy that he tipped over while attempting to run. The world spun in front of his eyes as he stumbled along but he shook his head and regained focus. This hallway looked exactly like the last one; the same red-and-white striped walls, same unmarked doors, same total absence of other people. He needed to find help so he stopped at a random door and knocked.

"Is anyone in there? Please, I've been kidnapped and I need help," Flea yelled as he knocked over and over. When nobody answered, he pounded even harder. When he could wait no longer, he tried the handle. Like the last handle he'd turned, this one was also unlocked. Inside, the room was painted the same bright red and green as Flea's room but was not nearly as empty. Instead, it was filled with toys, and not just simple ones: it looked like someone had robbed a toy store of its best stuff and set up the ideal room for a kid Flea's age. This certainly didn't look like a normal room at a hotel, no matter how large or fancy the place might be.

"Will you stop already?" the young man called out as he followed Flea down the hallway.

Flea ran on, trying several more doors, finding each room similarly filled with awesome toys. He had no idea what kind of strange hotel/toy warehouse he had been taken to. The young man was quickly gaining on Flea, who had never in his life exerted this much energy. His captor continued yelling for him to stop, though that only served as more motivation for Flea to keep running. He eventually saw another glass window ahead and looked through it long enough to see that he'd circled around the huge lobby again and ended up on the other side.

"You're really annoying me," the young man yelled. Unfortunately for Flea, his captor was not running out of breath. But he immediately realized that yelling threats was not the best way to make someone stop running. "No, wait, I'm sorry, I – "

Flea opened the nearest door expecting another 'slidewell' but found himself standing on a small platform, still several stories above the ground floor. He looked back at the closing door to see a picture of a trampoline on this one, as well as the label 'HOPWELL'. Again, Flea's fear of heights made it difficult for him to look over the edge of the platform but the sound of approaching footsteps gave him the courage he needed. Ten feet below, Flea saw a large trampoline. It wasn't exactly the most welcoming sight, but it was better than being caught. Flea took a deep breath before plunging off the platform. He landed on the center of the trampoline and immediately realized that it was tilted slightly forward. He struck the springy object and bounced up and forward, his body twisting in the air as he plunged toward the next trampoline another ten feet down. The trampolines were set up like a staircase – a bouncy staircase that flung his body uncontrollably toward the next 'step.'

Flea wished that he'd stuck with the 'slidewell.' After striking the second trampoline and being shot forward again, he was so off balance that his body completely flipped on the way down to the third step. As Flea completed his forward rotation, he spotted a blurry movement traveling *up* toward him. Flea worried that his captor had somehow gotten to the ground floor already and was now working his way up the 'hopwell' to catch him. Considering that Flea was so out of control, being caught by the young man might not be such a bad thing. But when he caught a quick view of this person's face, he knew right away that it wasn't the young man. This person was far older, though this old man *did* appear just as angry as the young man, not to mention his similarly sharp facial features.

"Watch where you're going," the old man yelled at Flea. Somehow the two narrowly avoided colliding, though that was because the old man had enough control to get out of Flea's way. "This hopwell is for going up *only*."

"Please, you have to help me," Flea called out to the old man though the two had already passed one another.

Flea continued bouncing end-over-end on his way down, yet he still heard the young man's voice call out from above.

"Sorry, Vork, he's very confused, he's not listening to me."

"You should do as he says, Flea," the older man – Vork – called out.

Obviously, the young man had at least one accomplice with the kidnapping and Flea suspected even more. As the world spun in front of Flea's eyes, he could tell that he was getting closer to the ground floor. He hit the last trampoline and was tossed five feet back into the air before finally crashing down on the hard ground, knocking the wind from his lungs. He rolled onto his back and tried to catch his breath. When he looked up at the 'hopwell' he saw that the young man was only two trampolines above him. *I don't have time to worry about breathing,* he thought as he got up and began to stumble away.

Now that Flea stood inside the lobby, it appeared even more cavernous than he'd first thought. In fact, considering that there was a roller coaster nearby – and a full-size one at that, complete with a track made out of ice and several loop-dee-loops – Flea wondered if this place was more like an indoor amusement park than a hotel lobby. No one seemed to be riding the coaster at the moment, though the empty cars continued to circle around and around the track. A few other smaller rides along with countless games were scattered about and Flea felt his mind going into sensory overload. He struggled to figure out where he was and why there weren't more people around this incredible room. In the distance, he spotted the snowy white light of the outside world and knew that he had to reach those glass exit doors.

As if the amusement-type atmosphere wasn't strange enough, the piles of wood and building materials scattered about the room were just as baffling. Flea ran as fast as his tired legs and empty lungs would let him. Since the young man had landed perfectly on his feet behind him, Flea considered grabbing a hammer from a pile of nearby tools in order to defend himself. But he could never hurt someone like that, not even someone who'd kidnapped him. Besides, he formulated a better escape plan upon spotting one of the other amusement rides.

A small, yet fast-moving train circled the entire lobby on icy tracks and was about to pass Flea on its way back toward the lobby's exit. The sight of the approaching train gave him the quick burst of energy he needed to leap over the railing that guarded the icy tracks. Unfortunately, he stumbled over a small stack of building supplies. Most of the train-cars passed by and the young man made up even more ground.

Just as the final train-car sped next to him, Flea squeezed the last bit of energy from his tiring legs and dived for the train's back railing. He breathed a sigh of relief when he grabbed hold. He started to pull himself onto the train, but his grip was nearly ripped free by a sudden heavy tugging at his legs. When he looked back to see the young man gripping his legs tightly, Flea knew that it was only a matter of time before the weight of them both was too much to hold.

"What are you doing? You don't understand, you have nothing to fear," the young man yelled as his body was dragged along the icy railroad track. "Just let go so we can talk about – "

But Flea didn't let him finish. He wriggled one of his legs free from the grip and placed his foot against the young man's face, thus interrupting his plea for Flea to stop running. The young man was very strong and continued to hold on until Flea pushed with all his might. Flea's captor rolled end over end along the icy track, cursing Flea the entire time.

Once free of the extra weight, Flea quickly pulled himself up and over the railing. He looked back in time to see the young man jump back to his feet and begin running after the train. It was clear that the train moved too quickly for him to catch and Flea felt momentary relieved knowing that he would reach the doors to the outside world in a matter of seconds. The young man suddenly stopped near a pile of building materials, but Flea soon learned that his captor was far from giving up.

Although Flea had not watched much television in his life, he saw plenty of cartoon fights between cats and dogs, which usually looked like a big cloud of dust with the occasional arm or leg sticking out. That description was exactly how the young man looked once he approached the pile of wood, nails and tools. Flea was amazed by the frenzy of building activity as the young man moved in a blur.

That must be what I look like when I build things, Flea thought. For the first time since waking up, Flea wondered if the young man wasn't who he seemed to be, if there *was* some sort of connection the two had in regards to their amazing ability to build. *But why would he kidnap me unless he wanted to hurt me?*

Flea's view of the young man lasted only seconds until the train sped out of sight. But moments later, he spotted another blur of movement, this one rapidly approaching the back of the train. Flea was shocked to see the young man speeding toward him, riding a wooden bike. The young man pedaled furiously and it became obvious to Flea that he would catch the train very soon. Flea looked ahead of the train and saw that it wouldn't be long until he reached the lobby's exit, but he was certain that the young man would catch the train in time.

At least the *back* part of the train.

With his captor just seconds away, Flea turned and climbed atop the oversized toy train, scrambling his way across the different cars. Flea felt far less steady now and knew that one tiny slip would send him toppling off the side of the train, which seemed like it was moving much faster than he first thought. He risked a glance back and saw the young man jump expertly onto the train; his newly built bike veered off and crashed into the protective fence, shattering the wood into thousands of tiny splinters. The young man jumped on top of the train and ran toward him without fear, jumping from one train-car to the next with graceful ease. In turn, Flea picked up his own speed. It wasn't long until he reached the front of the train and there was no place left to hide.

"Don't do anything stupid!" the young man yelled from just a few feet back.

The train approached the exit doors. Flea didn't know how to make the train stop; he didn't even know if it *could* stop. While jumping was an unpleasant thought, it was the only way he could get off. He spotted a candy cane-shaped light-post just beside the track and hoped it would provide an easier way to reach the ground. However, reaching the light-post was not going to be easy.

"Leave me alone!" Flea yelled back.

Before the kidnapper could close the gap between them, Flea leaped off the train. Right away, he realized that he'd misjudged the distance to the post, that he was going to come up well short. He knew his fall to the ground could possibly prove deadly but as soon as that fear kicked in, Flea felt a strange warmth from his ringed hand. A bright golden light suddenly shined and a strong wind pushed Flea forward and higher into the air, just enough for him to grab the top of the light-post and slide safely to the floor. He had no idea how he'd gotten so lucky – or if it was *more* than luck that helped him – but he glanced back in time to see that the young man had no such luck.

The kidnapper also jumped toward the huge candy-cane post but did not reach it, crashing down to the ground. Although the young man fell, he was even graceful in that movement and rolled several times to ease the brunt of the fall. Still, he was very slow to get up and though Flea felt bad for him, he did not hang around long enough to check on him. Instead, he threw open the lobby doors and ran into the outside world.

The first thing he noticed was snow, as several feet already covered the ground while plenty more fell from above. Strangely, Flea felt less cold on his skin than usual; it seemed more like room temperature out here than freezing. But he barely gave that a second thought. He was too focused on finding someone who could help him, or at least figuring out exactly where he was. Unfortunately, there was too much snow on the ground to figure out which street –

Wait, there are *no streets out here*, Flea quickly realized. Through the heavy sheets of falling snow, he saw numerous buildings – some of them huge, some of them smaller – spread out across the land. His rapidly beating heart seemed to come to a complete stop. Flea had never exactly been *here* before, yet he still recognized every single one of the buildings, especially the icy structure closest to the hotel.

It's not *a hotel,* Flea thought, knowing that his kidnapper had told him at least one thing that wasn't a lie. *It's a dormitory.*

Though Flea had already constructed the ice bank on TV, seeing the full-sized building just across the way caused his feet to skid to a halt. Flea was too shocked to keep running and there was no place for him to go anyway. Instead, he stood a few feet outside of the dormitory and stared in awe at his surroundings, not budging even when he heard the doors opening. The young man crunched in the snow behind Flea and when he spoke, he was out of breath, his words mixed with irritation and pain.

"I was hoping this introduction would be much easier," the young man said. "But welcome to the North Pole."

CHAPTER NINE
An Elf's New Home

Flea was too shocked to do much of anything but follow orders from the annoyed young man, who introduced himself as Niko.

"I still don't understand," Flea said slowly, his mind barely working. "Why am I here?"

"Isn't that obvious?" Niko answered, his voice oozing with condescension. "It's because you're an elf."

"An *elf*?" Flea asked. He could hardly believe he said that word, though it didn't seem like such nonsense when he considered what he'd just seen. "Well, where are all the other elves then?"

"Are you *kidding* me? Our busy season just started, the rest of the elves have *much* more important things to do then hang around the dorm," Niko said. "You should thank your lucky snowflakes that nobody was here to witness that little stunt of yours on the train. That was really stupid."

Although Flea had ten questions for every answer that Niko told him, he somehow knew exactly what he'd meant by 'that little stunt.' Flea glanced down at his ringed hand and still saw a slightly golden glow.

"Here, you're going to want to cover that hand at all times," Niko said, tossing Flea a glove.

"I don't know how that happened, the wind that is," Flea said. He tried to remove the gold ring from his finger but it wouldn't budge. It was as if the ring had become part of his skin. "I can't get it to come off."

"And that's exactly why I gave you the *glove*," Niko said. He shook his head, clearly annoyed, so Flea finally pulled the glove over his hand. "If the other elves saw your hand glowing, they'd probably be frightened of you – more so than they probably will be anyway."

"But I still don't understand why I'm here in the first place," Flea said. "This doesn't make any sense."

Niko sighed angrily and stopped walking. He turned to face Flea, looking very threatening as he did so.

"I'm only going to ask you these questions once and then I don't ever want to hear you question your heritage again. Do you understand?"

Flea nodded his head.

"Are you bothered by the cold weather?"

"No."

"Have you ever noticed that you have strange abilities when it comes to the snow and ice?"

"Yes, just recently I – "

"Are you good with your hands, more so than any other skill you might have?" Niko asked.

"Yeah, I'm *really* good at building things."

"And did anyone need to teach you *how* to build things?"

"No."

"Sounds like an elf to me," Niko said. He turned and continued walking to the heart of the lobby as Flea rushed to catch up. "Now please, no more dumb questions about whether or not you're an elf. Only a fool would question it further at this point, especially after seeing all of this around you."

Niko began to walk again, picking up his pace so that Flea had to jog just to keep up.

"Where are we going?"

"Back to your room," Niko said. "There's one order of business we have to take care of before you can leave the dorm. It would've been much easier – and far less *time-consuming* – if you'd just listened to me in the first place and didn't run all the way down here."

Flea's mind raced with countless questions about the existence of the North Pole and elves but decided not to push his luck. Instead, he tried to take in every detail of this amazing lobby. He wasn't quite sure how life as an elf would be – or if that was even the reason he'd been brought here – but Flea hoped to have some free time to spend in this lobby at some point. He'd never been to an amusement park before so having one to himself would be really cool. They quickly approached a part of the lobby that Flea wanted *nothing* to do with, though, especially considering what had happened the first time. He remembered the old man – *the old* elf, Flea reminded himself – saying that the 'hopwell' was used for going up. When he looked around the lobby, Flea saw no signs of a conventional elevator.

"You're going to have to show me a better way to use that thing," Flea said as they approached the staggered tower of trampolines. But Niko walked right past it, giving Flea hope that there would be a much less frightening way to reach his floor.

"We already wasted way too much time with our little *run* earlier," Niko said. "Like I said, I'm a very busy elf and I have a lot to do so we have to take the quicker way to the dorm's upper levels."

"So I guess you're some kind of toy-maker then? The way you made the bike from that stack of wood was pretty incredible," Flea said.

"If you're asking whether I'm a factory elf then the answer is *no*," Niko said. "Obviously, I'm a very good builder and if that was my full-time job then there's no doubt in my mind that I'd be top-of-the-tree level. But I was put in charge of a more important North Pole duty years ago."

"And what duty is that?" Flea asked.

"*That duty* is something *you* don't need to know about," Niko said bluntly. "Just remember that you're new here and my important business is not for the ears of bottom-of-the-tree level elves, let alone someone on no level at all."

Flea knew he shouldn't pester Niko with any more questions at the moment but they were quickly approaching a part of the lobby that held little else besides the icy roller coaster. Flea watched the coaster's train-cars go around several loops, which made his stomach sink.

"We aren't going to have to ride that, are we?" Flea asked. "Because I don't really like heights."

Niko muttered to himself and shook his head angrily, as if this had been the worst possible thing Flea could've said.

"Don't worry, we aren't going on the coaster, you have nothing to be afraid of," Niko said. For the first time, his voice softened with reassurance, though Flea knew fakeness when he heard it. "Actually, we'll be using *that* to travel to your floor."

In the corner was a large, black metal tube that reminded Flea of an oversized canon. The feeling of dread remained in his stomach at the sight of this huge tube but Niko walked straight into the tube's opening. Flea relaxed about the possible danger. He only hesitated a moment before entering, feeling much better upon seeing a row of lights lining the tube's inner wall. Flea wondered if the tube led to some kind of elevator system but quickly saw that it didn't. Instead, there were two seats at the back, the sight of which started Flea's stomach doing back-flips again. He suddenly had the feeling that the 'hopwell' would've been the better travel option.

"What is this thing?" Flea asked.

Niko sat down in one of the chairs and patted the other one next to him. Flea wanted to turn and run from this tube but his feet brought him forward and he sat down.

"Is there some kind of seatbelt on this thing?" he asked.

"That would sort of defeat the purpose, don't you think?" Niko asked. This time, the lighter tone to Niko's voice sounded genuine.

"Defeat the purpose of what?" Flea asked.

Niko lifted his hand and pressed his palm against a small square plate on the side of the tube. He told Flea to do the same, which Flea did against his better judgement. He heard a sudden *whirring* sound from behind his seat as the tube began to turn and tilt back. Once the *whirring* and movement stopped, the next sound was that of a metal coil being tightly wound. Even if Flea wanted to escape from the tube at this point, the sheer gravity of being pressed against the back of his seat would've stopped him. The new voice that spoke had a mechanical tone, which Flea understood to be a computer. What he *didn't* understand was the meaning of its words.

"The spring is ready."

Before Flea could ask, a large hologram appeared before his very eyes, a number '5' floating in the air in front of him. The holographic number soon changed to a '4' followed by a '3'.

"What is it counting down to?" Flea asked, panic filling his voice.

Niko merely chuckled in response, as he was clearly intent on letting Flea find that out for himself. Once the '1' faded away, Flea got his answer.

The spring released behind them and shot their chairs forward so quickly that Flea would've missed the trip through the tube had his eyes been able to blink. Flea was soaring through the air before he knew it, his body no longer attached to the seat that shot him out of the tube. Flea screamed in fear, his mind unable to process any words or thoughts at the moment as the two soared directly toward the speeding roller coaster. It looked like they might crash right into one of the track's loop-dee-loops but their flight through the air slowed just enough for Flea and Niko to pass perfectly through the center of the loop. Although that was one potential obstacle out of the way, Flea still zoomed straight toward the lobby wall.

Seconds before impact, two small holes appeared in the wall and they each soared perfectly into one of them. Flea was unaware that he was still screaming until he heard the sound of his voice echoing inside the narrow tunnel he now slid through. Before he could figure out what had happened, Flea's slide came to an abrupt end as he passed through a chute and tumbled clumsily onto the floor of a white-and-red striped hallway. He turned around just in time to see Niko emerge from the chute, though the elf landed perfectly on his feet. Flea's heart still pounded wildly. His head spun and he was in no condition to stand just yet. Niko, however, was not very sympathetic.

"There's no time for resting," the elf said. "How many times do I have to remind you that I'm in a rush?"

Niko took Flea by the arm and helped him to his feet. Flea's legs felt like rubber for his first few steps but Niko obviously didn't care as he continued walking quickly down the hallway. Flea's mind was still loopy but one thing about the hallway doors made even less sense to him now than when he'd first noticed.

"How can the elves tell the difference between rooms if they aren't numbered?" he asked as they walked past countless unmarked doors.

"They just *know*," Niko said. "Finding your room isn't rocket science."

Had Flea known there was no way to really tell, he would've started counting the doors the moment he stumbled out of the chute, even though his brain still rattled in his head and made *simple thinking* difficult let alone counting. As Flea passed each door, he listened for any sign of life, hoping that his quiet room might be easier to identify if it was the only one without noise. But the only thing he heard was his own pounding heart and Niko's footsteps.

"Where are the rest of the elves?" Flea asked. "This dorm seems way too big to have nobody else living here."

"Believe me, you'll wish this place were much bigger when the others are around, especially since you live on one of the highest floors. This is where we house some of the more… interesting characters," Niko said. "But the reason it's so quiet now is because one way or another, *all* of the elves are getting ready for Christmas."

This didn't make sense to Flea since he remembered one of the final things he'd seen in his bedroom before passing out.

"But it was 11:59 when I fell asleep and came here…or when you took me here. Actually, how did I get here?" Flea asked. Niko kept walking quickly and seemed in no hurry to discuss the kidnapping so Flea focused on his original line of questioning. "Are you already planning for *next* Christmas?"

"Time doesn't really work the same way at the North Pole as it does in your world, at least not on Christmas Eve. The night before the big holiday, certain… steps are taken to ensure that we have plenty of time to finish preparations," Niko explained.

"Steps? You mean like stopping time or something?" Flea asked. That idea would have seemed ridiculous to him a few hours earlier but Flea was quickly learning that *nothing* around here was impossible.

"Stopping time is impossible," Niko said. But before he explained any further, he stopped in front of a door that looked exactly like all the others. "Now enough with the questions, I'm sure you'll learn plenty when you go to school."

"School?" Flea asked.

Once again, he thought back to the buildings he'd created on *The Great Build-Off* and recalled one of the bigger ones near the back of the North Pole.

"Did you *really* think you would be given a free pass into the toy factory because of the limited amount of building you did in shop class?" Niko laughed, making Flea feel so stupid that he could think of no response. "Now I need you to go into your room and change into proper elf attire. But hurry up, you don't want to be late on your first day, do you?"

"And you're sure this is *my* room?" Flea asked when his hand touched the handle. He still had no idea how Niko could tell the difference and Flea didn't want to intrude on anyone else's personal space.

Niko sighed and opened the door to the empty room. After having seen the other rooms filled with toys, Flea felt sure that this empty room was indeed his. Niko closed the door and waited in the hallway while Flea looked around the empty room for his elf outfit. He was just about to ask Niko where to find his new clothes when he spotted a closet on the far side of the room. When he opened the closet door, Flea saw a single outfit on a hangar. He was shocked by what the clothes looked like. He took the hangar off the rack and laid the clothes – as well as the shoes – on his bed. Flea shook his head and walked back toward the door.

"Are you sure I can't wear what I already have on?" he called out.

"Do you *really* want to stick out like a sore thumb?" Niko answered from the other side of the closed door.

Having worn mismatched, second-hand clothes his entire life, Flea knew a thing or two about 'sticking out' on his first day. He hoped that wearing these clothes would help him fit in better so he quickly changed into them, shaking his head with every new piece of elf clothing that he put on.

CHAPTER TEN

Snowmen Problems

Flea felt ridiculous when he and Niko walked back outside. The snowfall had lightened enough for him to view more of the North Pole, though he still saw no other elves out and about. Although he was interested to meet some of the others, Flea wasn't exactly looking forward to anyone seeing him dressed like this, even though Niko promised it was the standard elf apparel.

I wonder if everyone else feels so itchy wearing this junk, Flea thought. The inside of his closet had contained a mirror, but Flea tried to forget the image of himself wearing this outfit. The ensemble consisted of a big green jacket over a white puffy shirt, bulging green shorts with high golden socks and silver shoes with curled tips and jangly silver balls at the end. It was all topped off with a large red Christmas hat that nearly hung over his entire face.

"Are you sure I don't remind you of a leprechaun?" Flea asked as he pulled up his golden socks for the tenth time.

"I've met plenty of leprechauns," Niko said. "Believe me, they dress *nothing* like that."

Flea was about to ask more about leprechauns, but he noticed a smile on Niko's face and figured he was joking. Unfortunately, Flea wasn't sure exactly *what* Niko was joking about. Despite snow soaking through the cloth-made shoes, Flea was able to enjoy his surroundings as they walked toward several of the life-sized buildings that he'd built in a smaller scale. The first was the ice bank, more beautiful in person than he could have imagined. Sunlight broke through the clouds as they walked past, causing light to reflect off the icy structure. Flea felt unusually drawn toward the building but when he wandered too close to it, a surge of snow rushed up from the ground and formed several snowmen guards.

"What's kept inside there?" Flea asked upon seeing the high level of protection around the building.

"That's information that *you* have no reason to know," Niko said. "Very few elves know about it. There are plenty who've been here for years and years that aren't privileged to such important North Pole secrets. You make sure you stay *far away* from that ice bank at all times. I promise you, there'll be serious trouble for you if you try to get near it."

Flea sensed the familiar feeling of being watched and he spotted one of the ice-bank snowmen looking at him with its strange green eyes.

"I know that snowman, or at least one just like it," Flea said excitedly as they walked beyond the bank. But before Niko could look, all of the snowmen dissolved back into the ground. "Was I being watched during the last couple weeks? I think I saw some of those snowmen outside my apartment."

"How should I know?" Niko asked, the angry tone returning to his voice. "Santa Claus doesn't tell me everything he sets up."

Flea couldn't believe that he'd been at the North Pole this long and hadn't even thought about Santa until now. The man in the big red suit was yet another topic about which Flea had so many questions. But he didn't get the chance to ask a single one before movement in the distance distracted him. He felt the slightest rumble beneath his feet as a huge rolling snowball quickly approached. Flea had no idea where the snowball came from but it was headed straight for them. He reacted accordingly.

"Watch out!" Flea yelled as he dived to the snowy ground. His huge hat nearly fell off and snow poured into his big green jacket in the process, but Flea preferred this to being crushed by a runaway snowball. When he looked up from the ground, he saw that Niko hadn't moved and was staring down at him with confusion.

"What are you *doing*?" Niko said, shaking his head.

The snowball slowed and came to a stop a few feet in front of Niko. Flea watched in amazement as the large snowball slowly separated into three different balls – each progressively smaller than the last – and proceeded to stack themselves atop one another. Two eyes, a nose and a mouth formed on the top snowball and Flea found himself staring into the face of yet another snowman, this one with a distinctly different look from the ice-bank ones.

"Did you trip?" the snowman asked, its voice low, slow and a bit dopey-sounding.

Flea hadn't even realized he was still sprawled on the ground, so he promptly jumped back to his feet.

"You can *actually* talk?" Flea asked.

A talking snowman was added to Flea's ever-expanding list of things he never expected to see in life. The snowman's eyebrows indented and turned downward and a frown formed on his face. Flea had clearly offended it.

"I'm the one with snow for brains but you're wearing *that*?" the snowman asked. "You must be new here."

"How did you –"

"Was there something you needed?" Niko asked, interrupting Flea's conversation with the snowman.

The snowman turned toward the larger elf but now appeared confused.

"I'm having trouble remembering but I think… yes, I think there *was* something," the snowman said, its words coming out at a snail's pace even though its brain seemed to move even slower. "Oh yeah, I remember that it was something important, too."

In the short time Flea had come to know Niko, he'd realized that the elf was short on patience and easily annoyed – at least that was how he'd acted toward Flea and his never-ending supply of questions. Flea expected Niko to explode on the simple-minded snowman but was therefore surprised when Niko smiled and spoke calmly to the snowy messenger.

"Well I told you to come and find me if there was a problem," Niko said softly. "*Is* there a problem?"

The snowman's brow remained scrunched up in confusion for several seconds until it finally relaxed and smiled.

"Yes, there is a problem," the snowman answered. He paused just long enough for Flea to doubt whether the snowman remembered exactly what the problem was but he finally continued. "There's been movement on the border since you've been gone."

"*Forward* movement? Like movement beyond the red line?" Niko asked.

"I wouldn't have rushed to find you if they'd gone *back*," the snowman said. "I'm not that dumb."

"I'm sorry for doubting you, I just don't understand how they could've moved beyond the red line," Niko said. For once, Flea heard fear in Niko's voice and wished he knew what the elf and the snowman were talking about. "I need to see this right away."

The snowman transformed back into a single large ball and rolled off in the direction he'd come from. Niko began to run behind him but stopped when he realized he wasn't alone.

"Well don't just stand there," Niko barked angrily at Flea. "Let's go!"

Flea ran after them, quickly falling behind since his shoes were terrible for running. The two silver balls *jingled* and *jangled* loudly with every step he took. They ran in a different direction from the school, instead heading to the huge building that Flea remembered as the toy factory. He looked up to see a huge clock face, its hands stopped just before twelve. *It's like they're stuck on 11:59,* Flea thought. *The clock must be broken.* When they got closer to the factory, Flea tried to look through the large glass doors but saw very little except for bright colors and a few flashes of movement. He only needed this brief glance to understand that the factory was the center of the North Pole's main activity.

They finally reached a tiny building on the outskirts of the village. It was the first place that was truly a mystery to Flea, as this building hadn't been part of the North Pole display he'd built on TV. The snowman entered the guarded doors and Niko began to follow before he stopped and turned to Flea.

"I need you to wait out here for a few minutes, I'll be right back," Niko ordered. "*Don't* wander off."

"Why can't I come inside with you?" Flea asked. The two large snowmen guarding the entrance made Flea feel uncomfortable. Plus, he felt a slight chill the farther away he got from the rest of the North Pole. "What is this building? I don't recognize it."

"Secrecy is necessary to deal with North Pole security so I'm not going to answer that," Niko said before turning to the pair of guards. "Whatever you do, don't let him leave the North Pole border."

"Yes, sir," the guards answered in unison.

For several minutes, Flea waited outside the security building, staring in awe at his surroundings from another point of view. He had a moment to reflect on the crazy things that had happened to him today and with those thoughts came so many new questions. Impatience had never been a problem for him before now but that was probably because he never had anything exciting happen to him. When Flea could no longer stare at the village in front of him, he looked at the barren landscape beyond the security building. There was nothing out there but empty, snowy land. He felt a cool breeze blowing from that direction and had a bad feeling about what lay beyond the North Pole's borders. Something had obviously worried Niko and Flea would've bet that whatever 'problem' Niko had been warned about came from somewhere out there. Flea took a step in that direction but felt a sudden warmth from his ringed hand. When he looked down, he saw a faint golden glow coming from underneath the red glove he wore.

A warning, Flea somehow knew.

"Sir, please do not walk any farther in that direction," said one of the snowman guards.

Flea wasn't so stupid that he'd head off and look for trouble so he felt annoyed that Niko had ordered these guards to baby-sit him. The glowing ring worried him and he wanted to tell Niko, he didn't want to stand around and wait any longer. Flea approached the entrance and tried to summon the strength he needed to sound threatening.

"I need to go inside," he said, his attempt at firmness sounding audibly weak. Flea knew the snowmen weren't likely to step aside because they feared him so he hoped that they would listen to reason. "I have something important I – "

"Yes, sir," the guards said in unison, sliding apart to let Flea through.

Flea tried to hide his surprise as he rushed through the entrance before the guards could change their minds. Just inside the door was a small hallway that Flea followed to the end. He saw a bluish light shining and heard Niko's distinctively angry voice.

"I guess it's a good thing that *he* didn't stay with the rest of them for too long but I still don't understand how this can be happening," Niko said, a twinge of fear mixed in with his frustration. "The Army has been moving at the same slow, steady pace for years, now suddenly they're able to take this giant leap forward? It just doesn't make sense."

"They began to move a few hours ago, not too long after you left to go on the secret mission with – "

Niko angrily interrupted the slow-speaking snowman, who'd apparently shed some sort of light on the mystery.

"It's the *kid*," Niko said with certainty. Flea felt his stomach turn as *he* was apparently the 'kid' to which Niko was referring. "I *knew* he never should have been brought here. How can Santa expect me to successfully manage North Pole security if he's not going to take my advice about such important matters?"

Although Niko apparently hated him, Flea still felt guilty about eavesdropping and decided now was the time to tell him about his glowing ring. Flea walked into the room ready to warn Niko but found the elf and the snowman turned away from him. The moment Flea saw what the two were looking at, he completely forgot what he was going to say. Against the far wall was a massive holographic image that reminded Flea of a futuristic video game. But he quickly realized it was some sort of map, one that showed rows upon rows of snowmen lined up in perfect battle formation. It was clear that these snowmen were nothing like the two kinds that Flea had already encountered here at the North Pole.

These battle snowmen were clad in armor made of sticks, were armed with sharp icicle-weapons and had bright red eyes that Flea recognized as evil. A red holographic line made up some sort of boundary but several rows of snowmen in the front were well beyond the red line, which was apparently Niko's main cause for concern. But the snowmen weren't alone in making up this massive Army. Pacing back and forth in front of the first row of snowmen was a huge white creature.

The creature was some sort of animal yet it managed to walk on two feet, which appeared quite unnatural. Just at that moment, the animal – which was clearly the leader – pointed to one of the snowmen in the front row and waved it forward. Flea watched as the snowman nervously shuffled forward. The holographic map had no sound but Flea could see that the animal yelled for the snowman to continue forward. The Army snowman followed orders, but once it proceeded a few feet beyond the animal, it suddenly disintegrated into a puff of snowy fog.

Niko's slow-speaking snowman shivered.

"At least they can't pass our borders," the snowman said. "The Army is still a long way off from putting us in danger."

But Niko was not satisfied.

"It should've been *months* until the Army could cross that red line," the elf said. "This is not good, not good at all."

Flea couldn't stay silent any longer.

"How did that snowman just explode like that?" he asked.

Although Niko's snowman might have been slow when it came to talking or thinking, he *wasn't* slow when it came to reacting. In a split second, he stepped defensively in front of Niko, sharp icy edges forming at the ends of his arms. Niko was also surprised to see Flea standing there. He immediately waved his hand through the hologram and made it disappear.

"Who are you and what are you doing here?" the snowman asked, his voice still slow but somehow more menacing than humorous this time.

"It's okay, remember you just met him outside with me?" Niko asked. "Flea is the new elf at the North Pole."

The security snowman relaxed, its sharp-edged arms turning back to their normal stubs. "Oh yeah, the one with the clothes. What do the others think of him?"

"Most don't know yet," Niko said. "Wait here, I'll be back soon."

Niko grabbed Flea by the elbow and guided him out of the building.

"How did you get inside?" Niko asked but he didn't wait for an answer before continuing to complain. "Never mind, I don't know and I don't care. I have more important things to worry about. You need to do something that'll keep you busy and out of trouble. You aren't going to be any trouble for me, are you?"

"No, I don't – "

"Good, because you've been enough trouble already," Niko said. "And whatever you might have overheard back there, *don't* bother asking me any questions about it."

Niko intended to get rid of Flea by dropping him off at the school, which was where they were quickly headed. As Flea approached the big building, his stomach churned as it did every time he was about to start a new school yet again.

"Great, another new school," he muttered to himself. If Niko heard what Flea said, he didn't mention it. Flea never got used to entering a new school, but for the first time that he could remember, his usual emotional soup of fear and anxiety also had a dash of hope mixed in with it. Flea didn't know exactly what went on inside this elf school but there was a chance that he might actually fit in for once, something he never thought would happen.

"Think you can make it the rest of the way or do I need to hold your hand through *everything*?" Niko asked. "Look, I have way too much to do. The elves are getting their orders and now I have this new security issue to deal with. I don't know what you think you saw back there but if you know what's good for you, you won't say a word about it to *anyone*. Believe me, your appearance at the North Pole will already be enough to worry some of the elves, you don't want to give them anything else to be concerned about."

Niko sure had a way of sucking the hope right out of Flea, who suddenly doubted all the positive feelings he'd just been experiencing. Niko turned and began to march away when Flea realized that there was still so much he needed to find out before entering the school.

"But I don't know where to go," Flea said.

"It's the first door, that shouldn't be hard, even for someone like *you*," Niko said.

"What about books or school supplies?" Flea called out as Niko got farther away. "I don't have *any* of that stuff."

"You won't need them!" Niko said.

Once on his own, Flea walked the rest of the way to the school, pausing in front of the doors, taking his traditional deep breath before entering the unknown. He expected to see more brightness like the elf dormitory and activity like the factory, but when he opened the doors, Flea discovered that he was wrong on both accounts.

CHAPTER ELEVEN
Back to School

Inside, the school was rundown. Dark and dirty and dusty, the place looked like it hadn't been used in many years. Dozens of broken and poorly-made toys were strewn about the hallway, the sight of which gave Flea the creeps. He was tempted to turn around and head out of the doors, to call out to Niko that there was a problem, but the elf was already too far away and wasn't likely to have much sympathy – or answers – for Flea. Instead, Flea carefully tiptoed around the old toys (afraid that they might come to life and attack him at any moment) and entered the first door he came across. The classroom was dark and empty but Flea found the light-switch just inside the door and flipped it on. A string of red and green Christmas tree lights ran along the ceiling like track lighting and illuminated the room with a crimson haze.

Unlike every other classroom Flea had ever seen, this one didn't have any blackboards or paper or desks. Several large tables were scattered haphazardly around the room, with partially-built toys littering every surface. But the strangest part was the lack of any other people – *make that any other elves,* Flea thought – which made Flea feel like he might be in some sort of trouble. Flea hoped he simply had the wrong room but before he had the chance to walk out and search the surrounding classrooms, the door opened and a small elf entered.

"Have you learned not to hop *down* the hopwell yet?" the elf asked.

Flea recognized the condescending voice, not to mention the elf's face. While Flea hadn't been able to gauge Niko's age, it was clear that this particular elf was *old*. The elderly elf had the same sharp features as Flea and Niko but that was the end of the similarities. The rest of his face was covered with wrinkles and there was a small patch of white hair atop his head. His glasses were extra thick and he seemed so frail that Flea was shocked that the old elf used the 'hopwell.'

"Your name is Vork, right?" Flea asked, remembering the name Niko called out earlier.

"If I am going to be your teacher, then you will call me *Mister* Vork," the old elf said. "Doesn't anyone have manners anymore?"

Vork was apparently just as cranky as Niko, though a smile appeared on his face for the briefest of moments.

"I see that you're wearing the traditional elf-in-training attire," Vork said. "It's a very *subtle* way of showing that you're new to the North Pole."

Vork wore similar black clothing to Niko's, though he didn't wear a large red Christmas hat like the younger elf. The sight of yet another elf dressed differently from him made Flea nervous, especially considering how ridiculous he looked.

"Niko told me that *all* elves wore this kind of outfit. Why aren't you?" Flea asked suspiciously.

"Fashion is for the young, I'm old and prefer a more boring style," Vork said. He looked toward the door and then at the clock hanging just above it, which read 11:59. "I know it's been years since I last taught but elves in my day were more respectful about showing up on time." The old elf sighed. "Well, I'm guessing that you have lots of general questions about the North Pole so you might as well waste my time and ask away before the others show up."

Vork seemed just as annoyed by Flea's mere presence as Niko had been.

"Why don't you like me?" Flea asked.

"Of all the North Pole's amazing mysteries and wonders, *that's* the idiotic question you choose to ask?" Vork asked, slowly shaking his head. "Fine, you'll get your answer. You are *new* and you are *different*, two qualities that most elves don't like in others. I don't exactly know if that's fair but that's just how it is so you better get used to it."

Maybe this school won't be that different from the others, Flea thought with disappointment.

"Then why was I even brought here?" he asked.

"You *are* an elf, that much is obvious, so you *belong* at the North Pole...at least that's what someone very important here seems to think," Vork said. "Plus, your line of products is already in high demand for this Christmas season."

"*My* line of products?" Flea asked.

"For someone with very limited time to ask questions, you sure are missing the big picture," Vork said.

Flea knew he was right and quickly focused on the most important things he'd been wondering about.

"Fine, tell me how Christmas hasn't already past. Niko explained that time is slowed down everywhere across the world except the North Pole."

"*And* the South Pole," Vork quickly interceded. "The South Pole experiences the same time slowdown that we do. You must never forget the importance of balance on Earth."

"Okay, balance, that's great, but *how* is time slowed down?" Flea wanted to know.

"That information is known only by Santa Claus and a few of the most elderly and important elves – neither of which *you* happen to be," Vork said. "For now, you can know exactly what the rest of the elves know: Santa leaves at 11:58 aboard his sleigh and returns at 11:59, at which point the world's time has officially slowed."

"Why wait until the last minute to complete all of the work?" Flea asked. "Why not start months earlier to give yourselves plenty of time to finish?"

"If you've been asking such foolish questions all day, then I understand why Niko became so frustrated with you," Vork said. "Sometimes a little bit of thought can go a long way. The answer to that question is quite obvious."

Flea pleaded with his brain to come up with an answer but the harder he thought, the fewer possibilities came to mind. Niko and Vork were obviously highly intelligent and left Flea suddenly nervous that he would be the dumbest elf at the North Pole, a *third* quality that would give others reason to dislike him.

"I'm sorry, I can't think of – "

"*Lists,*" Vork said angrily. "We need to wait until the very last minute to make sure that both of our lists are finalized."

"Both?"

"Wishlists and the Naughty/Nice list," Vork explained. "If a child changes what he or she wants at the last minute, we have to be ready to make him or her happy on Christmas morning. And consequently, we need to have an updated naughty list to determine how much coal we need."

"Where do those lists come from?"

"From the Deet-Deets of course," Vork said, as if this was common knowledge to anyone not a total fool.

"Did I hear you right? Did you say *Deet-Deets*?"

"I guess you might know them better as Christmas decorations," Vork explained. "Most parents put them around their house and think they're getting into the holiday spirit. But what they don't know – and more importantly, what the *kids* don't know – is that the Deet-Deets are watching over them and transmitting information to the North Pole computer systems."

Flea immediately thought back to his apartment and wondered if the bent-branched plastic tree had been judging whether he'd been naughty or nice this year. Considering that Flea disobeyed Miss Mabel and caused her great disappointment, he didn't expect to find much under the tree this year.

I don't even know if I'll ever be returning to Miss Mabel or that apartment again, Flea thought. But before he had the chance to ask, Vork held up a finger for silence and listened at the door.

"Question time is over, you'll just have to figure out some things on your own. The others are on their way. Take your place behind one of the tables so we can get started right away," Vork said.

Vork hobbled just outside the open door. Even though Flea didn't hear anyone coming, he still felt nervous to meet other students. The classroom was large and he expected it to fill with elf students; he wished for at least one friendly face in the bunch. Flea hoped that not *all* of them would be as resentful toward him as Niko and Vork.

"Hurry up, you're late," Vork called to someone in the hallway.

"Sorry, Mr. Vork."

Moments later, the first student strolled into the classroom. He tried to give Vork a high-five but the older elf just shook his head. While Niko and Vork were both very thin and looked miserable, this new elf had neither of those two characteristics. He still had the same pointy elf features but his face was pudgy and he wore a wide grin. He certainly looked friendly enough but there was one thing about him that worried Flea: his outfit. The elf's clothes looked nothing like Flea's, despite the fact that it was still a very strange ensemble. The pudgy elf wore a big green shirt with a picture of a Christmas tree on it that actually had blinking lights –

the first article of clothing Flea had ever seen with working lights. As if the shirt wasn't weird enough, the rest of his outfit consisted of red-and-white striped pants (the pattern exactly like the color scheme of the dormitory's hallways) and a pair of shoes that were shaped like old-fashioned wooden sleds. The elf was quite a sight and at least Flea felt like he wasn't the worst-dressed elf in the class – unless that was how *all* the others elves dressed.

The new elf walked over to Flea, who instinctively backed away when he thought he was about to be attacked. But Flea couldn't escape the elf's grip. He was lifted off his feet in a tight bear hug, the most unlikely welcome that Flea ever received.

"I *like* your style," the elf said when he put Flea down and looked over the odd elf outfit. "I know a lot of the other elves might be freaked out by you being here but it's just about the best thing that's ever happened to me."

Flea didn't quite know what to say to this goofy elf, who upon closer inspection seemed to have a few wispy patches of facial hair above and below his big smile.

"Thanks, I think," Flea finally said. "My name is Flea."

"I'm Minko," the bigger elf said. "It's great to meet you, Flea. I can't *wait* for class to start." Minko was so excited that he could hardly stand still. He reminded Flea of a kid he'd gone to school with who was diagnosed with Attention Deficit Disorder. Minko must have realized that he was acting too hyper because he suddenly calmed down, the ever-present smile on his face finally disappearing. "I just hope it goes much better than the *last time* I was here."

"What do you mean the *last* time?" Flea asked as he became worried by Minko's mood swing toward gloom.

"Someone else is coming," Vork said.

While Flea hadn't heard Minko's approach until he was just outside the door, the next student's voice echoed down the hallway.

"This isn't fair, I shouldn't be here," she complained loudly enough so that *Flea* blushed from her tirade. "I already know everything!"

"Uh oh, I know who *that* is," Minko whispered to Flea.

Since Minko sounded so nervous, Flea expected a big-and-bad she-elf to come stomping in. Flea had been tortured by his fair share of females bullies over the years – in fact, girls were usually far more brutal to deal with than boys.

"You are an elf and since you don't have any other special ability useful to the North Pole, your first priority should be building," Vork told her.

"Whatever," she said and swept past the older elf and into the classroom.

Flea was instantly dumbfounded by her beauty, as her elfish features were much softer than any other elf Flea had seen so far. She also wore fashionable (and therefore expensive) clothes just like all the other popular girls with whom Flea had ever gone to school, though she was by far the prettiest Flea had ever seen. Unfortunately, she didn't look quite as beautiful with her nose turned up and a sneer across her face, which was her reaction the moment she saw Flea and Minko.

"Are you sure there's not *another* class I could possibly take?" she asked Vork sweetly. The old elf was far too wise to fall for her sudden kindness, as she was obviously accustomed to getting her way.

"This is the only one, now please take a place behind one of the tables."

The girl groaned in displeasure before walking dejectedly toward the table farthest away from Flea and Minko.

"Don't worry about her, she's just embarrassed because her style isn't as good as ours," Minko whispered to Flea.

At first, Flea thought the bigger elf was joking but Minko's face did not contain the slightest hint that he was anything but serious. The three students wondered if any more students would arrive but Vork closed the door and walked toward the front of the class.

"Okay, it's time to begin class."

The girl elf breathed sharply and Flea saw that she was staring with dread at the two other students in the room with her.

"*Pleeeease* don't say it's just me, the weirdo and the new guy," she said.

"Hey, I'm not new," Minko responded, clearly offended by what she'd said.

"Duh," she shot back at him.

"That's enough. In this classroom, I will not respond to any questions or comments when you haven't first raised your hand," Vork said. "Now I'm going to start by taking attendance."

"Attendance for only three of us?" she asked.

Vork ignored the question and read the first name. "Flea?"

Flea raised his hand.

"Your name is *Flea*?" she asked, barely able to suppress a mocking laugh. Flea wanted to explain that it was only a nickname but she didn't give him the chance. "What a dumb name but I guess it matches that outfit you're wearing."

"Minko?" Vork asked, still looking down at the attendance list on his clipboard. Minko dutifully raised his hand before Vork read off the last of the three names. "Rome?"

The girl sighed but didn't raise her name until Vork repeated it five times. With attendance taken, Vork put down the clipboard.

"Let's get started," Vork said. "Anyone in the mood for a pop quiz?"

CHAPTER TWELVE

Making First Impressions

Vork clapped his hands and Flea watched as the tabletop in front of him flipped open, revealing a number of simple building materials: wood, nails, a hammer, a saw, paint and a brush. The idea of a pop quiz caused Flea's heart to pound, as he remembered that Niko built a bike with even fewer supplies, a task that Flea felt totally unable to tackle. He forced himself to take a deep breath and hoped this quiz would be much easier.

"I know that *some* of you have taken this class before…" Flea looked around to see that Minko and Rome both blushed. "…but I need to judge how much everyone knows already or if maybe *some* of us have gotten better over the years since he last had class," Vork said.

Minko – who had seemed ready to talk about anything before – suddenly avoided meeting Flea's questioning gaze.

"It's been *years* since you last had class?" Flea whispered to Minko.

The bigger elf did not answer the question and instead pointed to the front of the class. "Shhh, you should pay attention to this."

"I'm about to show an image of a product that I expect you to reproduce," Vork explained. "Pay careful attention to every possible detail."

The elderly elf pushed a button on the front table and a huge hologram of a toy chest appeared in the center of the room. The image quickly rotated a single time but the chest appeared simple to Flea, whose mind instinctively registered the intricate details of the woodwork. Flea glanced over at Minko to see the big elf staring intently – almost desperately – at the hologram. And even though Rome tried to appear cool and indifferent, she kept her eyes aimed directly at the hologram the entire time. After only a few seconds, the three-dimensional image of the toy chest disappeared, replaced by a large holographic zero.

"We need more time to study it," Rome complained.

"*Real* builder elves wouldn't have needed nearly as much time as I gave so consider yourselves lucky," Vork said. "It's time to start building…" The older elf swept his hand through the big zero, thus starting the timer. "…*now*."

For the first five seconds, Flea watched as the hologram counted up to five. He didn't realize the sense of urgency until he glanced over at Minko and Rome and saw that they were both rushing to begin. Flea started by grabbing a piece of wood and some nails but he was so nervous that he nearly dropped the hammer on his foot. But once he focused on the picture of the toy chest in his mind, his instincts kicked in and his hands began moving as if on their own.

Though Flea had been on a TV show watched by millions of viewers across the country, he never felt as much pressure as right now with the clock running and Vork watching his every move.

Flea's mind and hands were focused on the task, but this was the first time he was ever in his 'building zone' when other thoughts came to him, worried thoughts about what he might be doing wrong. He hammered and sawed and nailed and painted exclusively with his right hand, as his left served more of a support role in picking up materials or steadying them while he worked. Flea realized that his left hand should be playing a more active role in the building process but when he tried to hammer with it, he struck the nail at a bad angle, causing it to jut awkwardly out of the side of the toy chest.

Flea glanced up to see that Vork was watching him closely so he fixed his mistake by pulling out the nail and hammering it in correctly with his right hand. He abandoned the left-hand idea and focused on building the toy chest as quickly and accurately as possible, allowing his natural ability to completely take over. Several times, Flea was tempted to peek over at Rome and Minko to see how far along they were but those were important seconds he could not afford to waste, especially since he already had to fix one mistake. He just hoped that the other two didn't finish so long before him that Vork ruled that Flea was unworthy to remain at the North Pole. Once he was finished building, he hurried through the paint job, which never took very long. The toy box was soon complete. Unfortunately, Flea was in such a rush to put down his paintbrush that he sat it too close to the edge of his table and it promptly fell off.

Flea reached for the falling brush but his reaction time was not quick enough. But the brush never did hit the floor. Flea's worry was instantly followed by a surge of warmth in his hand. The slightest of breezes shot up from the ground and propelled the paintbrush into his hand. Flea quickly glanced around but nobody seemed to have noticed what just happened. No one, that is, except Vork, whose eyes were drawn toward Flea's hand – and for good reason. As Flea carefully placed the brush back on his worktable, he saw the faint golden light once again through his gloved hand. Thankfully, Vork didn't speak about the glow. The older elf swept his hand through the holographic timer and pushed the stopped number over Flea's toy chest.

Four minutes, thirty seconds, Flea saw proudly, especially when he had the chance to study his toy chest, which looked better than he could've hoped.

He finally looked at the other two students, both of whom were still busily working. The timer at the front of the room continued to run as Rome and Minko were far behind, not to mention that neither of their toy chests looked as good as his. Flea felt better knowing that at least he belonged here, though a part of him felt bad to see the other two struggling. Minko finally finished but Vork waited just a few more seconds before he brought the timer – and Rome – to a stop. The large holographic number blinked continuously having reached the ten-minute mark.

"That's enough, I can't take any more of this," Vork said as he shook his head. "Let's get this over with already."

The old elf approached Rome's work station in the back corner of the room. Rome's problem was immediately clear to Flea:

she was way too slow. In ten minutes, she had only completed two sides of the toy chest. To be fair, Flea had to admit that they looked perfectly done. Vork, however, was in no mood to point out the positives.

"If you concentrated on your building skills as much as your clothes and hair, you might've actually been able to finish on time," Vork said. "You're an elf, *not* a runway model. Your main concern shouldn't be trying to look perfect; it should be trying to complete projects in a shorter amount of time without worrying about messing up your outfit or your nails – and the nails I mean are those at the end of your fingers. I've seen piles of snow rise quicker than you work and I *don't* mean during a snowstorm."

Rome looked to be on the verge of tears following the tongue-lashing and Flea actually felt bad for her, despite her attitude problem. True to her form, Rome's face hardened when she noticed Flea and Minko staring at her. She shot them both an angry look, as though they'd been responsible for Vork's criticism. The teacher turned away from her and headed toward the two boys on the other side of the room. Flea's breath came in quicker rasps and he broke into a cold sweat imagining what Vork would say to him. But the teacher first stopped in front of Minko's desk, over which the holographic time read 9:58. Minko might have finished before the time limit ended, but Flea could hardly believe that a North Pole elf had built the… product in front of him.

"Where is your toy chest?" Vork asked.

Minko was clearly confused and looked to Flea for an answer, but Flea could only shrug his shoulders.

"Umm, it's right here," Minko said tentatively.

Vork looked at Minko's table but ignored the box-like object on it. The teacher walked all around the table, making a show of not seeing the 'toy chest', which he asked for several more times. It eventually dawned on Minko exactly what Vork was trying to tell him about his work. Minko's face turned bright red and Rome snickered from across the room. Vork's cruelty simultaneously worried and angered Flea, though he could fully understand why the teacher was so perplexed when he looked at Minko's work. With the exception of having four sides, a top and a bottom, Minko's project looked *nothing* like the holographic image of the toy chest. Anything that *could* have been messed up *was* messed up. Flea could see that Minko's toy chest was tilting severely to the front, the result of four sides of totally different size. Dozens of nails stuck out at random angles, none of the intricate details in the woodwork had even been attempted and the paint job was a complete mess, as though Minko had simply closed his eyes and thrown the entire contents of a paint can over the chest without the use of a brush.

Flea liked the friendly elf but not even Minko's personality could persuade Flea to find a single positive aspect of his work. Vork started to give him several different critiques but he stopped each time, shaking his head with disturbed amazement. Vork was clearly at a loss for words.

"You have a long way to go, Minko," Vork said. "A *long* way."

Minko nodded his head and tried to force a smile. "Well, it wasn't *that* bad considering it was the first thing I've built in... a *lot* of years."

Rome burst into laughter. She stared at Minko's monstrosity and cackled loudly.

"Not *that* bad?" she asked between fits of laughter. "Please tell me you aren't that delusional. I doubt you could put a feather inside that thing without it falling apart."

Minko looked to the teacher for support but Vork simply smiled.

"I think she's being a bit generous with that assessment," Vork said. "I figure a stiff breeze would send it to pieces."

Flea might have smiled if Minko didn't look so upset. The pudgy elf turned away from Vork and focused his embarrassed anger on Rome, who still laughed at Vork's insult toward Minko.

"At least I was able to *finish* in time," Minko said to her. "Maybe you could've made an entire toy chest if he'd given us another hour or two."

This immediately wiped the smile from Rome's face, which skewed in anger again. "Well if I really wanted, I could have made at least *five* chests as terrible as yours, though I'd have to concentrate to be *that* bad."

"Okay, okay, that's enough," Vork said, finally interceding before Minko and Rome broke into an all-out war. "You're both equally terrible in your own ways. Now please shut up so I can evaluate our last entry."

Vork approached Flea's table and for the first time, the other students noticed his toy chest.

"Oh, no," Minko whispered to himself.

"Are you trying to make us look bad, new guy?" Rome asked.

She clearly wasn't happy, but that made Flea feel better knowing that his level of quality threatened her. Flea didn't exactly feel good about making Minko look bad but the bigger elf wasn't as jealous as Rome.

"Leave him alone," Minko snapped at her, though his voice and body language both revealed that he was deflated. "It's not his fault that he's a natural. Good job, Flea, that looks awesome."

"Whatever," Rome said. "I didn't want to take this stupid class anyway. Hopefully Fly can bring an end to this class nice and quick for all of us."

Flea smiled and nodded his thanks to Minko. The goofy elf had no idea how much his kind words meant to him. Hearing that he was a natural made Flea feel a sense of confidence he'd never known and he watched with pride as Vork quietly examined his work. Several minutes passed without Vork saying a single word, which only raised Flea's self-confidence. He figured the teacher could not find a single thing to complain about.

Maybe I am good, Flea hoped as a smile splayed across his face.

"You're not as good as you think," Vork said, thus wiping the grin from Flea's face. Vork clapped twice and the holographic toy chest reappeared, slowly floating across the room until it superimposed itself directly over Flea's rendition. "As you can see right away, your toy chest is several inches longer and taller than the actual model, which would make it worthy of rejection if you tried passing this off in the toy factory."

"That seems awfully picky to me," Minko added.

"You don't care about specific details?" Vork asked Minko, his voice oozing with sarcasm. "Why doesn't *that* surprise me?"

"It's okay, he's right, Minko," Flea said, trying to accept criticism in the hope that it would make him a better builder one day. Besides, Flea had no problem dealing with his first effort only being a few inches from perfection.

Unfortunately, the mis-measured dimensions were only the beginning of a lengthy list of mistakes that Flea made. Although he had done significantly better than Minko and Rome, the teacher spent more time ripping apart Flea's work detail by tiny little detail. He ended his critique with a story.

"Just imagine an excited little child rushing downstairs on Christmas morning and opening *that* piece of junk. I wouldn't be surprised if he or she threw the rest of the presents straight into the fireplace out of sheer disappointment," Vork said. "On top of the pathetic outcome of your toy chest, I also noticed numerous flaws in your building technique. First off, you were very slow."

"Slow?" Rome asked, more of out shock than an attempt at solidarity with the two other failures.

"Yes, *slow*. Flea might've moved like a speeding snowball compared to the two of you but that's not saying much *at all*," Vork said. "A big reason for this is that you were only able to work with your right hand. And as *glowing* a job you might've done with that, you proved to be mistake-prone with your left."

"I thought I did a pretty good job of covering up that error," Flea admitted.

"Well you thought *wrong*," Vork countered. "Any elf worth his weight in snow is ambidextrous but I'd be willing to bet that Minko here could defeat you in a race if the two of you were limited to just your left hands."

Flea turned and forced a smile at Minko, who shrugged his shoulders. Flea was upset that his only talent in life wasn't nearly as good as he'd started to think. But Minko continued to prove that he was always an optimist.

"I think your toy chest looks awesome," Minko said. "And I took a glance at you while we were building and it was definitely the fastest I've ever seen someone work."

Before Flea had a chance to thank him, Rome just *had* to add her two cents, though her main target continued to be Minko.

"That's because you've never even stepped foot inside the toy factory to see *real* elves at work," she said.

"How do you know where I've been?" Minko shot back.

"It's pretty hard to miss someone who's always blinking," Rome said, pointing to Minko's shirt. "Besides, who around the North Pole *doesn't* know about the poor pathetic *card elf?*"

Minko blushed and turned away from her, the first time she'd clearly gotten under his skin.

"At least I *do* my own work," Minko muttered, though Flea doubted whether Rome had heard him.

Vork hobbled to the front of the classroom and pushed a button on his table, revealing his own pile of supplies and tools.

"If you two lovebirds are done bickering, I'll show you how this is done," the teacher said. The old elf appeared so frail that Flea doubted he could even pick up the hammer let alone build the huge toy chest. But Flea reminded himself that Vork had no trouble using the 'hopwell' so it probably wasn't wise to underestimate him. Vork reset the holographic timer and started it, cracking his knuckles several times and wasting nearly five seconds. "Watch and learn."

What followed was an amazing sight that Flea would not forget as long as he lived. The feeble old elf moved so quickly and efficiently that the three students could barely see his exact actions. Vork moved like a blur as his replica of the toy chest seemed to spring up from the table. Had Flea not seen similar lightning-quick movements from Niko earlier, he would've been convinced that he was watching some sort of illusion or magic trick. But Vork proved to be just as adept a builder and when he finished and swept his hand through the timer, the mouths of all three students hung open in shock.

"Forty seconds?" Minko asked, clearly in awe.

The image of the toy chest reappeared and floated over Vork's rendition. The two matched perfectly but the old elf still shook his head slowly.

"I know, forty seconds is a disgrace," Vork said, much to his students' surprise. "I'm a lot slower than I used to be but let's see how fast *you* three move when you're a century or two past your 500th birthday."

Flea was most shocked to hear of Vork's age but Minko and Rome both nodded their heads in understanding.

"Okay, I'm ending class early now that I've evaluated each of you," the teacher said. "Now comes the hard part for me: trying to figure out how to make all of you better." Vork shook his head again. "I don't know what I've gotten myself into, *always* attempting the impossible. You better head off to your regular job posts until I come up with a plan."

Rome didn't need to be told twice as she quickly headed for the door. Minko seemed disappointed that class was ending so soon but he also left the room, leaving Flea alone with the teacher yet again.

"Excuse me, sir, but I don't *have* a regular job post," Flea said.

Vork nodded his head. "Then you'd better catch up with the other two and hope that one of them will let you tag along for a while," the teacher said.

Flea rushed out of the classroom, hoping to catch up with Minko or Rome before they were gone and left him alone in the North Pole grounds.

CHAPTER THIRTEEN
Blocked Entrance

"Don't think you're coming with me, little Fly, especially not dressed in that nerdy costume," Rome said.

Flea caught up with the two of them just outside the school. Rome had been trying to rush away from Minko but the pudgy elf was following in her footsteps, satisfied that his mere presence was making her mad. She'd been yelling at Minko to leave her alone – to make sure none of her friends saw him near her – when Flea found them and explained that he needed to tag along with one of them until it was time for their next class. Rome's reaction was what he'd expected but fate interceded and punished her for her meanness. She stepped in a small hole in the snowy surface and stumbled to the ground.

Minko immediately tried to help her up but Rome smacked his hand away.

"Don't touch me, weirdo," she snapped. Rome got to her feet and carefully wiped the snow off her clothes, spending much more time doing so than Flea would have.

"I was only trying to help," Minko said. "You might want to try being nicer to us since we'll all be spending so much time together." Rome turned away from them but Minko saw something attached to her back that didn't belong. He grabbed the long piece of clear tape and pulled it off her shirt. "And you might want to try to keep the tape off of yourself... unless that's some cool new accessory to your outfit."

Rome snatched the piece of tape out of Minko's hand but her face immediately softened, which only made her look more beautiful.

"Thanks," she said quietly. It was the first word Flea had heard from her that didn't sound angry or mean. "And anyway, it's not like we'll be in class much longer if your friend here keeps building the way he did today. Vork will graduate him in no time and that'll be the end of our lessons."

Minko nodded his head solemnly and for a moment, he and Rome looked like two friends sharing a common pain.

"What do you mean?" Flea asked.

Minko and Rome explained that in order for the elf school to be open, three students in need of learning were required. Once one of them was past through the class – as Rome and Minko both expected Flea to be very soon – the school would be closed again with the two others returning to their menial jobs.

"It's been years since the last time any new elves were here to go to school. And I don't know about Minko, but I was starting to doubt that it would ever be opened again, that I would ever get another chance," Rome explained. "But now that you're zipping through the work and will probably graduate within another class or two, it seems almost like a tease that the school was reopened at all."

"But I thought you didn't even want to be there," Flea said. "You said you didn't care about the class."

"*Of course* I want to be there," Rome snapped. "I'm an elf. Do you know how embarrassing it is not to be able to build like everyone else?'

"Not exactly," Flea admitted. "But I *do* know what it feels like not to fit in because I'm different."

Flea meant to come across as understanding but Rome obviously didn't take it that way.

"Well I *do* fit in regardless of how I build," she said. An idea must've suddenly come to Rome, who became much sweeter when she spoke to Flea. "If you really wanted to help me… and I guess Minko, too… you could always purposely do bad in class to give us more time to improve. Maybe Vork would graduate all of us at the same time – or at least you and me."

When Rome smiled and batted her eyelids, she could have suggested *anything* and it would have sounded like a good idea to Flea. Thankfully, Minko wasn't quite as entranced by her beauty – or at least not that he let on.

"Don't listen to her, Flea, cheating is not a very elfish thing to do," Minko said. "Rome is being selfish and only looking out for her own best interests. You shouldn't hold yourself back for anyone."

Flea nodded, as the sound of Minko's voice brought him back to reality and allowed his mind to think clearly again. While Flea would have loved to help these two get through school to become full-fledged builder elves, he was worried about what would happen to him if he intentionally did poorly in class. It seemed obvious that he was *supposed* to succeed in school, so if that didn't happen soon, Flea wondered if those responsible for bringing him to the North Pole would change their minds. Besides, if Flea were kicked out of school and the North Pole, then Minko and Rome would be out of luck anyway.

Flea was starting to learn that he might not be able to trust Rome. If he purposely did bad and Rome quickly improved, there was a chance that only *she* would pass, leaving Flea and Minko stuck in elfish purgatory.

"I think you two are giving me much more credit than I deserve," Flea said, attempting to ease Rome's concerns without exactly rejecting her plan. "You saw how long Vork bashed my toy chest. I'm sure I still have a long way to go, too."

"Based on how you did today, I have no doubt you'll be a top-of-the-tree level builder in no time," Minko said. "And with a talent like yours, you deserve that chance as soon as possible. You better make sure you try your hardest in class at all times."

"*Fine*, be a *card elf* for the rest of your life," Rome snapped at the pudgy elf, as if it was Minko's fault that Flea had such talent. "But just imagine being Vork's age without ever having seen the inside of the toy factory. It's really amazing inside, you don't know what you're missing."

With that, Rome took a Christmas tree ball from her pocket and wore it like a necklace, which seemed strange to Flea since it didn't match her outfit very well. She marched away from the two boys, who watched her enter the big glass doors of the nearby toy factory.

"That was just mean," Minko said matter-of-factly, though Flea was sure the pudgy elf never would've admitted that if Rome were still standing with them.

"How is she allowed access to the toy factory if she never graduated from elf school?" Flea asked. "It doesn't seem fair that she can go inside if you can't."

Minko shrugged his shoulders, not nearly as upset by this fact as Rome would've been had the roles been reversed.

"I guess she gets special treatment since she's friends with important elves like Niko. He's very close with the boss, you know, so he can bend the rules if he wants. And since some of the others seem to think that Rome is attractive, I'm sure that helps her cause," Minko said as he continued to stare longingly at the toy factory. "But I'm pretty sure Rome doesn't do any real work in there. I don't know about you but I wouldn't want to be in the toy factory if they only gave me idiot-proof jobs, like building yo-yos or something."

Minko started to walk again but Flea couldn't pull his eyes away from the bright colors just inside the factory doors.

"You've *never* been inside?" Flea asked. "Not even once?"

"I've heard plenty of stories but I don't have access," Minko said. "It's not *all* bad, though. Sometimes, the other elves sneak out some of the coolest and most popular toys for me, so it's not like my dorm room is missing anything that cool. One of them even brought me this shirt, which just so happens to be the hottest fashion trend from what I've heard. This shirt here is an original but I've made myself a couple others just like it."

"Those shirts are the hottest trend *here*? At the North Pole?" Flea asked.

Minko stopped for a moment, visibly deep in thought.

"Actually, no," he said, surprised by this realization. "The other elves told me that these shirts are the hottest trend in the *human* world. I guess none of them can pull off a human look like I can."

Flea had a bad feeling that Minko had been the target of a cruel joke by the other elves. Minko seemed too happy about the blinking shirts, though, so Flea didn't want to burst his bubble. Besides, Flea had more important questions he wanted answered.

"I don't understand why you just don't walk into the factory and take a look around," Flea said, glancing around the North Pole to see that nobody was watching them.

"I wish it was that easy," Minko chuckled. "But come on, *you* can give it a try."

The two walked toward the factory but when they got close, Minko stopped and gestured for Flea to continue toward the entrance. Flea hesitated at first – he didn't want to start any trouble but Minko assured him it was okay – before walking the last few feet to the door. He never reached his destination, however. Another groundswell of snow shot up, creating a blockade of faceless, connected snowmen in front of the door. The way they suddenly formed from the snowy ground reminded Flea of the snowmen guarding the ice bank. But that was the end of any similarities between the two varieties of snowmen. Flea tried to climb up and over and between the blockade but the snow shifted with his every movement; he obviously wasn't getting past them.

Flea took a step back from the blockade and was surprised when a snowball soared past him and exploded the faceless head of a nearby snowman. Upset, Flea turned just in time to see Minko toss another snowball at the blockade. Minko threw just about as well as he built, but his snowballs still traveled fast enough to blast another hole in the blockade.

"What are you doing?" Flea asked.

Minko could see that he was upsetting Flea so he pointed to the blockade. "Look, it doesn't bother them."

Flea turned back to see that both holes in the blockade had refilled already. Minko explained that he would never attack any of the smarter snowmen and that the blockade's only function was to stop those elves not permitted into the factory.

"Aren't *you* the only one not permitted to enter?" Flea asked.

"I *was* until you showed up here," Minko said. "But we would need nothing short of a snow-bomb or two to blast through the blockade and I've never even held one of them. Besides, even if we managed to sneak into the factory and get past the secretary in the front, the other elves would notice us right away since they'd be jealous of our style."

"Just so I get this straight, the other elves *don't* wear the same outfit as mine?" Flea asked.

"Nope, most of them wear plain clothes like Vork or those strange outfits like Rome," Minko said.

It was now obvious that Niko had tricked Flea into wearing this ridiculous outfit. Flea figured it was his punishment for having led Niko on the wild chase through the elf dorm. Flea no longer wanted to hang around the factory to meet elves so he convinced Minko to show him other parts of the North Pole – *empty* parts – and the location of his job post. As they walked through the deserted village, Minko explained that the elves had only received their first work orders a few hours ago so it would be a *long* time before most of them emerged from the factory.

"Some of them don't take a single break until all of their orders have been filled," Minko explained. "Finishing first is a prestigious honor that the top-level elves aim for, especially when they win Santa's prize. In human time, those elves build for weeks straight without taking a single break."

"*Weeks?* How can they do that without collapsing from exhaustion?" Flea wondered.

"Building season is the time of the year that elves are most excited about – at least the rest of the elves who contribute to Christmas," Minko said glumly, as he wasn't part of that group. "Everyone sleeps for several weeks straight before Christmas Eve to be ready for building time. 11:59 is the start of our year."

Flea glanced back to the toy factory clock, as the time served as a reminder about how late it was and how tired he felt. He certainly hadn't hibernated for the last few weeks so his body still ran on human time. It had been more than twenty-four hours since he slept last. If Flea had a bed near him, he had little doubt that he could lie down and pass out from exhaustion in a matter of seconds. But he still had way too much to see and learn before he could seriously consider resting. Plus, a part of his mind couldn't escape the idea that this was all a dream – albeit a very *detailed* dream – and Flea didn't want to take the risk of waking up just yet.

"Speaking of 11:59, how does Santa actually slow down time?" Flea asked.

Minko suddenly stopped walking and a serious expression formed on his face. The pudgy elf looked all around to make sure that nobody could hear them before he leaned in much closer to Flea. When he spoke, his usually boisterous voice was no louder than a whisper.

"I probably shouldn't be telling you this since you're new and all, but you seem like the kind of elf I can trust," Minko said. Flea nodded his head in agreement but the pudgy elf still glanced around one more time. "You didn't hear this from me, but Santa stops time by using...magic."

Flea was tempted to laugh until he realized that Minko wasn't being sarcastic.

"I figured it was magic, but what *kind* of magic? What exactly does Santa do?" Flea asked.

Minko broke into his usual smile again.

"If I'm not even allowed inside the toy factory, do you think they would trust me with the secret to Santa's magic?" Minko laughed.

In the distance, Flea spotted the tiny security building and wondered if Minko could shine any light on the North Pole's security issue or the army of snowmen crossing the red holographic line. But Flea remembered Niko's warning to keep his mouth shut about what he'd seen and he highly doubted whether Minko knew anything important about security. Instead, Flea returned his focus to the other North Pole building that most intrigued him.

"Tell me about the ice bank then."

Minko's knowledge of the ice bank was also very limited, as he knew little information beyond the stories he'd heard from other elves. The ice bank was the most heavily guarded of the North Pole buildings, despite the rumors that it only protected a single object. Unfortunately, nobody knew exactly what that object was. The only elves allowed entrance to the ice bank were Santa and his family, though the main guard sprung up regardless of who got close.

"Wait, did you say Santa's *family*?" Flea asked.

"Yes, of course."

"I didn't know that Santa had a family," Flea said, as he tried to think through all the popular Christmas songs. He couldn't recall any mention of Santa's family.

"Really? Because you've already met Santa's son," Minko said. "I can't believe that Niko didn't tell you that Santa Claus is his father."

CHAPTER FOURTEEN
Tight Security

"*Niko?*"

"How else did you think he would get such an important job around here?" Minko asked. "That's why Rome flirted with him, so she could gain access to the toy factory. Niko is related to Santa, that's why he's so important around here even though he's the youngest elf at the North Pole. Wait, how old are *you*?"

"Ten," Flea answered, still in shock to find out about Niko's relation. He couldn't quite comprehend how someone so cranky could be the son of the world's most jolly character.

"Then I guess that makes Niko the *second* youngest but only by a handful of years. Still, the way he bosses around elves you might think that he was just as old as Vork or the other North Pole elders," Minko said.

"Does Santa have any *other* children?"

"Nope, just the one."

"So what's the story with Mrs. Claus?" Flea wondered.

When Minko stopped walking and looked around again, Flea expected to hear another 'secret.' But the pudgy elf wore a look of complete seriousness that bordered on anger. For someone wearing such a festive blinking shirt, Minko's expression seemed out of place.

"We don't *ever* talk about Mrs. Claus around here, not to anyone, not even in whispers amongst ourselves," Minko said. "So do us both a favor and never ask me about her again."

Minko turned and marched off. Flea was so shocked by Minko's reaction that he turned bright red and muttered an apology, though he wasn't totally sure *why* he was so sorry. Flea worried that he had just ruined his first real chance of making a friend. He realized now that Minko's friendliness was the only part of his North Pole experience that didn't make him feel awkward and unwanted. For some unknown reason, mentioning Mrs. Claus was a big no-no here and Flea wondered if he'd given the elves yet another reason to demand that he leave the North Pole.

But Minko did not get very far before he stopped and turned back toward Flea.

"Don't just stand there, I have much more to show you here," Minko said, his voice and facial expression having softened. Flea hurried to catch up and saw that the pudgy elf had also blushed. "I'm sorry for snapping. I've never really met any *new* elves before. I have to keep reminding myself that you don't know about these kinds of things. And I guess it's actually good that you asked me and not someone else about Mrs..... about her, especially Niko. The elves around here can get a bit sensitive about that subject."

Flea nodded, not wanting to make another mention about Mrs. Claus. He was suddenly very thankful that this subject hadn't come up earlier with Niko, that this wasn't one of the dozens of questions he'd pestered him with. More than anything else, Flea realized that maybe he needed to heed Niko's earlier advice about not asking so many questions in the future.

For several minutes, the only sound Flea and Minko made was the *crunching* of their footsteps in the snow. The silence between them grew awkward until Minko stopped just beyond the ice bank and picked up a handful of snow.

"You wanted to know more about the ice bank so watch this," he said. "You better take a few steps back, though. Since you're new, the guards won't know you so they better know that *I'm* the one doing this." Minko carefully formed the handful of snow into a large, perfectly formed snowball. "Like I said, only Santa or his family can enter the ice bank. *This* is what would happen if anyone else tried to break in."

Minko lobbed the snowball high toward the ice bank but before it reached the building, an icy arrow intercepted it and caused the snowball to explode. Flea looked down to see an entire line of snowmen encircling the ice bank, though these *weren't* simply the blockade variety. The green-eyed snowman leader of the bank security force stared directly at Flea and Minko, both of whom backed away upon seeing the squad of well-armed snowmen ready to strike.

"What did you do?" Flea whispered. "It looks like they're going to attack us."

"Don't worry, they know who I am and that we're not a threat," Minko said, though he didn't sound very convincing. "Still, I wouldn't make any sudden movements if I were you."

Once the two elves stepped farther back and made no further threatening moves, most of the armed-snowmen melted back into the snowy ground. Still, the leader continued to watch them, the familiar green-eyes boring a hole directly into Flea.

"Why were the ice bank guards up?" Niko called out as he rushed toward them from the security building. Niko ran so quickly that his big red Christmas hat nearly flew off several times, though he was careful to keep a tight hold of it against his head. Santa's son glanced toward the barren landscape beyond the village.

"I'm sorry, Niko, I was… I was just showing Flea why he should stay away from the ice bank," Minko stuttered. He was clearly worried about getting in trouble, especially when he saw how angry Niko appeared. But luckily for the pudgy elf, Santa's son seemed totally focused on Flea.

"Did you try to enter the ice bank?" Niko demanded to know. Though the tone of his voice sounded angry, Flea thought he also detected a bit of panic in it as well. "I *told* you there'd be trouble if you tried to get close to it. It's barely been a few hours and you've *already* disobeyed the only direct order I gave you."

"It wasn't him, I pr-… I promise Flea had nothing to do with it," Minko said. "I was just trying to show off and – "

Without taking his eyes away from Flea, Niko held up a finger to Minko, who instantly stopped talking.

"Walk away right now, Minko," Niko said. Once the pudgy elf was out of earshot, Niko continued to hiss angrily at Flea. "I thought the North Pole was under attack. How could you let that fool do something so stupid when you saw what was happening in the security building?"

"I didn't know what he was doing," Flea countered. "Besides, you didn't *explain* to me what I saw in there."

"And you're proving that you don't deserve to know *anything* important that's going on around here," Niko said. He stormed back to the security building, but not before issuing one final warning. "*Stay away* from the ice bank, don't make me have to warn you a third time."

Minko apologized profusely when Flea caught up. Flea told him not worry about it even though he was concerned that Santa – or whoever else was in charge of making decisions here – had yet another reason to boot him out of the North Pole. Flea had little time to focus on his misfortune though, as the two passed yet another one of the main buildings that Flea had previously built.

"Welcome to the reindeer stable," Minko said.

The stable resembled a large brown barn, a building that seemed out of place here at the North Pole. The stable lacked bright colors and looked like it was straight out of the human world. Flea again traced his knowledge of the North Pole back to famous Christmas tunes, as he remembered that nine reindeer pulled Santa's sleigh. While Flea was no expert on the subject of animal care, the stable looked way too big to house only nine reindeer. He was just about to ask Minko about this when he reminded himself that learning on his own – whenever that might happen – might be the better option. Besides, the symphony of strange sounds that emerged from the reindeer stable made Flea forget his previous questions, as a whole new set of them suddenly came to mind.

What the heck is going on in there? Flea wondered. As he walked along the length of the stable, he heard every distinct noise, each sound totally different from the last. The *stomping* of hooves perfectly in tune with loud music. The *clinking* of metal against metal over and over again, each time followed by a thunderous *grunting*. A high-pitched, *whiny* voice that screamed "but I'm a superstar!" moments before a door slammed. Finally, soft piano music. And those were the only noises that he could distinguish from one another. Flea had no idea what these strange noises were but the reindeer stable sounded nothing short of crazy. Once Flea and Minko were beyond the stable and away from the noise, they could finally talk again.

"I realize that getting yelled at by Niko was a real downer, but I know how I can make it up to you," Minko said. "I'll show you one of the coolest parts of the North Pole and introduce you to two of the coolest elves I know."

"You really don't have to do anything special on my behalf," Flea said. "Maybe we should just get to your job post and avoid any more… complications with your work schedule."

Flea knew he was already on thin ice around here and was starting to get the feeling that trouble followed Minko. But the pudgy elf seemed oblivious to Flea's concerns and told him that this would only take a few minutes.

"First, notice that the factory is there…" Minko said, pointing at the large building. He then drew a straight line in the air toward a smaller building, another one that Flea hadn't built on *The Great Build-Off*. "…and the garage is over there. The two are connected but I'll tell you why later. Come on, we're going to the garage."

Along the way, Minko warned Flea not to trip over a hatch in the ground. The hatch was halfway between the two buildings but when Flea asked what it was, Minko told him that he would explain later.

"There are cars at the North Pole?" Flea wondered, as he could think of no other explanation why a garage would be needed.

"Cars? On ground covered with this much snow?" Minko said. "I don't think so. The garage holds something *much* better than a car, though you might not want to tell anyone that I brought you here. Technically, I'm not sure that anyone else is supposed to see this right now, not even me."

When the two reached the smaller building, they found that the rolling garage door was raised only about a foot off the ground. It clearly wasn't a sign to Flea of an open invitation to enter, though that wasn't about to stop Minko. The pudgy elf lay flat on the ground and wiggled his way under the opening. Once he squeezed his way inside, he whispered to Flea to follow him.

How do I always end up getting myself in these positions? Flea wondered. He looked around the North Pole and saw that nobody was watching, although that didn't make him feel any better as he climbed to the ground and shimmied his way into the garage.

CHAPTER FIFTEEN
Wrench and Grinder

"And you're *sure* we're allowed in here?" Flea asked once he got to his feet and brushed the snow off of his clothes.

"Don't worry so much," Minko said. "I'm friends with the mechanics who work here. They are really cool elves, can't you tell already?"

It was hard to tell *anything* inside the dark garage. A small amount of light trickled in from the outside and allowed Flea to see a long ramp leading downward, though he couldn't tell exactly how deep it went. However, he saw an eerie reddish glow and heard loud pounding music coming from down the ramp that made him seriously doubt whether coming here was a good idea. Minko carefully stepped over a red laser beam at ground level and Flea did the same.

"Actually, I *can't* tell," Flea said.

"I guess you'll just have to trust me then," Minko said.

Had there been enough light to see, Minko might've noticed the doubtful expression on Flea's face: brow creased, one raised eyebrow, lips curled downward. But the pudgy elf took off down the ramp and Flea followed closely behind against his better judgement. Thankfully, Flea soon discovered the identities of the glowing lights and loud music, neither of which were quite as bad as his overactive imagination made them out to be. Dozens of strings of Christmas lights hung everywhere inside the garage and at the bottom of the ramp. The lights blinked in perfect unison with the rock 'n' roll tune – "Rockin' Around the Christmas Tree" – that blared so loudly Flea couldn't hear himself think. He even saw that the nearby walls were plastered with posters of pretty elf girls wearing Santa-suit bikinis. Flea was so busy staring at the posters that he didn't notice Minko step over yet another laser beam near the ground. As Flea stepped from the ramp and entered the actual garage part of the building, his foot passed directly through the beam.

The sudden change couldn't have been more dramatic. The crazy blinking lights were instantly replaced by soft white spotlights overhead, the loud rock 'n' roll by a relaxing orchestral version of "White Christmas." Even the walls completely changed, as rolls of Christmas-themed wrapping paper unrolled from the ceiling and covered all of the posters.

"How did you do that?" Flea asked.

"*I* didn't," Minko said. "I'm sorry, I should have told you to watch out for the second security beam. You must've set it off."

Before Flea could become upset about causing more trouble, he noticed what took up most of the space inside the garage. Minko was right about one thing: this was *way* more impressive than any simple car. Flea stared at the back of a huge sleigh, which was nearly ten feet high and just as wide. He slowly began to circle around the ornately designed sleigh, gawking at the sheer majesty of its beauty. Like nearly everything else Flea had experienced so far at the North Pole, the sleigh was far more amazing than any Christmas tale had ever described. He was so focused on it that he almost didn't hear the whistling and singing of an elf on the other side of the sleigh.

"La la la, working on the sleigh," the voice sang nervously. Flea and Minko came face-to-face with a masked elf holding some sort of fire-breathing tool that Flea had never seen before. When the elf saw who was in his garage, he sighed in relief and yelled up toward the sleigh. "Don't worry, Grinder, it's not the big man."

The elf turned off the modified blowtorch and removed his mask. While he had the same sharp facial features as other elves, two things about this new elf immediately stood out to Flea. First, he wore clothing nearly as strange as Minko's, minus the blinking lights. His tracksuit was a shiny metallic silver that seemed to make him shine. But even more distinct was his hair, bright red with huge spikes (which must've required more hair gel than Flea could've imagined). The red-spiked elf tossed the tool over his shoulder and it exploded in a fiery burst near the back wall, which nobody seemed too concerned about.

"Sorry to frighten you, Wrench, but I saw the garage door open so I thought it would be okay to come down and say hi," Minko said.

The elf named Wrench stared at Flea as if deep in thought, unable to make up his mind about something.

"We needed to get some cool air circulating in here because *someone* has been playing with fire for the last few hours," another voice said from well above them.

Flea looked up just in time to see a second elf inside the front part of the sleigh. Even though there was a ladder leading up the ten feet, he jumped off the sleigh and landed just inches next to Wrench.

"I wasn't *playing,* I was *testing,*" Wrench bickered. "There's a difference between the two, even an idiot would know *that.*"

The second elf was clearly Wrench's brother and with the exception of a few details, Flea could tell they were twins. While Wrench's spiky hair was bright red, his brother's was an equally bright green. He also wore a tracksuit, though its velvety black color was far less flashy than Wrench's metallic silver. Flea wasn't normally one to judge people (or elves) based upon their appearance – after all, *he'd* been judged so many times in life himself – but the twins reminded him of surfers. Wrench walked over to the wall and opened a hidden box.

"Since you aren't Santa, we may as well get this place back to how we like it," the red-spiked elf said. He flipped a switch and the blinking lights and rock music returned in full force. "We don't think the big man would appreciate our style too much, we're not into the typical elf stuff. So Minko, who's your friend?"

"I guess the rumors of a newcomer are true," the green-haired twin said.

"Wrench and Grinder, I'd like to introduce you to Flea."

"Wrench and Grinder?" Flea asked as he shook hands with them. "Are those your *real* names?"

"Is Flea *yours*?" Grinder wondered.

Wrench explained that he and his brother preferred their nicknames to their real ones, Russ and Guss.

"Besides, our nicknames and hair colors make it easier for the other elves to tell us apart," Wrench said. "Grinder and green both start with the letter 'g.' Red and Wrench both start with 'r' so that's easy to remember, too."

"Uh, but doesn't Wrench really start with a 'w'?" Flea asked.

The twins – and Minko, for that matter – looked confused as their minds tried to figure out what Flea had said. Finally, Grinder winked at Flea and the other two began to laugh.

"See? Isn't he funny?" Minko asked.

"Funny and Flea, both start with 'f'," Wrench said. "I'll never forget that now."

Flea wasn't sure if the twins were being serious but he decided not to push the subject of spelling any further.

"Wrench and Grinder are genius mechanics," Minko said. "They make sure that Santa's sleigh is running smoothly at all times."

"That's only one of our duties," Wrench said. "Our other duty is much more interesting; it's the one that makes the annual sleigh unveiling one of the highlights of the year."

Over the sound of loud rock music, Flea heard the distant echo of a *bang* coming from the back of the sleigh. He looked up and for the first time realized that there was a large chute sticking out of the wall, its conveyor belt coming to an end directly above the sleigh's massive cargo area. A seemingly endless supply of wrapped

Christmas presents tumbled off the belt and into the sleigh. Each time a new present dropped, Flea saw a puff of tiny sparkles bloom above the cargo hold.

"How long does it take before the sleigh fills up?" Flea asked.

Wrench and Grinder looked at each other and started to laugh until they realized that Flea's wasn't joking.

"I think he's being serious," Grinder said.

"Funny Flea ain't the smartest new guy they could've brought to the North Pole," Wrench said. "You see, Santa stopped by a while ago with one of...*them*."

"*Them*?" Flea asked.

"Yes, *them*," Wrench answered, offering no further explanation of the vague term. "Anyway, Santa and the *other one* completed the yearly routine to make sure all the gifts fit. But like usual, they made me and my brother wait outside first. But I might be able to let you in on part of the secret that I *do* know. Can I trust you with this information, Funny Flea?"

"If it's important for you to keep the secret then maybe you shouldn't – "

"Of course you can trust him," Minko interrupted before Flea could talk Wrench out of telling him any secrets.

Flea was quickly learning that it might be better to know less around here, that knowing too much could get him into trouble. But Minko and the twins seemed like they wanted him to know. They all stepped in closer to Flea after suspiciously glancing around the rest of the garage.

"Don't tell anyone I told you this, but Santa is able to make all of the presents fit in the sleigh by using..." Wrench started, before lowering his voice to nothing more than a whisper. "...by using *magic*."

"Ahhh," Minko said knowingly, nodding his head. Flea nodded his head as well, as if this revelation had proven very informative. "So, any idea on what the big change to the sleigh will be this year?"

"You're just going to have to wait and find out like everyone else," Grinder said.

"I don't know why you would change a single thing about the sleigh," Flea said, as he continued to stare in awe at the huge vehicle. "It really is amazing."

When nobody said anything for several seconds, Flea looked back toward the twins, both of whom appeared offended. Flea didn't know what he'd said to insult them but Minko immediately jumped in on his behalf.

"You don't understand, Flea. This change is the interesting part of the job that Wrench mentioned earlier," Minko explained. "The twins work non-stop on one big modification every year and it's unveiled to all of the elves just before Santa takes off to deliver the presents. We all get super excited for it every time, it's a perfect way to reward us elves for all of our hard work."

Flea still didn't think the sleigh should be altered in any way but he wasn't about to say that now.

"That's awesome, I really can't wait to see what you guys do," Flea said a bit too enthusiastically. Grinder seemed suspicious by Flea's sudden change of heart but Wrench broke into a wide, satisfied grin.

"Okay, it's time for you two to go," Wrench said. "We have our plan ready so it's time for us to get to work. Take one last look at the sleigh, Funny Flea, it'll never look like this again."

The twins donned their masks and each grabbed a blowtorch. Grinder told them to shut the garage door when they left and Minko gave him the thumbs-up as he led Flea back toward the ramp. Flea nearly slipped on the dusty floor and silently cursed the cloth elf shoes, which *jangled* all the way back to the surface. Flea asked Minko what change he thought the twins might make to the sleigh but Minko didn't even want to venture a guess.

"The sleigh change really *is* an exciting part of Santa's launch but I have to admit, it's not quite as important as Wrench seems to think," Minko said once they crawled back outside and lowered the garage door. "The twins are great guys but I'm sure you could tell that they were a little on the strange side. It might have to do with the fact that they're separated from the rest of the elves for such a long period of time, stuck down in that tiny garage. But it might also be due to inhaling too much of the sleigh's exhaust fumes, if you know what I mean."

Flea didn't know what Minko meant but it seemed awfully peculiar that an elf wearing a shirt with blinking lights would say that someone *else* was strange.

"I guess I've put off working long enough," Minko said. "It's time that I – or should I say *we* – contribute to Christmas."

Minko brought Flea back to the hatch in the ground located precisely halfway between the garage and the toy factory. He opened the lid and climbed down a long ladder. Once again, Flea felt uncomfortable about going underground. As he descended, his mind filled with all kinds of strange ideas about where Minko was taking him, but what he found was nothing short of boring. The ladder led to a plain room. He heard the *whirring* of a motor long before he spotted a conveyor belt on the far side of the wall. The belt moved very quickly as presents streamed in through an opening on one end of the room and streamed out through an opening on the opposite side. The conveyor slowed only long enough for each present to hesitate a split second in front of a machine that shot out some sort of laser.

"Whoa, that laser looks pretty cool," Flea said. "Your job can't be all that bad if you get to play with that thing."

Flea knew that Minko didn't like his job so he said this to make his new friend feel better about working down here. Unfortunately, his words had the opposite effect and Minko frowned. He walked across the room and pushed the power button on the machine, thus shutting off the laser. This also brought the conveyor belt to a total standstill.

"Actually, I get to use something a little less interesting than a laser," Minko said. He reached into his pocket and pulled out two pens, one of which he handed over to Flea. "The laser-writer is my replacement whenever I'm not here."

Minko rolled a pair of chairs over to the conveyor belt and turned on a television monitor located on the wall just in front of them. Flea didn't think that working would be so bad if they could watch TV but it soon became apparent that there were no shows for them to watch. Instead, the name 'Edward' appeared on the screen. Minko picked up the first wrapped-present and located the blank card taped to it.

"The name on the screen corresponds to the name we write in the card," Minko said, as he printed the name 'Edward' in much neater handwriting than Flea expected from him. "Just make sure your writing is legible or else there could be mix-ups during deliveries. Also, be sure to keep up. There are a lot of cards to write and if we go too slow, then the present tunnels can get clogged with packages."

Flea nodded his head in understanding. He grabbed the first present and hurriedly wrote 'Edward', which he did on dozens of subsequent gifts as the name continued to stay on the monitor.

"As you'll see, some kids are more spoiled than others," Minko said.

Flea hurried to keep up with the never-ending supply of gifts. He struggled to stay concentrated on writing neatly and spelling names correctly while trying to find the tiny cards on some of the larger boxes. Minko was moving slower than usual and while he didn't pester Flea to hurry, he whistled Christmas songs every time Flea started to fall behind. Flea barely worked for twenty minutes before his hand started to cramp and his writing suffered. Eventually, Flea pushed away from the conveyor belt and let Minko take over on his own, as the pudgy elf accomplished more by himself than when the two worked together.

"I don't understand, if a machine can just write out all the cards, why waste your time doing this?" Flea asked while he massaged his hand.

Flea spoke mostly out of frustration and didn't intend to sound so demeaning, but Minko became visibly upset.

"Because I'm an *elf* and I'm not allowed to build in the toy factory," he said quietly. "So if writing names in cards is the only way I can contribute to Christmas, then that's what I'll do, even if I'm stuck down here for several *more* centuries."

Several more centuries? Flea wondered. He knew that Minko was older than Niko but the pudgy elf's personality made him seem very young. Still, if Minko really had spent centuries down here, then Flea's assumption of his age was way off.

"How old *are* you?" he asked, too curious to stop himself from asking such a personal question.

"I'm not *that* old, jeez," Minko said. "In fact, I'm one of the youngest elves at the North Pole – not even a hundred years old yet. But I guess seventy years of being the worst elf in the North Pole isn't very impressive."

"Don't worry, things will get better for you," Flea said.

Flea sensed a deeper pain in his new friend and swore to himself that he would do everything possible to get Minko out of this hole in the ground. Flea didn't quite know what else to say so he picked up his pen and rolled back over to the conveyor belt, where the two continued to work in silence.

- - - - - - - - - - -

- - - -

Filling out name cards was possibly the worst boredom Flea ever had to endure. The two worked and worked and worked and Flea quickly lost track of time as the presents continued to stream in and out of the tiny underground room. Fatigue began to seriously wear him down but he continued to fight through the pain for as long as he could. But once his work began to suffer, Flea could no longer work in silence and he asked how long they'd been writing.

"Only about ten hours," Minko said, his voice still sounding somewhat downtrodden yet totally fresh, as though he'd only begun writing a few minutes earlier. "But if you're too tired to continue, you should go back to the dorms and get some rest. Don't worry, I can handle this on my own...it wouldn't be the first time."

Flea hated to abandon a job that wasn't complete but knew there was just no way he could be much help anymore. He promised Minko that he would return after taking a quick nap. He trudged back to the surface and headed toward the elf dormitory, too tired to enjoy his surroundings. At one point, Flea spotted Niko heading toward Santa's cabin at the back of the North Pole. Flea stopped and waited to see if Santa would emerge from the cabin but he didn't. Instead, Niko walked through the front door. Flea wanted to go and introduce himself to Santa Claus – he wanted to see him in person and thank him for giving permission to be here – but was too tired to walk all the way over there. Besides, Flea thought twice about overstepping his boundaries so soon.

The North Pole was still mostly empty but once he reached the dorm's huge lobby, he spotted a few elves riding the icy roller coaster. Flea stopped in front of the 'hopwell' but didn't have the energy to bounce all the way up to his floor, especially since he didn't know exactly which floor he was supposed to be on. Instead, he stumbled over to the canon elevator and climbed inside, despite how much he hated the insane ride he was about to take. He sat in the seat and pressed his palm against the hand plate, thus shooting himself through the air. Flea again feared that he would splat against the wall but he soared straight into an opening. He slid through the chute and didn't wipe out nearly as bad as the first time.

He walked down the hallway and hopelessly tried to recognize the door to his room, though everything still looked exactly the same. He got about halfway down the hall before again realizing that he should have counted the doors, yet he was too tired to turn around and go back. Eventually, Flea became so desperate that he started opening doors at random. He stumbled into dozens of wrong rooms, nearly all of which were filled with the newest and coolest toys. Only one room was different, as it looked strangely like a museum dedicated to simple, old-fashioned toys, at least those that weren't broken and littering the floor.

Fortunately, Flea didn't have much time to think about the strange room because he opened the next door and finally found an empty room. He saw his old clothes lying on the floor and was so relieved that he crashed onto his bed. Within seconds, Flea was passed out, without having removed a single article of his elf outfit. His shoes *jingled* and *jangled* every time he rolled over in his sleep…

CHAPTER SIXTEEN
Red-Robe

Flea awoke to a pounding on the door, the same pounding noise that
Miss Mabel usually made to get him up in the morning for school.
Flea was so tired that his eyes refused to budge, his mind begging
him to drift back to sleep.

"Just a few more minutes, Miss Mabel," Flea muttered,
though the pounding continued, increasing in intensity so that Flea
almost expected the door to break in half. He suddenly remembered
his vivid dream of the North Pole and his eyes snapped open. The
brightly-colored walls of the big empty room made Flea quickly
realize that this was no dream. He climbed out of bed and found that
his cloth elf-shoes must have fallen off when he was sleeping. Flea
tried to grab the door handle but he could hardly grip it because his
hand was so cramped. When he opened the door, he saw Minko
standing there, looking frantic.

"Thank Claus you're here, I was starting to get worried,"
Minko said. "I thought you might've tried to leave the North Pole
after our card-writing party."

"How long ago was that?" Flea wondered, as he rubbed his
eyes and massaged his hand. He felt so tired that he was convinced
his new friend had let him nap for only an hour or two. Minko rolled
up his sleeve and looked down at his wrist, though he wore no
watch.

"About twenty hours, give or take a few," Minko said. "I got a *lot* of work done in that time."

Flea was shocked that anyone could work so many hours in a row and still look as awake and energetic as Minko.

"But never mind that, you have to hurry up and come with me," Minko said, grabbing Flea's wrist and pulling him into the hallway. Flea stopped Minko and pointed to his feet.

"I need to put on some shoes and change my clothes," he said, not wanting to take the risk of anyone else seeing him in this ridiculous outfit.

"Okay, you can get your shoes but there's no time for you to change," Minko said frantically. "We waited for you in the classroom for half an hour before Vork sent me to find you. I'm afraid he might postpone our lesson or cancel altogether if we don't get back soon."

This information instantly brought Flea to full alertness, as he felt terrible for causing yet another problem. He rushed into his room but bypassed the elf shoes for his usual beat-up sneakers.

"I'm sorry, I had no idea that we had class right now," Flea said as he pulled on the sneakers over his high golden socks. "How did you find out about it?"

"Niko came and told me, I'm sure he went to the factory to let Rome know, too. He didn't come here?"

"No, I'm starting to get the feeling like he's trying to stop me from doing well here," Flea complained. "I *really* don't think he likes me and wants me kicked out of the North Pole."

With his sneakers on, Flea removed the big green elf jacket and rolled up the sleeves to the white puffy shirt, hoping he looked a *little* more normal. He wanted to ditch his gloves, too, but knew the unpredictable gold ring made the gloves important. A part of Flea wanted to march over to the security building and ask Niko what his problem was but he knew he lacked the courage. Besides, he saw Minko bend over and pick up a tiny scrap of paper just inside the door.

"It looks like he *did* try to tell you," Minko said. "At least sort of."

Minko handed over the piece of paper, which was no larger than a gum wrapper. Flea squinted to read the single word written so small that he could hardly see: CLASS. Flea crumpled the scrap and angrily tossed it into the hallway. A burst of determination exploded within him and he never felt a greater urge to succeed than right now. He marched out of his room and down the hallway before he remembered to do something else. He returned to his door and ripped a long piece of cloth from his shirtsleeve.

"What are you doing?" Minko asked, clearly appalled to see Flea ruin such a 'stylish' shirt.

"I'm making sure I know which room is mine," he said. He tied the piece of white cloth to his door handle.

Flea and Minko rushed down the hallway and slid down the spiraling 'slidewell.' The ride was much more enjoyable for Flea now that he knew to lay flat and keep his head down the whole way. Still, he rushed down yet again because of Niko. When they reached the lobby's ground floor, Flea walked quickly in the direction of the exit when Minko asked him to stop. His friend looked apologetic and desperate at the same time, as Flea was about to learn another of his new friend's very strange habits.

"I'm sorry, I need to ride the roller coaster," Minko called out as he rushed through the empty, roped-off line leading to the coaster.

"Aren't we supposed to be in a hurry?" Flea asked.

"I know, I know, if you want to head off to the school without me, I totally understand," Minko said. "But I've *never* been able to walk past the roller coaster without taking it for a ride. Besides, there's *always* a long line of elves so I have to take advantage when nobody is around."

Minko's quirkiness was so odd that Flea had a hard time taking him serious. But wearing blinking shirts and faking an attack on the most-guarded North Pole building were only the start of a long list of crazy things about Minko, a list that was growing by the minute. Flea watched his friend climb into the first of a long train of cars. The ride started moving moments later, picking up speed as the cars reached the first of many loops. Although the anxiety of being late to class – and maybe getting kicked out of the North Pole – made Flea's stomach feel like it was also going around loops, he couldn't help but smile at the sound of Minko's terrified *whoops,* which echoed throughout the entire lobby.

As Flea waited for the long roller coaster ride to come to an end, he felt a sudden warmth in his ringed-hand – which he was quickly learning meant some kind of warning – and looked down to see a glow coming from inside his glove. He also had the feeling that he was being watched. When he spun around, Flea saw that he was right. Regardless of the style or age differences that Flea had noticed from the elves he'd met so far, they all appeared somewhat similar in the way they looked. But the elf staring at him now was clearly of a different breed.

If that is *even an elf,* Flea wondered. Flea tried not to stare back so he turned his attention back to the roller coaster, hoping that Minko's ride would soon be over. But as the train of cars finally looped back to the start, Flea was surprised to see it continue through for a second trip around. Minko, however, didn't seem quite as concerned as he *whooped* in joy to see his ride prolonged.

Flea still felt the hair standing on the back of his neck, and when he glanced behind, he saw the creepy elf approaching him. This elf had similar pointy facial features but his skin was snow-white, his hair long and stringy and his eyes glowed a brilliant – yet unnatural – green. He also appeared ancient and frail, even more so than Vork, as his face was so wrinkled it actually looked painful. And as strange as Minko and the twins might've dressed, the long silken red robe worn by this elf was even more inexplicable. Flea felt his heart beating faster as the red-robed elf came closer. Red-robe's feet were hidden beneath the flowing robe, making him appear to be floating. The strange elf glided to a stop a few feet from Flea and continued to stare, which obviously made Flea nervous and uncomfortable.

"Hi," Flea finally mumbled to break the silence between them. Red-robe didn't speak a single word, nor did his eyes budge from Flea.

Minko's cries of joy made Flea glance toward the coaster again, where his friend was having a grand old time, apparently at Flea's expense. He didn't want to turn away from the coaster but he *knew* the red-robed elf was still staring at him. Finally, Flea couldn't ignore that any longer.

"I'm just waiting for my friend to finish," Flea babbled. "Were you going to ride the coaster next?"

The idea of this frail elf riding the coaster was almost laughable and Flea wasn't sure why he said it. But while red-robe continued to stare at him, Flea became more talkative as his level of discomfort grew.

"I'm sorry, should I not be standing here?" he asked.

The elf raised his hand and Flea instinctively recoiled, though there was nowhere for him to go since he was standing right against the lined ropes leading to the coaster. For a brief moment, Flea thought the old elf was actually going to hit him. But instead, red-robe waved his hand in a semi-circular gesture just above Flea's head. Flea became confused and his entire body grew heavy. The sound of the sliding roller coaster grew slower and more distant. His eyes barely stayed open enough for him to notice that the world around him now appeared sparkly.

"Only you can save her," red-robe said with his strange voice, which almost sounded like the noise made by a croaking frog.

But Flea hardly noticed how strained the voice was, as red-robe repeated, "Only you can save her."

Flea was in such a trance that his mind couldn't fathom a single question or even *realize* that he had no idea what the elf meant.

"Only *I* can save her," Flea said. "Only *I* can save her."

The sparkles in front of his eyes subsided before Flea realized that he was still muttering to himself. Minko was suddenly standing where red-robe had just been, a look of confusion etched on his pudgy face.

"Are you crazy?" Minko asked. "Why were you talking to *him*?"

Flea's head cleared and he turned to see the red-robed elf quickly gliding away.

"*He* approached *me*, not the other way around," Flea said, as the elf's warning continued to replay in his mind.

"I've never seen one of *them* inside the dorm," Minko said. The strange elf disappeared through the lobby doors in the distance and Minko explained that they better get to class now. Although the two should've been in a rush, neither walked very quickly. They took no chance of catching up with red-robe.

"Only I can save her," Flea repeated.

"Huh?"

"Only I can save her," he said again. "After that strange elf put me in some sort of trance, he gave me that warning over and over. Any idea what it means?"

Minko slowly shook his head. "I doubt *anyone* would understand something one of *them* said. *Those* elves are very old and mysterious, I'm pretty sure they play a big role in Santa's…" Minko lowered his voice to a whisper. "…Santa's magic. I don't know where *they* live or stay and I've never spoken to *them*. In fact, I've gone years before without seeing a single one of *them*."

"He said *her*, only I can save *her*," Flea said. "Which *her* could he possibly mean?"

"I have no idea," Minko said when they reached the lobby doors. They both glanced around the North Pole grounds and saw no trace of red-robe. "But if we don't get back to school soon, we'll have to worry more about saving *ourselves*."

As they jogged toward the school, Flea noticed that a few more elves were out and about, most of them standing just outside the toy factory. The elves just stood around, undoubtedly enjoying the fresh air after being stuck inside the factory for countless hours. Many of the elves stared openly at Flea and whispered to one another but he didn't have time to worry about this – *or* to worry that they were all dressed similarly to Niko, minus for the big red hat. Flea just kept thinking about red-robe's warning and more specifically, about which 'her' he was referring to. But once they entered the school and walked into the classroom, Flea realized that he'd only met one 'her' so far.

CHAPTER SEVENTEEN
Vork's Three Gifts

"Take you long enough?" Rome asked. "I've been waiting over an *hour* for you."

She looked very mad but Flea could only smile at her. He suddenly knew the course of action he needed to take (although he still didn't know *why* he had to take it). Flea turned to his teacher, who didn't appear nearly as annoyed as Rome to have been left waiting for so long.

"I'm really sorry, Mr. Vork. I was sleeping and never received word from Niko about having class again."

"Sleeping *already*? You sure are new," Vork said. "And you could be weeks late to this class for all I care. It doesn't matter to me if the three of you *ever* become proper builder elves."

"Well it matters to me," Rome said angrily. She ran her fingers through her hair to make sure it was perfectly in place, but suddenly pulled out a long piece of colored paper. For some reason, Rome blushed as she crumpled up the paper and threw it toward the two boys. "Now hurry up and get to your tables so we can start already."

Flea followed her orders and rushed to his table. Minko, however, stood in place for several long seconds before casually strolling away.

"I'm not going to my table because *you* told me to," he said to Rome. "I'm going to my table because I *want* to."

Vork looked at the two bickering students and shook his head.

"Now that we're all here and ready, class can begin," Vork said. "After considering your initial evaluations, I've come up with three presents that will help each of you improve your building skills."

Three similarly wrapped gifts sat on the table at the front of the classroom, two smaller boxes and one significantly larger. Vork picked up the first present and handed it to Rome.

"Thank you," said a surprised Rome. She shook the box and apparently liked the sound as a huge grin appeared on her face. "I know clothes when I hear them."

"Open it," Vork instructed.

The teacher walked away from Rome's desk while she ripped off the wrapping paper. Flea noticed a sly grin appear on Vork's face and knew this was going to be bad for her even before she opened the box. Rome frowned.

"You *must* be joking," Rome said. For the first time, she spoke to Vork using the same annoyed tone she normally reserved for Flea and Minko.

"What did you get?" Minko asked excitedly.

"I'm *not* joking," Vork said. "Go ahead and take out your present so your classmates can see." Rome hesitated and looked desperately to her teacher, though Vork was unaffected by her beauty *or* her pouting. "They're going to see you wearing it anyway."

Rome sighed and pulled out an outfit that looked similar to the ridiculous elf costume that Flea wore.

"Finally, you'll have some style like Flea and me," Minko said.

Rome made a noise somewhere between a frustrated grunt and an angry shriek before she dropped the clothes back into the box. "There's no way I'm going to wear that, no *possible* way."

"Yes, you will," Vork said. "Because if you don't wear it, you'll be expelled from this school. If that happens, there won't be enough students left for this class and *none of you* will graduate."

"Come on, just wear it already," Minko snapped at her. "Don't make all of us suffer because you're selfish."

Rome crossed her arms and stared stone-faced at her fellow students. Minko's insults obviously weren't about to convince her.

"Please, Rome, it really doesn't look *that* bad on me, does it?" Flea asked.

"Yes, as a matter of fact it does," she said without hesitation. She remained silent for nearly a minute, waiting for Vork to say something else. But the teacher already mentioned that he was in no rush for anything. Rome eventually conceded defeat in the war of silence. "Fine, I'll wear it when you need me to."

"Good, right now will do," Vork said.

"Seriously?" she asked incredulously.

The teacher nodded and Rome sighed before snatching the box off her table and storming out of the classroom. She returned moments later wearing the ridiculous outfit and an expression of utter misery.

"The *entire* outfit, please," Vork said.

Rome made the same annoyed grunt/shriek noise again. She reached into the box and pulled out the oversized Christmas hat, which she placed carefully over her perfect hair. Minko made no attempt to subdue his laughter. Flea smiled at her in an attempt to convey his thanks for her doing this. Rome, however, couldn't tell the difference between the reactions from both boys.

"If either of you ever mention this to the other elves, I'll *personally* shove you in a box bound for Antarctica," she warned.

Vork waited for Rome to return to her table before addressing her.

"In order for you to succeed, you'll have to focus on being an *elf,* not a fashion model," the teacher said. "And believe me, nothing could be further from a fashion model than *that* outfit."

Vork returned to the front table and picked up the next wrapped gift. He headed toward the two boys but beyond Minko's table. He dropped the box in front of Flea, causing a loud metallic *clang.* Flea opened the box and discovered a single metal glove inside, which looked like it was from a medieval suit of armor.

"What do I do with this?" Flea asked as he studied the metal glove.

"Obviously, you wear it," Vork said. "On your *right* hand."

Despite the glove being so big and heavy, its opening was surprisingly small as he squeezed his hand through. The glove was barely on his hand for a few seconds before Vork grabbed a hammer off his desk.

"Catch!" the teacher said as he hurled the hammer in Flea's direction.

Flea instinctively tried to catch the hammer with his right hand. He was barely able to lift the heavy metal glove in time to stop the hammer from hitting him. It ricocheted off the glove and smashed into his foot, causing Flea to yelp in pain.

"In order to maximize efficiency while building, *real* elves are taught to use both hands equally," Vork explained. "Your left hand has a *lot* of catching up to do with the right."

"Yes, sir," Flea said.

Vork finally gave the largest of the presents to Minko, who excitedly ripped off the wrapping paper and spilled the contents onto his table. While Minko might have been satisfied with either of the first two presents Vork handed out, he was clearly confused and underwhelmed by what he received.

"A bunch of nails and a piece of wood?" he asked.

"That's right, but it's not just *any* piece of wood," Vork explained. "You're not looking at it closely enough."

Minko picked up the wood and examined it more in depth, though he discovered only a simple difference.

"Okay, it's a piece of wood with a bunch of little circles drawn on it," Minko said.

"Now you're getting somewhere," Vork said. "Flip it over and look on the other side."

Minko did as he was told but still wasn't impressed.

"More circles," he said.

"Those circles are drawn in *exactly* the same spots on both sides of that wood," Vork explained. "You've never learned the basic fundamentals of building. I guess that instinct didn't come quite so naturally to *you*. The most important thing you must learn first is to nail straight. In order to successfully hammer a nail straight through that board, it must go through the circle on one side and come out its corresponding circle on the other side. Once you can complete that entire board in less than thirty seconds, then you can move on to more difficult tasks."

"Only thirty *seconds*?" Minko asked. "But there are too many circles drawn on this thing."

"There are sixty circles – two per second – so you better get practicing."

Minko glanced at Flea and shrugged his shoulders, apparently willing to give this a shot. He picked up his hammer and placed a nail over the first circle, perfectly driving it through the circle on the other side of the wood. Minko smiled as the nail turned green with success and he quickly moved on to the next one, not spending nearly as much time lining it up. From the next table over, Flea could tell that his friend hadn't placed the nail straight enough even as he swung the hammer down. As soon as the nail went crooked, they all heard a loud *buzz* followed immediately by Minko's yelp. He dropped the hammer as all of his hair now stuck straight up. As if being shocked wasn't bad enough, the one green nail he'd already successfully hammered returned to its usual silver color and fell out of the wood, its circle quickly filling back in.

"What the – "

"I forgot to mention that any mistakes will be promptly punished," Vork said with a smile. "I hope that will provide you the proper motivation to improve."

Minko tried a few more nails before he messed up another one. A buzz, a yelp and a new hair-do later, it was Rome's turn to laugh at Minko's misfortune.

"I love what you've done to your hair," she said.

Minko tried to smooth his hair flat but it shot straight back up every time, much to Rome's enjoyment.

"If I only had a big, ugly red hat to cover it," Minko shot back at her, though he quickly realized that Rome wasn't the only one wearing such a hat. "Sorry, Flea, your hat looks really good."

Vork waved Flea over to the table next to Rome's in the corner of the room. While Minko continued working on his hammering drill, the teacher decided it was time for the two better builders to retry the toy chest challenge under their new conditions. At first, Flea had a lot of trouble working with only his left hand. Even the simple task of holding a nail steady was nearly impossible to do with the metal glove. But after only a few hours of practice, Flea was surprised by how easily he adapted. His left had improved and he built toy chest after toy chest, though nothing he completed seemed to rise to Vork's incredibly high standards. Rome had the same trouble impressing their teacher, although Flea noticed that she was building much quicker than before.

A loud crack of electricity exploded from Minko's direction and a bright flash of blue light momentarily illuminated the classroom. Minko yelled even louder than usual as the wood clattered against the floor, nails shooting across the room.

"He must've overloaded it," Vork said. Minko stood completely still, a shocked look on his face. A tiny bit of smoke floated above his head. "I've never seen any elf take this long to master such a simple skill. I better make sure the wooden board isn't about to blow up."

Minko burst into a stream of excuses as the teacher approached him. Flea couldn't help joining Rome in laughter but the two soon got back to work while Minko gathered the nails strewn about the room. Flea was only a few steps away from completing his best toy chest yet, one he was determined to impress Vork with.

"You really *are* as good as the other elves," Rome said as she stole a glance toward Flea's work. She'd stopped working just long enough to brush dust off her clothes and fix her hair.

"Thanks, I really appreciate that," Flea said. "It looks like you're getting much better, too."

Rome casually shrugged her shoulders. "Too bad I'm not getting better quickly enough. You'll graduate way before your weird friend or I will be good enough to pass. At least when Minko and I return to our horrible jobs, we can take this little bit of gained knowledge with us. Maybe we'll even get another chance to pass this class in a few *more* centuries. Maybe."

Flea knew exactly what Rome was trying to do. But he'd already planned what to do about this class, guided by red-robe's warning that 'only he could save her.' Still, that didn't mean Flea had to let Rome know about his plans, especially since she continued to prove how selfish she could be. Minko yelped again and Flea glanced over to see his friend still hammering nails into the fixed piece of wood. Minko seemed more determined than ever to get better and leave his card-writing job forever.

Hopefully I can save him while I'm saving her, too, Flea thought.

Vork returned to the front of the class where he pushed a button at his desk. Flea's perfectly-built toy chest – along with Rome's project and Minko's wooden board – fell apart in front of him, leaving him with just a stack of raw materials.

"While this class has been real fun, I think we all deserve a break for a while," Vork said. The three students sighed in relief, as Minko's hair, Rome's sense of style and Flea's tired left hand all needed a break. But the teacher wasn't about to make it *that* easy for them to escape the classroom. "Class can come to an end once Minko finishes his hammering challenge in less than thirty seconds…" (This announcement caused Rome to groan loudly.) "…*and* either Flea or Rome can build a toy chest – to *my* standards – in less than three minutes."

Rome clearly looked deflated at the thought of such a difficult task but Flea whispered words of support to her. "We can *do* this, *both* of us."

The holographic image of the toy chest replayed at the front of the room for only a few seconds before being replaced by the timer, which blinked 3:00…

CHAPTER EIGHTEEN
Flea's Reward for Helping

"Go!" Vork called out.

He swept his hand through the timer and it started counting back from three minutes. Flea started to work with his left hand, which now moved just as smoothly and instinctively as his right. He'd even grown accustomed to working with the clunky metal glove on his other hand. Flea progressed quickly through his project and when he saw that he was halfway finished, he stole a quick glance at the holographic timer.

2:01...2:00...1:59...

Flea was amazed that so little time had passed, but when he looked over at Rome's toy chest, he saw that she was still far behind.

Only I can save her, Flea thought. *Only I can save Rome from a lifetime of humiliation about not being a proper builder elf.*

Flea heard Minko curse a second time as another one of his thirty-second time periods past. Minko and Rome both needed his help so Flea was purposely errant when he struck the next nail, causing it to poke out of the side of his toy chest. It was the same mistake he'd made the first time he tried hammering with his left hand, so he hoped Vork wouldn't become too suspicious of it happening again. Flea didn't slow his working speed but by the time he removed the errant nail and covered up his 'error', the three minutes expired and left him well short of completion. His and

Rome's toy chests momentarily turned green before falling apart into raw materials again.

"Try again," Vork said and restarted the timer.

Flea and Rome started over. Flea slowed his pace so that he came just short of finishing when the timer reached zero. This same pattern continued for several hours, as Flea built slowly enough to barely miss finishing or he made small mistakes that took him too long to correct. While Rome came closer to finishing each time, she eventually hit a wall where her work was not progressing any further. She clearly became frustrated and Flea's words of encouragement between each round of building soon annoyed her.

"Don't worry, you can do this," Flea said after one occasion when she came close to finishing.

"You don't know *anything* so *stop* talking to me," she snapped. Rome looked remorseful for a brief moment but Vork started the timer again before she had the chance to apologize.

Soon after restarting, Minko called Vork over to his table, leaving Flea and Rome alone. Flea knew he might not get another opportunity like this so he glanced over at Rome to see which section she started to build. At this point, her hair was all over the place and her face was covered with a layer of dust but she didn't seem to care, as she was too focused on the task at hand. Flea didn't feel proud of what he was about to do but Rome was obviously following Vork's advice to focus on building and she deserved to be rewarded. With Vork concentrated completely on Minko, Flea started to build his chest at the exact opposite part of Rome. Flea knew that Minko's test only lasted thirty seconds but he made significant progress in that limited amount of time. He took his partially built section and placed it on Rome's table, taking back some of her materials in return. She looked at him with confusion but Flea merely nodded, silently telling her to hurry up.

Flea returned to his table and saw that Vork was still preoccupied but that didn't last much longer. By the time Vork returned with only a minute remaining, Flea was much further behind than usual. He could feel Vork's suspicious glare though Flea refused to make eye contact, worrying that the guilty expression he wore would give him away. A light-bulb went off in Flea's head. He mis-hit another nail, sending it out the side of the chest. He grunted angrily – though he hoped not *too* angrily.

"That's the second time in the last minute," he muttered to himself, loudly enough for his teacher to hear.

Though Flea had sacrificed so much of his allotted time to help Rome – not to mention fixing his 'mistake' – he still came very close to completing his toy chest when the timer ran out and his project fell to pieces yet again. But when he looked at Rome's table, he saw that her toy chest remained intact and a wide grin appeared on her face.

"Has a *miracle* finally happened?" Vork asked. He closely examined Rome's project as she ran her hands through her hair and wiped the dust from her face. Vork nodded his head approvingly but when he looked in Flea's direction, Flea quickly turned away, unable to stop himself from blushing. Though Vork must have undoubtedly suspected something amiss, he said nothing – at least nothing about Rome's sudden success. "It looks like the prized newcomer is our only failure."

Flea and Rome both looked over to Minko, who held up his board full of green nails, the stopped holographic timer flashing at the one-second mark. Minko was clearly happy but he tried not to smile *too* much when he looked toward Flea.

"You better learn as quickly as your classmates or you might not be needed here after all," Vork warned. "Class dismissed."

\- \- \- \- \- \- \- \- \- \- \-
\- \- \- \-

While Vork's warning worried Flea, he was happy to hear Minko talk so excitedly about the moment he finished his hammering challenge. As the two walked down the school's dark hallway, they heard the sound of running footsteps behind them.

"Hey guys, wait up!" Rome called out.

She'd already changed out of the elf costume and prettied herself up, but Rome still wore the big red Christmas hat. For the first time since Flea met her, Rome appeared totally relaxed, not annoyed or angry or upset. She finally looked like a real person – or a real *elf* – and not some phony who was more concerned about her looks and image. To someone who didn't know better, the three students might have actually looked like a group of friends walking the halls.

"I still like the elf costume more," Minko said as he looked over Rome's fashionable clothes.

She was about to argue with him, but instead chuckled and slowly shook her head. "You *would* think that," she said before turning to Flea. "I just wanted to say thanks for helping me back there. I know I might seem selfish sometimes but I *am* appreciative for what you did."

"Why is she thanking you, Flea? What did you do?" Minko asked.

"Nothing," Flea said quickly. He was certain that his friend would be angry if he found out that he and Rome had technically cheated. "It wasn't really a big deal. I just tried to keep both of us positive the whole time so we wouldn't grow discouraged."

"Yeah, that was a nice thing to do even though I haven't exactly been the nicest elf to you," Rome said.

"I'm new here so I'm sure there'll be times when I need help from *both* of you," Flea said. "I still understand so little around here, I can't even find my room in the dorm. I actually had to rip a piece of my shirt and tie it around the handle to remember which room was mine."

Rome chuckled, her smile so radiant that Flea had a hard time walking without tripping over his own two feet. The students walked out the door and into the outside world, where the snow continued to fall lightly.

"Don't worry, if you lived in the human world for so many years, it won't take long to get used to this place," Rome said.

As they approached the toy factory, Flea and Minko expected Rome to head off on her own, especially since even more elves hung out near the factory's entrance. But she didn't distance herself from them. In fact, she even allowed the other elves to see her talking to them.

"So, what are you two going to do until our next class?" she asked.

"Why do you care?" Minko asked defensively.

"I don't know, I just – "

Rome never got the chance to finish that thought.

"Rome!" a voice called out near the factory.

A group of youngish-looking elves – all of them as well-dressed as Rome – stood apart from the rest of the elves near the factory. This group looked at Flea and Minko with total disdain, especially the guy in the front. He stood with his hands on his hips, angrily glaring, his hair tousled in an unnatural way that must've required plenty of time to get just right. He was clearly the leader of the group and was just as handsome as Rome was beautiful. But it didn't take long to show that he had a mean streak that cut even deeper than hers.

"You're actually hanging out with the card elf and the weird new guy?" the leader asked Rome.

Rome frowned at Flea and Minko in an apologetic way before her expression changed back to its usual snobby sneer.

"Of course not," Rome said as she jogged over to her group of friends. "I'm being *forced* to take that stupid class. Trust me, I can't wait until it's over."

Flea and Minko watched as a few of the 'cool elves' pointed at Rome's red hat and laughed. She immediately turned red and took it off, smoothing out her hair in the process. Flea suddenly understood why she'd been so adamant about not telling her friends about the elf outfit she was forced to wear in class. Despite Rome's sudden attitude change toward him, a part of Flea actually felt bad for her. Her 'friends' didn't seem to treat her very well and Flea certainly knew how it felt to be the outsider in a group.

"Let's go, I don't feel like listening to this any more," Minko whispered.

When Flea turned to follow him toward the hatch, he thought he spotted red-robe just outside Santa's cabin but when he blinked his eyes, he saw nothing there. He wondered if the saving that Rome required went beyond just graduating from elf school. Minko, however, had little sympathy for her.

"I *knew* she didn't change," Minko said. "She would never do anything to anger Artimus Maximus, he's the leader of that little group. He can be a real pain in the ice. If it wasn't for his entourage never leaving his side – especially the big guys, Orby and Roc – I would... I would do *something,* that's for sure."

"Why does Rome feel the need to hang out with them?" Flea asked.

"She's just trying to convince herself that she's not in love with me," Minko said.

Flea chuckled but when his friend looked at him, Minko appeared totally serious. Just as Minko broke into a grin, there was a loud *thud* as a snowball smashed against the back of his head and caused him to stumble forward and crash to the ground. Flea spun around just in time to see a snowball *whizzing* directly toward his face. He felt the warmth in his hand and raised it to cover himself. A breeze blew just hard enough to push the snowball off its path, missing him by inches. In the distance, Flea saw the group of elves laughing just as Artimus – and his perfect hair – unleashed a fastball headed right for him. This time, Flea held his hand up and watched as the snowball instantly melted before it could hit him.

The crowd of onlookers – consisting of more than just Rome's group of friends – gasped upon seeing Flea's ability to stop the snow in mid-flight. Many were visibly disturbed and some even went so far as to rush back into the toy factory. Artimus, however, seemed more bothered by Flea.

"Freak!" he yelled out. "The new guy is a *freak!*"

Artimus ordered Rome and the rest of his group back into the toy factory. Minko pulled himself to his feet and picked up his own snowball, launching it in the group's direction. Unfortunately, it came up well short. Minko unleashed a torrent of threats toward Artimus and the group but they were all inside by the time the first words left his mouth. With the rest of the elves still staring at Flea, he grabbed his friend by the arm and convinced Minko that it was time to cool off and head to the card-writing station.

\-   -   -   -   -   -   -   -   -   -   -

\-   -   -   -

Flea and Minko put in another marathon session of card writing. At first, the work wasn't so bad since Flea was finally able to use his right hand again. He listened to Minko complain about Artimus and Rome and everything else at the North Pole that made his life difficult.

"You can add being friends with me to that list," Flea said. "They all think I'm a freak now."

"Artimus and his friends have been calling me a freak for *decades* now so don't worry about them. They're just jealous of the amazing abilities you have," Minko said. "Besides, the way I figure, it's better to have the elf with freakish abilities on *my* side."

Flea eventually grew tired and needed sleep again, as his body had not yet acclimated to life at the North Pole. Minko was still wide-eyed and energized from his success in class so he stayed behind at his card-writing post. Deep down, he hoped this was the last Christmas season that he'd hold *this* job.

"If I'm still asleep when you find out about our next class, make sure you come and find me *right away*," Flea said. "My room is the one with the piece of white cloth tied around the door handle."

Flea headed back to the elf dorm, passing numerous elves along the way. Word had apparently circulated about what he'd done during the snowball attack and many elves stared at him with a combination of apprehension and fear. This was a new feeling for Flea, as the students in his new schools usually looked at him because they thought he was strange. He suddenly wasn't so sure which way was worse.

Flea headed straight for the canon elevator inside the dorm, soaring up to his floor with hardly a worry during the flight. He rode the chute and landed perfectly on his feet in the hallway, proud of himself for finally learning to do something right. *Maybe it* won't *be so hard to get used to living here,* Flea thought. But as he started to walk down the hall, his day quickly took a turn for the worse. There was something different about the first unmarked door: a white strip of cloth was tied around the handle. At first, Flea was confused and wondered if this was merely a coincidence, if other lost elves had caught on to the trick of locating his room. But when he approached the next door – and the next one and the next one after that – he saw that *every* door in this hallway had the same piece of white cloth dangling from the handle.

Then Flea heard the laughter. The sound echoed from somewhere down the hallway and he knew it was at his expense. Usually he would've tried to avoid any sort of confrontation, but he was so angry that he didn't hesitate to run toward the noise, determined to find those responsible for torturing him. Miss Mabel was no longer here to hold Flea back from sticking up for himself, which was exactly what he planned to do now. He sprinted all the way down the hallway – nearly slipping several times on small patches of snow scattered about – until he reached the other end. There, he saw Artimus Maximus and his group of well-dressed friends huddled around the final door before the 'slidewell.' The group continued to laugh even when Flea came into view and stopped just a few doors down.

"Here comes the freak!" one of the girl elves shrieked. "Let's get out of here."

Though most of the group quickly headed for the slidewell – with some of the bigger guys pushing aside the smaller girls so they could escape first – Artimus stood in place and stared at Flea, smiling his wicked grin. This so enraged Flea that he sprinted toward the much bigger elf, wanting to tear him limb from limb even though he'd never fought anyone in his entire life.

Artimus flinched first.

"Don't you leave until you're finished," Artimus yelled at the lone elf still huddled by the final door. The group leader then followed the rest of his friends into the slidewell. Flea considered taking out his frustration on the last elf left behind but decided that following Artimus down the slide would be far more satisfying. But he didn't make it to the final door when he heard Artimus call out from the slidewell. "Hurry up, Rome!"

Flea stopped dead in his tracks and looked at the final elf in the hallway with him. He'd been so focused on reaching Artimus that he hadn't realized it was *Rome* tying the white cloth to the last door handle. As she turned to look at Flea and their eyes met, it dawned on him that this must have been Rome's idea, that he had *just* told her about the way he marked his door. For a brief moment, Flea thought he saw a spark of regret in her eyes. But despite the fact that none of her friends were around, Rome didn't apologize. She said nothing before rushing into the slidewell.

Minko was right, Flea thought sadly. *She* hasn't *changed.*

Flea's disappointment took away his desire to track down Artimus. Besides, he had the feeling that this wouldn't be the last run-in he'd have with the cruel group of 'cool elves.' Flea's sprint down the hallway had made him even more tired so he headed back toward his room, having to search for it all over again.

With each room he found full of toys, Flea angrily ripped the white piece of cloth from the handle. He had two handfuls of cloth by the time he stopped in front of another door and grabbed the handle. He paused because it felt cold to the touch. Although Flea had no idea why the handle felt like ice, he somehow knew that he'd found his room. He turned the handle but when he gently pushed the door, it didn't budge an inch. Flea had to throw his entire weight against it and when the door finally opened, an avalanche of snow poured into the hallway from his room. Snow filled the inside of his room from floor to ceiling, and directly in the middle of that snowy wall were dozens of pieces of coal, aligned to form a single word: FREAK.

CHAPTER NINETEEN
The Gift Wrapper

Flea yawned as he rushed to keep up with Minko. On their way to
the elf school, Minko walked with an extra pep in his step, fueled by
anger at how he'd just found Flea. Rome waited inside the entrance
and immediately rushed over to Flea.

"I'm so sorry about what happened, Flea. That wasn't my
idea," Rome said.

"Tying the white cloth to every single door handle wasn't
your idea?" Flea asked.

"Well, maybe *that* part was, but it was only supposed to be a
joke," she said. "Believe me, as soon as I told my friends about the
way you marked your door, I instantly regretted it. I had no idea they
were going to do the whole snow thing until it was too late to stop
them. I think you really embarrassed Artimus when you stopped his
snowball. We've never seen anyone do something like that and I
guess he wanted revenge."

Minko looked so angry that he shook with rage, though he
remained quiet and allowed Flea to address Rome first.

"That's okay, don't worry about it," Flea said, not wanting
any awkwardness in class. He'd slept off most of his anger toward
Rome. Besides, he truly didn't think that filling his room with snow
had been her idea, though she'd obviously done nothing to stop it.

Minko was not so forgiving.

"Do you know where I just found Flea?" Minko yelled.

Flea tried to grab his friend's arm to hold him back but Minko easily pulled himself free and stepped just inches from Rome.

"It's okay, Minko, really," Flea said, trying to calm him down. Minko backed away about a foot but wasn't going to just drop the subject.

"It's *not* okay, Flea. *Nobody* treats my friends that way. *Nobody* should have to sleep on the floor in the middle of the hallway because a bunch of iceblock-heads filled his room with snow," Minko growled. "Just because you and your friends are the youngest elves here, that doesn't mean you should act like mean little children, like you're only fifty years old."

Flea expected Rome to explode on Minko, who she seemed to hate more than anyone else. The two of them usually looked for any reason to battle and Flea was certain that this was about to turn ugly. But Rome surprised both of them by hanging her head and nodding in agreement.

"You're right, it was really mean and you didn't deserve that, Flea. I'm really sorry that Artimus and my other friends – myself included – can be such jerks," Rome said with utmost sincerity.

"Why do you even bother hanging out with them?" Flea asked. "You're so much better than they are."

Rome shrugged. "I don't know. We all grew up and went to school together and they accept me even though I didn't graduate and now I'm just a… well, I'm not a real builder."

"But it seems like they're really mean to you, too," Flea said.

"It's not that bad," Rome said unconvincingly. "They just joke around a lot, they always have and I'm sure they always will."

Vork stuck his head out of the nearby room and told the three students to end their therapy session and get to class.

-    -   -   -   -   -   -   -   -   -   -

-    -   -   -

Although the toy factory clock – and thus the entire world – remained stuck on 11:59, the equivalent of a month's worth of time passed at the North Pole. Flea, Minko and Rome spent a majority of that time in the classroom, honing their skills (though in Flea's case, he made sure to hone a bit more slowly). Every time they left school, Rome ditched the two of them for her 'friends', who seemed to spend more and more time hanging out in front of the toy factory, waiting to harass Flea and Minko. Artimus and his goons hurled snowballs at them but Flea was able to stop them all, as well as keep Minko from fighting back. Flea wasn't sure if he'd lost his ability to *throw* snowballs as well as he could stop them, but he was content with laying low and staying out of trouble. He just wished that Minko wouldn't complain so much about Rome. After all, she'd never joined her friends in throwing snowballs at them.

The route they took to the card-writing station passed by the garage, where they always saw sparks through the garage door window and heard the *grinding* of serious metal work. As much as Flea and Minko both wanted to peek at the twins' progress on the sleigh, they always resisted the urge to spy on Wrench and Grinder.

Minko promised that staying away would make the big unveiling all the more exciting. But considering how much effort the twins seemed to be putting into the sleigh, Flea doubted he would recognize it the next time he saw it.

Eventually, Flea's body required less and less sleep as he grew accustomed to life at the North Pole. Unfortunately, that meant spending more time writing cards, a task that Flea hated more each time he had to climb down the ladder to the small underground station. Flea often grew so bored while writing that his thoughts returned to Miss Mabel, who he started to miss even though no time had passed for her in the human world. Even Minko had stopped trying to convince him that writing names 'wasn't that bad.' As Minko's building skills improved, he became less content with the idea of staying at this job much longer.

Flea and Minko were in the middle of yet another long work session when they heard the hatch door *squeak* open.

"Niko ordered me to tell you two that it's time for class now," said the slow-speaking voice of one of the security building snowmen.

Flea and Minko looked at each other with relief and jumped out of their seats, both of them sore from sitting in the same spot for so long. This had been one of the longest breaks between classes that they'd ever endured and both started to worry that there was a problem. Minko quickly flipped on the laser-writer and the two rushed toward the school. As usual, Artimus and his friends were waiting, heavily armed with snowballs. But one of the girls rushed

over to them and whispered something, causing them to drop their
snowy weapons. The bullies played innocent just as Flea spotted
Niko emerging from the school and heading in his direction.

"Hey, Niko," Artimus called out. "How's your father?"

Niko glanced nervously toward Flea before shaking hands
with Artimus and speaking to him so softly that Flea couldn't hear.
Not surprisingly, it seemed as though Niko and Artimus were
friendly enough with one another. After a brief exchange, Artimus
rejoined his friends and Niko called out to Rome and Minko that
they should head off to class.

"Have fun with your *buddies,* Rome," Artimus called out,
garnering several chuckles amongst his group.

Flea continued toward the school alongside Minko but Niko
stopped him and said he needed to talk.

"Is everything okay with the North Pole's security?" Flea
asked once he and Niko were alone.

"No, as a matter of fact everything *isn't* okay with security
but that's none of your concern," Niko said. "I just visited with Vork
and received an update about your class. I was very disappointed to
learn that you've been underachieving. The North Pole is being put
in more danger because you're here and *failure* is the best you can
do?"

Flea glanced around the North Pole village but didn't see any
signs of impending attack from the Army of snowmen.

"I still don't understand how *me* being here puts the North
Pole in more danger," Flea said.

"And that's something you don't *need* to understand so spare me your attitude and fifty questions," Niko said. "Maybe you should concentrate more on not allowing the card-writer and gift-wrapper to beat you in class."

"The gift wrapper?" Flea asked.

Niko sighed and slowly shook his head, clearly annoyed.

"That's what Rome does inside the toy factory. She begged me for the job even though there are machines that can do it," Niko explained. "And *she's* doing better than you?"

Flea couldn't admit to Niko that he was taking it easy in class for Minko and Rome's benefit, though he *wanted* to give a reason why he should stay at the North Pole. But his mind drifted to Rome and the news that she was even farther down the totem pole than she'd let on, reinforcing his need to 'save her.'

"Nothing to say for yourself?" Niko asked. "I'm too busy to stand here and watch you stare off into space, you know."

"I'm sorry, I'll try to do better," Flea said weakly. He tried to sound firmer when he spoke again. "I *promise* I'll do better, I won't disappoint you *or* your father."

This was the first time that Niko looked genuinely surprised.

"You know that Santa's my father?" he asked.

"I've picked up *some* common knowledge since I've been here. I'm not quite as dumb as you seem to think," Flea said. "Is there any possibility that you could introduce me to Santa? I need him to understand how serious I am about being the best elf I can be."

"I'm not sure an introduction is such a good idea right now," Niko said. A sudden gust of wind nearly blew off his hat and he was careful to keep it pulled down low on his head. "Besides, Santa is very busy this time of the year and frankly, you're just some new elf not worthy of his time. I've also heard around the village that you've had some trouble with Artimus and his friends, is that true?"

"Minko and I seem to be their favorite targets for throwing snowballs. But I've figured out a way to deal with the situation and avoid making trouble," Flea said, hoping that his responsibility would gain him some credit.

It didn't.

"No respectable elf would take such abuse without tossing a few snowballs back," Niko said. "You were brought here for a reason and *any* sign of weakness gives Santa second thoughts about your character. Fight back, prove that you aren't anybody's target. And as far as your schooling goes, you'll soon have the chance to prove your worthiness. You better not disappoint or you'll get a one-way ticket back to the human world."

Niko walked away without another word. Artimus and his friends continued watching Flea, as they were undoubtedly waiting for Niko to leave before attacking. Now that Flea had permission to fight back, he was tempted to stay right there and give the bullies a taste of their own medicine. But Flea no longer had to fight his battles alone and knew that Minko would not want to miss any of the action. He ran off toward school, excited to tell his best friend that they could finally fight back.

But when Flea rushed into the first classroom – the only one in the entire school where they'd ever had practice – he found it empty.

CHAPTER TWENTY
Final Exams

"Over here, Flea!" Vork called out from somewhere down the school's long, dark hallway. "Get moving, we don't have all day!"

Flea was surprised that they'd be having class elsewhere.

"Mr. Vork, I have to get my metal glove!" Flea called back.

"Leave it!"

Farther down the hallway, Flea found less light and more broken toys littering the floor. Vork, Minko and Rome waited inside one of the final classrooms, which Flea discovered wasn't as small or simple as the other one. In fact, this place looked less like a classroom and more like a production center. It held a seemingly endless supply of materials as well as an old conveyor belt. There were a pair of machines at the end of the conveyor belt, one of which looked exactly like the laser card-writer.

"We are here today because Minko has completed most of the basic fundamentals tests and Flea and Rome clearly know how to...*work together* to get things done on a timetable," Vork said. Flea and Rome looked at each other, both wearing similar expressions of guilt. "Did you really think I wouldn't figure out what you two were doing?"

"What *were* you two doing?" Minko asked.

"Flea was helping me get better," Rome said, oversimplifying their cheating.

"If Flea was smart, he would've worried about helping *himself* do better, setting *himself* apart from you two to make sure that he graduated," Vork lectured, causing Flea to blush. "But because of your dishonest actions, it has been decided that all three of you will either pass or fail *together*."

"Then I'm sure Minko and I will step up and help Flea," Rome said confidently. "We can *do* this, guys, I know we can."

Flea turned and smiled at Rome, who seemed self*less* instead of self*ish* for the first time.

"The two of you *better* because neither of you has as much to lose if you fail," Vork said cryptically. "You two will always have a place here, regardless of the terrible jobs you'll return to. Flea, however, will lose his chance to stay at the North Pole. It's just too dangerous for him to be here if he's unable to prove himself useful. Do the three of you understand what's on the line?"

Rome and Minko nodded though Vork's words had a much greater impact on Flea. This sudden change had undoubtedly been Niko's doing and Flea felt pressured to perform up Vork's lofty expectations. Now that there was no threat of him graduating alone and leaving Minko and Rome behind, Flea didn't have to hold back.

"So what do we have to do?" he asked.

"The orders for some of the most sought-after gifts this holiday season came during the last few days before Christmas Eve," Vork explained. "These orders were the direct result of a television program that aired in the human world a few days ago, a show that introduced a new line of products."

"*The Great Build-Off,*" Flea interrupted. He already knew where this was headed.

"That's correct. The entire elf building-force has been working on the rest of the world's orders – and have made *serious* progress toward finishing – but they haven't yet touched any of the products offered at www.shopteachergoods.com. So in order to pass elf school *and* prove your worthiness to build in Santa's toy factory, the three of you must complete all of these orders before the factory-whistle blows, ending the Christmas building season."

"And when will that be?" Flea asked.

"We'll never know," Rome answered. "It will be whenever the last elf finishes his or her last order."

"So we'll be left guessing the whole time?" Flea asked, his stomach already beginning to churn with anxiety.

"The Christmas Tree ceremony will be our only hint," Minko added. "When the village center is filled with elves and the North Pole's Christmas Tree is covered with ornaments, we'll know that time is almost up."

Flea knew nothing about tree ceremonies or hanging ornaments but Rome and Minko both seemed to know what they were talking about.

"If I were you three, I'd spend less time talking and more time building," Vork said.

"How do we begin?" Flea asked.

The teacher called Rome to him and demanded that she hand over her access pass to the toy factory. She hesitantly gave her small

Christmas ornament to Vork, who smashed it on the floor. "You'll either never step foot in the factory again or you'll become a proper elf." Vork then looked straight at Flea. "Maybe Rome can help *you* for once."

Vork handed her three Christmas balls, each of them very plain-looking. Rome accepted them with awe though, and Minko quickly rushed to her side. Neither seemed to notice when their teacher left the room without further instruction. When Flea came closer, he thought he saw Minko's eyes glistening.

"Which one is mine? How do we know?" Minko asked.

"I'm not totally sure, I've never had one of these before," Rome said. "My old ornament was nothing more than a pass to get by the blockade snowmen guarding the factory. I can't get a clear feeling about one while I'm holding all three."

Rome rushed over to a nearby table and gently placed down the three Christmas balls – one red, one green, one blue.

Although the two North Pole elves stared at the simple ornaments like excited little children on Christmas morning, Minko pulled himself away from the table and turned to his friend. Flea was clearly confused.

"I think Flea should choose first," Minko said. "If it wasn't for him, neither of us would have this opportunity."

Rome had trouble pulling her eyes away from the Christmas balls but she eventually stepped aside.

"You're right," she said quietly. "Besides, it doesn't matter which one of us goes first. Only one of the ornaments is destined for each of us. Still, you need to hurry up and choose, Flea. I've been waiting for this moment so long, I don't know if I can hold out much longer."

"How do I know which one is mine?" Flea asked.

"From what I've heard from my friends, you'll *know* when you're holding your ornament," Rome said.

Flea approached the table but didn't understand all the fuss about the ornaments. He picked up the blue one and held it for several seconds.

"Well?" Minko asked.

"Nothing, at least not that I can feel," Flea answered.

"Trust me, you'll *feel* it. Choose another one," Rome said.

Flea picked up the red one but still nothing so he finally tried the green Christmas ball. Flea's head tilted back as warmth rushed throughout his entire body. A blinding white light shined from above and flowed directly into the ornament in his hand. Once his eyes adjusted to the brilliant light, he noticed a stream of translucent toys within the bright whiteness. When the last of the light was sucked into his Christmas ball, Flea's surroundings came back into focus and he realized that he'd been holding his breath.

"Whoa," he said after taking a deep gulp of air.

"Now *that* is your ornament," Rome said. "Yours forever."

Rome quickly picked up the blue ornament and Minko the red one but it was obvious that neither had a reaction. When they switched, though, both had amazed expressions on their faces. Flea couldn't see their white lights and figured that only the ornament's owner could witness the bright spectacle. Once Rome and Minko took their deep breaths, all of the ornaments simultaneously flickered to life. Hovering just inches above Flea's green Christmas ball was a tiny holographic image of a birdhouse, one that was very similar to those he'd built in shop class for Mr. Strick. In human time, that had only been a few days earlier but Flea had done so much since then and felt like a completely new person.

A completely new elf, he corrected himself.

Flea looked at Minko and Rome and saw that both of their ornaments also displayed similarly tiny holographic images. Rome tapped her hologram with a single finger and the image became much bigger, allowing her to better see every detail. When she swept her hand through the image of – shockingly enough – a toy chest, the image returned to its much smaller form. Flea tried to do the same with his hologram and was impressed by how well the image responded to the lightest of touches. These ornaments were amazing but Flea still didn't quite understand their purpose.

"These Christmas balls aren't *just* your pass into the toy factory," Rome said. "They're what provides gift orders to proper builder elves."

"So I have to build this?" Flea asked.

"We *all* have to build what appears from our ornaments," Rome said. "And there's no time to waste. Minko, start the conveyor belt."

Minko followed Rome's order and within moments, the conveyor belt coughed to life and slowly began to turn. Minko also powered on the card-writer but he didn't know how to work the other machine. Rome approached that machine and instantly turned it on.

"How'd you know how to do that?" Minko asked.

Rome blushed but didn't answer. Instead, each of them retrieved the supplies they needed to build their first orders. Flea only required a brief glance at his hologram to mentally process every detail but he second-guessed himself and touched the image to make it bigger. Both Rome and Minko started their orders before Flea even picked up a hammer and nail. Now that he truly had something to lose, he found himself incredibly nervous to make the first simple move. But he thought about Rome's words of encouragement – the same words he'd said to her long ago – and eventually picked up the first piece of wood and started to build.

No longer weighed down by the clunky metal glove, Flea built quicker than ever as his right and left hands worked together seamlessly. His natural building instincts almost had trouble keeping up with the speed of his hands and it wasn't long before Flea's first birdhouse was completed. His movements had been such a blur to him that Flea was ready to closely compare his work with the holographic image. But he didn't even get the chance to enlarge the tiny hologram. The image grew to full size on its own and drifted over the actual birdhouse, the two aligning perfectly. The hologram promptly disappeared and when Flea looked back toward his ornament, a new image was being displayed.

"What should I do with an order I've finished?" Flea asked the others.

Minko and Rome both looked at him – and the completed birdhouse – in shocked awe. They'd gotten a head-start on Flea but Rome was barely halfway through her project and Minko was even further behind.

"Put it on the conveyor belt," Minko said. "It leads into the tunnel system that ends at Santa's sleigh. Congratulations, you've officially contributed a gift to this Christmas season."

Minko got back to work as Flea carefully carried the birdhouse to the belt. Minko's words sunk into Flea's mind. He could hardly believe that this birdhouse – something he'd made with his own two hands – would be opened by someone on Christmas morning. The conveyor belt was moving quickly but the birdhouse remained steady as it swept toward the first machine. Flea watched it disappear inside, followed by the *crinkling* sound of paper. A second later, it emerged perfectly wrapped. Next, it moved on to the laser, which printed the recipient's name on the attached card. From there, the present sped through the hole in the wall and disappeared, not to reappear until Santa placed it under someone's tree. Flea now understood why Rome had known how to turn on the gift-wrapping machine.

Flea proceeded to build his next birdhouse even quicker than the first, despite this one having additional details. As he brought it to the conveyor belt, Flea noticed that Minko was having trouble with his first assignment and was quickly growing frustrated. Rome had also slowed down and Flea watched her stop building to fix her hair and brush sawdust off her fancy shirt. They were barely a few minutes into the most important job of their lives and the three had already reverted back to their form from the very first day of class.

"Is everything okay?" Flea asked his friend on the way back. Minko's hands shook from a combination of nerves and frustration.

"I don't think I can do this, look at how complicated this rocking horse is," he said, pointing to his hologram. "I don't even know why I'm trying to do this. I'm a failure and I always will be. "

Flea hated to see his usually happy friend defeated so quickly.

"No, you are an *elf* and you'll be a great builder one day," Flea said firmly. "But that has to start *now*. This rocking horse might seem difficult as a whole but you have to look at it as a bunch of smaller parts." Flea sawed and hammered and sanded as he talked and in a matter of seconds, he had several key components already built. But he refused to put them together, leaving that part for Minko. "All of the individual skills you learned in class can be applied here as long as you stay relaxed and focused."

His friend nodded and smiled. As Flea walked away, he watched proudly as Minko took a deep breath and continued to work much more confidently. Rome, however, didn't lack the skills or confidence to be doing so poorly. Vork's 'present' to Rome was just inside the door to the production room; Flea quickly reached inside.

"Do you want to be a gift wrapper forever?" he whispered to her. Flea held out the big red hat. "Don't worry, Minko and I still think you look perfect even if your hair and clothes aren't perfect."

"Don't tell Minko about the gift-wrapping thing, he'll never let me hear the end of it," Rome said as she took the hat.

"Your secret is safe with me," Flea promised, "as long as you stop worrying what you look like."

Rome smiled and in a symbol of good faith, she ripped the sleeve of her designer shirt. "You're right. Now I'll look like a mess no matter what," she said, though she still looked sadly at her ruined shirt, as though she'd lost a good friend. But she pulled her hat over her hair and returned to building, successfully finishing the toy chest before Flea got back to his workstation.

The three built for countless hours without so much as a single visit from Vork or Niko to check on their progress. Flea continued to produce the most gifts but Rome wasn't too far behind his production level. Even Minko – whose orders were easier to build than the others' – improved and maintained a respectable building pace. But order after order appeared above Flea's Christmas ball and his body eventually reminded him that it wasn't *completely* accustomed to the elf schedule just yet.

"There's no end in sight, is there?" Flea asked, breaking the silence that had lasted during several hours.

"Welcome to the life of an elf during the Christmas season," Rome said, stifling a yawn as she finished yet another order.

"I love it," Minko said with a wide smile. There wasn't the slightest hint of fatigue on his face.

"We're weeks behind the rest of the elves. It would be nice to know exactly how many orders we have," Flea said. "Oww!"

He dropped his hammer to the floor and grabbed his right pinkie finger, which exploded in pain. This was the first mistake Flea had ever made – at least the first *accidental* mistake – and the other two elves were just as shocked as Flea.

"Are you okay?" Minko asked.

"Yeah," Flea said, clearly embarrassed. "Guess I'm getting a bit tired. Kind of wish I had that metal glove on right about now."

Flea forced a smile, but got back to work right away. With his finger still throbbing, it was hard for him to clear his mind and let his instincts take over while building. His progress slowed dramatically and it wasn't long before Rome started producing just as quickly as him. But she had also grown very tired and soon the two of them were making as many mistakes as Minko.

"Maybe you should both get some rest," Minko suggested, "or at least some fresh air. There's no point struggling through your orders right now if you can come back fresh and refocused."

"What about you?" Rome asked. "You've been making mistakes, maybe you should get some rest, too."

Minko chuckled, clearly as energetic as always.

"Unfortunately, my mistakes have nothing to do with fatigue," he said. "I want to pull my own weight around here and since I'm much slower than the two of you, that just means I have to work longer."

"This isn't a contest, you don't have to feel the need to do as much as us," Rome told him. "We're all in this together and regardless of what happens, I'm proud of the incredible progress you've made."

Minko looked at Rome suspiciously, as if waiting for the punch line of what surely must be a joke. After all, these were the first kind words she'd ever directed at Minko. But when no joke came, Minko blushed and continued to focus on his construction.

"Thanks, but if this is the only chance I ever get to be a builder, I want to take full advantage of it and not waste a single second," Minko said.

Flea and Rome left the elf school's small production center – at least small when compared with the toy factory – and headed down the dark hallway and outside. The fresh air definitely felt great to Flea but it quickly became obvious that his body needed sleep to recover.

"Don't forget to take your hat off," Flea said as they approached the toy factory. Like usual, there was a large group of elves near the huge building and Flea guessed that Rome's friends were among them. "You don't want your friends to see you wearing it."

"You know what? I don't care what they think anymore," she said. "I've realized that there are things way more important than having Artimus and the others accept me. For so many years, I was the odd elf out because I couldn't build, so the only way I could fit in with my friends was by doing whatever they said. But because of the risk that you took so that Minko and I could learn more in school, I know that I don't have to listen to my mean friends anymore and I can be who I am supposed – "

Rome's hat suddenly exploded off the top of her head, as snow sprayed against her and Flea. Rome looked shocked when she turned around to see Artimus and the others laughing at her.

"That hat makes you look like a *loser*, just like your two new *pals*," Artimus called out to her. "Now hurry up and come over here. You've been spending too much time recently with the freak show."

Rome turned to Flea and frowned apologetically, the same expression she usually wore right before ditching him for Artimus and her other friends.

"It's okay, go on," Flea said, not wanting to make the situation any harder for her than it already was. "I don't want to cause any trouble for you."

Rome nodded before picking up her hat and starting toward her friends. Flea was used to this and didn't think twice as he headed off toward the elf dorm. But when he heard the sound of Rome's voice – her tone oozing with attitude that she normally reserved for Minko only – Flea turned around and was shocked to see her addressing Artimus in such a manner.

"Don't you elves *ever* work or is waiting for me your only activity?" she asked.

Rome brushed the snow off her red Christmas hat and proudly pulled it back onto her head. She crossed her arms defiantly and stared at Artimus, who was momentarily surprised by her sudden attitude change. But he quickly recovered and fired at the sorest spot in Rome's life.

"Who do you think you're talking to like that, *gift wrapper?*" Artimus yelled for all the elves to hear. "Now take off that ugly hat and get over here or you can forget ever being friends with us again."

"Yeah, *gift wrapper*," one of the bigger elves from the group said. "Nobody else would be friends with you."

"That's right," Artimus agreed. "We're all that you've got so you better not talk to us like that."

"I already have two *real* friends who don't care if I can build or not," Rome said. "They accept me for who I am and don't need to bully me to make themselves feel better. They aren't as pathetic as you, Artimus."

Rome turned her back on her friends and began walking back to Flea.

"You'll come crawling back to us," Artimus Maximus yelled. "And you'll hate what we'll make you do to become part of us again."

Rome appeared concerned by Artimus's warning but she did not turn back toward him, which only made the group leader angrier. Flea had hoped all along that Rome would change and was so proud that she finally had. But he had little time to enjoy this moment because he saw Artimus bend down to the ground. Knowing there was no way to reach Rome in time to save her, Flea quickly scooped up his own snowball. Artimus wound up and threw his projectile toward the back of Rome's head. For a brief moment, everything around Flea seemed to slow down and he focused solely on the speeding snowball. Without a thought, Flea launched his own snowball.

Since Rome's back was turned to Artimus, she didn't even know that she was under attack and looked surprised to see Flea throwing snow in her direction. His snowball whizzed by the side of her head – missing her ear by mere inches – and hit the other snowball just behind her, causing an explosion of snow in mid-air. Flea was just as amazed by his throw as the rest of the elves watching.

Obviously, he hadn't lost his other ability. Rome spun around and quickly realized what had just happened.

"You better not try that again, Artimus," Rome warned.

Flea didn't think that threatening Artimus was the way to get him to back off so he quickly joined Rome's side. As expected, Artimus did the opposite of what Rome said and reached to the snowy ground for another weapon. Flea and Rome grabbed snowballs of their own, as did the rest of the elves from Artimus's crowd. Flea and Rome found themselves in a showdown against numbers that were not in their favor.

"You got lucky with that first throw, freak," Artimus yelled.

"You don't want to test that theory," Flea called back, which only enraged Artimus more. The group leader turned to his well-armed friends and waved for them to fan out. Within seconds, Rome and Flea were nearly surrounded, though the two of them remained focused on Artimus, who was calling the shots. Red-Robe's warning to 'save her' again came to mind and Flea valiantly stepped in front of Rome, shielding her from whatever Artimus was about to do.

"You should have just stayed out of our business, freak," Artimus said.

Artimus pulled his arm back, ready to throw, but that arm never got the chance to move forward. He was suddenly drilled in the chest with a snowball and went down hard. Rome and Flea turned simultaneously and were both shocked to see the identity of the thrower.

CHAPTER TWENTY-ONE

No Trespassing

"Don't you *ever* throw anything at her again!" Minko yelled at the stunned elves, many of whom rushed to Artimus's side.

"Get away from me!" Artimus ordered his friends, his breath short and words pained from the direct hit he suffered. "Don't just stand there, fight back!"

The stunned elves might have hesitated to attack, but Rome had no such uncertainty. She took aim at the largest elf still surrounding them – that being Artimus's friend, Roc – and let her snowball fly, scoring a direct hit. Following her lead, Flea took aim at another elf and struck his target. The impact threw the elf – Orby – to the ground five feet back from where he stood. Rome's remaining friends – now her *former* friends – recovered from the shock and made a feeble attempt to fight back. With their three strongest elves down, though, the counterattack was weak. By the time Artimus pulled himself together and struggled to his feet, other outside elves – most with no idea about the animosity – gathered around in what they thought was some sort of game.

"Sweet! A snowball fight! Hurry up, Grinder, we have to get in on this!" Wrench excitedly called out from the open garage nearby.

The spiky-haired twins picked up snowballs and rushed toward the growing crowd of elves, all of who joined the 'fun' snowball fight. The scene quickly turned chaotic as snowballs flew all over the place. Artimus and his gang attempted to attack Flea and Rome with ferocity but everyone was being pelted from all sides. With Flea's superior aim and incredible arm, he struck only the bullies with his hardest thrown snowballs while he tossed much smaller, lighter shots at the others. Had this not started out as a battle with the mean group of 'cool elves,' the big snowball fight might have actually been fun.

During the snowy bedlam, Minko made his way to Flea and Rome, who continued to hold off Artimus and his friends. Minko wasn't just amazed by how well Flea threw, but also by Rome's ability to protect herself in a fight.

"The three of us could *definitely* beat the penguins in Snow Wars," Minko said while the three continued to hurl snowball after snowball.

"The penguins?" Flea asked before he realized his friend had said *two* things he didn't quite understand. "The *Snow Wars?*"

Before Minko could explain, a snowball whizzed between him and Flea, missing them both by a matter of inches. Across the way, they spotted Artimus banding together with his group of friends, who fought through the other elves and quickly made progress toward their three enemies. Minko and Flea were more than happy to stand there and fight, but Rome knew better and grabbed each of their hands.

"Come on, they're not worth it," Rome said, pulling them away. Minko was a bit more reluctant to leave but he eventually followed Flea's lead. "How did you know we were in trouble? I thought you were staying behind to keep building."

"Yeah, well, I just wanted to make sure you got back to the dorm safely," Minko said. Flea glanced at his two friends and saw them both blushing. Rome stopped and looked at Minko, who quickly added to his reasoning. "I couldn't let anything bad happen to you or else only me and Flea would be left and then class would get cancelled."

In the midst of all the chaos, Rome stared at Minko and saw him in a whole new way. Flea felt awkward standing there with the two of them so he quietly took a few steps away. Minko's face blushed red, too embarrassed to look at Rome. Flea came back to reality before either of his friends and he looked up just in time to see that Artimus had finally emerged from the hectic snowball brawl. His formerly perfect hair was now a snowy mess, another reason he appeared so focused on revenge.

"Look out!" Flea yelled as he saw Artimus launch a snowball directly toward Rome. It was too late for Flea to throw his own snowball to intercept it and he was too far away from Rome to melt the snowball. But while Rome remained frozen in fear, Minko sprang to action for the second time in minutes. He threw himself in the path of the speeding snowball and was promptly thrown off his feet and down to the ground. Flea fired another snowball back at Artimus but the bully dived out of the way before being hit. Artimus took cover behind a small snowbank, though Flea quickly picked it apart with a few well-placed throws. He was only another snowball or two away from destroying the snowbank and exposing Artimus when a number of his friends emerged from the big snowball fight and rushed to his defense.

"Come on, Flea!" Rome yelled behind him. "Forget about Artimus, he'll get what's coming to him later!"

Flea turned to see that Rome had already helped up Minko, who looked pained and out of breath, his hair and face covered in snow. There was a big white mark in the middle of his shirt and many of the blinking lights were now extinguished. But he somehow forced a smile – especially since Rome had an arm wrapped around his waist to keep him standing. Flea nearly started to laugh but a snowball barely missed his head and got his mind back on track. He launched one final snowball toward the group of elves before taking off with his friends.

Minko still hadn't totally recovered from the direct hit and it was a major effort for Rome to help the much bigger elf. Flea got on the other side of his friend and tried to help drag Minko along but that just slowed all *three* of them and took away their only means of defense. They wanted to reach the safety of the dorm, where Artimus and his group wouldn't dare continue the snowball fight. But it was obvious that they would never get there while half-dragging Minko, especially since snowballs were slamming to the ground all around their running feet.

"Just leave me," Minko said valiantly. "Give me a few snowballs and I'll slow them down for you."

"And let them turn you into a living Popsicle?" Rome asked. "Don't be ridiculous, this isn't some cheesy old war movie."

"He's right about one thing," Flea said as another snowball barely missed them. "There's no way we're reaching the dorm before they catch us. You two go ahead, I'll try to distract them and lead them away from here."

"But Flea, you don't know how mean Artimus can be if he catches you," Rome said.

"Actually, I *do*," he said. "But don't worry, I can take care of myself. I have plenty of experience dealing with bullies and snowball fights. Now hurry up, I'll try to hold them off long enough."

Flea released Minko and Rome continued to lead him away. With Artimus and his gang of ten running toward him, Flea bent over and grabbed a large handful of snow. Though there were plenty of targets to choose from, he took aim at his biggest enemy and threw. Artimus dived to the ground again and Flea's snowball connected with the elf behind him. The entire group paused as Flea threw several more snowballs in rapid succession, as he was less concerned with hitting the elves than giving his friends more time to escape.

"Don't be afraid of the freak!" Artimus called out to his crew. At that moment, Artimus barely dodged another snowball that Flea hurled in his direction. "There's only one of him and *ten* of us."

The group of elves collectively regained their confidence and soon there were ten snowballs soaring toward Flea. He dropped his own snowy weapon and put his hand up. He melted the first few snowballs, but they were coming from so many different angles that a couple partially intact balls made their way beyond his defense. The snow stung but did not budge Flea, who stood strong and watched the others reload. He unleashed a few more snowballs of his own but another round was soon coming his way. Again, he was able to stop most of the attack but a few more snowy fragments got by, one of them striking the side of his head, momentarily stunning him.

"See! The freak isn't as powerful as he tries to convince us!" Artimus yelled. The group leader picked up more snow but instead of throwing it, he waved the rest of his friends forward. Flea glanced back to see that Rome and Minko had made up a lot of ground toward the elf dorm but they could still be caught if Flea led the gang that way. He only had one option left.

"Nice hair, now who's the *freak*?" he yelled at Artimus. Flea threw one final snowball at the nearest elf before turning to run in the opposite direction of the elf dorm.

"Don't let him get away!" Artimus yelled.

I guess his hair really is *important to him,* Flea thought with a smile as the others followed him. Unfortunately, that smile didn't last very long. Flea's natural abilities to throw well and melt snowballs had proven indispensable in a fight so far but he hadn't acquired the skill of running fast. Artimus quickly gained on him and Flea knew it wouldn't be long until the angry group caught up and made him pay for his 'hair' comment. Snowballs crashed to the ground all around him and he expected one to slam into his back at any moment. Flea considered heading toward the security building but he almost preferred to take whatever punishment was coming from Artimus than turn to Niko for help.

Flea was eventually struck from behind and he crashed to the ground, though he absorbed the impact by rolling and quickly got back to his feet. Snow covered his face and got into his eyes but he kept running through blurred vision. He glanced behind again but could only see the shapes of several elves bearing down on him. Without realizing exactly where he was, Flea rushed to the nearest building and hid around the corner. He expected the others to round the corner and catch him at any second but nobody showed up. After brushing the snow from his hair and wiping it out of his eyes, Flea could finally see clearly again. He peeked around the corner to figure out why Artimus and the others had stopped their pursuit. The panting group of elves – including their leader – stood a few dozen feet away, all of them wearing shocked expressions. Artimus tried to play it cool by running his hands through his hair but Flea wasn't fooled: Artimus was surprised by *something*.

Then, Flea saw why. Standing a few feet in front of Artimus was the green-eyed snowman, leader of the security force. Flea hadn't noticed the snowman when he ran past. A chill ran down his spine, which had nothing to do with the freezing cold vapors that oozed from the building's walls – walls made of ice.

The ice bank, Flea realized. *That's why they all stopped.*

He had no idea how he'd been able to get so close to the building without being stopped – *or* attacked – by the security force.

Flea considered running away but was afraid of making a single move to alert the green-eyed snowman of his presence. *But the snowman had to have seen me approaching, I ran right by,* Flea thought. He spotted his footprints in the snow just a few feet next to the security leader.

Just in case the snowman *had* somehow missed Flea, there was one elf more than ready to point him out.

"Hey, snow brain! You aren't doing your job very well," Artimus called out to the snowman, though he still kept his distance. "You let someone by, he's standing right behind you!"

Flea was ready to take off at the first sign of movement from the snowman but it stayed completely still. Based upon the lone display Flea had seen from the security force, he was pretty sure they didn't miss much. Artimus turned away from the guard and addressed Flea.

"That's quite a trick you just pulled. How did you get that close to the ice bank?" he asked.

Flea could tell that it was killing Artimus to have to ask him a question. But while Flea had no idea how he'd gotten by the snowman, he wasn't about to give Artimus the satisfaction of admitting this. Although Flea was afraid that talking would alert the security force, the chance to further anger Artimus seemed worth the risk.

"Just because I'm new to the North Pole doesn't mean I'm totally clueless," Flea said, trying to sound as bold and confident as possible. "In fact, I'm surprised that *you've* been here so long and don't know how to get past the snowmen. Guess you might be spending too much time on your hair."

A couple of the girl elves in Artimus's group chuckled, although they stopped when he spun around to glare at them. Flea was quite satisfied with himself, even more so when Artimus turned back to him and looked like he was ready to explode with rage.

"You can't stay there forever, *freak*! Now why don't you come over here already!" Artimus yelled.

"Why don't you come make me?" Flea asked, before he knew what he was even saying. After all, if *he* could have somehow gotten by the snowman, then he saw no reason why Artimus wouldn't be able to as well. Still, Flea couldn't stop himself from antagonizing the North Pole's biggest bully.

"I'm not coming over there because we're not supposed to," Artimus said.

"If you ask me, it sounds like you're afraid," Flea said.

Artimus turned to his group and yelled at them to attack Flea, to go and drag him away from the ice bank. But not even Roc or Orby budged while the rest of his friends shook their heads.

"Rome and Minko might not be builders but they have *way* more courage than you," Flea taunted, wondering the whole time he spoke whether he was making a mistake. He was soon about to find out.

"You're all *cowards*!" Artimus yelled at his friends, none of whom budged. He picked up a huge handful of snow and started forward. "I'm going to make you *eat* this snowball when I get my hands on you."

Flea's heart pounded as Artimus hesitantly walked ahead. All elf eyes – Flea's and Artimus's especially – were on the snowman, who remained totally still the entire time. Artimus slowed down as he passed the snowman but when nothing happened, a wide grin crossed his face and he stared at Flea with evil intent. Flea swallowed hard and considered taking off but knew he couldn't run forever.

At least I'm thirsty from all that running, Flea thought as he eyed the big snowball that Artimus was about to force-feed him.

Suddenly, a wall of security snowmen sprung out of the ground. Running was no longer an option for Flea so he pressed himself tightly against the icy walls of the ice bank and hoped he could blend in. But the security force paid him no attention, as nearly a dozen snowmen descended upon Artimus, who stupidly tried to fight back and run away. He didn't get very far, however, before two of the snowmen restrained his arms. The leader of the security force finally slid in front of Artimus, who refused to calm down.

"What are you doing? Let me go! Don't you know who I am?" he yelled.

"I know who you *aren't*," the security leader said with a British accent. The voice sounded strange coming from a snowman.

"But I'm not the only one here, why aren't you – "

The security leader didn't let Artimus finish as he nodded his head toward the rest of the security force. Like a pack of hungry wolves eyeing a single piece of meat, the snowmen charged Artimus and totally engulfed him, the sound of the cocky elf's screams quickly cutting off. The security leader returned to his normal post, causing Artimus's friends to scatter in fear. Flea felt guilty; he obviously didn't like Artimus but he didn't exactly want anything *too* bad to happen to him. But when the security force eventually backed away and returned to their posts surrounding the ice bank, Flea laughed with relief.

CHAPTER TWENTY-TWO
The North Pole's Enemy

Where Artimus last stood was now a massive block of snow.
Sticking out the top of the snow block was Artimus's head, still red
with anger as he yelled for the snowmen to let him go. Even funnier
to Flea was the fact that the bully's perfect hair was plastered down
on the top of his head with snow. In the distance, the 'fun' snowball
fight had broken up. Many of the elves took notice to the security
snowmen still surrounding the ice bank. Flea knew that some elves
would be worried by this and would certainly have questions about
what had happened, questions to which he didn't have the answers.
Flea considered rushing into the ice bank's nearby entrance to hide
but figured he'd already pushed his luck with the snowmen and
didn't want to become his own block of snow. So as the rest of the
elves rushed to the icy building, Flea decided it was time to flee.

He slowly walked by the snowmen, which moved aside and
let him pass without a problem. Flea felt Artimus's eyes following
his every movement and he couldn't stop himself from smiling.

"I'm going to get you for this," said the voice from within the
snow block. "You *and* your friends are going to pay."

Flea was already tempting fate by not rushing away as
quickly as possible but there was one more thing he just *had* to do.
He picked up a final snowball and stared directly at Artimus, who
went quiet for the first time. Flea paced back and forth in front of
Artimus's snow block and tossed the snowball in his hand up and

down, up and down. Flea's torturer was such an easy target and he knew that had the roles been reversed, there was no *way* Artimus would have turned down such an opportunity.

"It's a good thing I'm *nothing* like you," Flea said.

He started to walk away but suddenly turned and fired the snowball as hard as he could at the huge block of snow. Artimus squealed in fear – a sound Flea would never forget as long as he lived – but the snowball struck well below his exposed face and head. The impact of Flea's throw cracked the heavy snow block and Artimus slowly freed his arms from their snowy binds. Flea could have thrown a few more snowballs to make it easier on Artimus but he wanted his enemy to spend plenty of time digging himself free, to spend plenty of time thinking about how Flea had shown him mercy.

Flea also wanted plenty of time to escape, as the first of the elves began to show up and ask what had happened.

"I'm not sure, but I wouldn't believe anything Artimus says," Flea told them. "I think he took a few too many snowballs to the head and decided to challenge the ice bank's security force."

Flea considered rushing to the dorm to check on his friends but knew that he'd given Rome and Minko plenty of time to get to safety. Instead, there was one elf that would need to know exactly what happened at the ice bank. In fact, Flea was surprised that Niko hadn't already rushed to the scene considering how quickly he'd arrived the first time he thought there was trouble with the security snowmen. Flea hoped that Santa's son wasn't dealing with bigger problems for the North Pole and decided to head to the security building to find out.

Besides, Flea wondered if Niko might have the answer as to why he could get close to the ice bank while others couldn't. When he reached the tiny building at the outskirts of the North Pole village, he once again found the entrance guarded by a pair of dim-witted snowmen – *very* different from the snowmen he'd just watched. Still, the snowmen did not budge until Flea spoke to them.

"I need to go inside and talk to Niko."

"Yes, sir," the two said in unison, sliding out of Flea's way.

Knowing that Niko was Santa's son made Flea much more nervous about angering him, so he knew better than to try sneaking into the security building's map room again. Instead, he stayed in the small hallway and called out that he was there and needed to speak with Niko. Only when several long moments passed without response did Flea cross the hallway and enter the security building's most important room. Niko was nowhere to be found and the holographic map was turned off yet the slow-talking snowman remained at his post.

"What are you doing here?" the snowman asked Flea.

"I came here about the North Pole's security," Flea said.

"Oh no! I was supposed to be keeping watch on that," the snowman said. It rushed over to the map and turned the large hologram on. "Please don't tell Niko that I forgot to do the one job he left for me."

"Don't worry, your secret is safe with me," Flea said.

When the holographic image of the snowman Army appeared on-screen, Flea was shocked that they were much farther beyond the red line than the first time he'd seen. Though Flea didn't exactly understand the Army or its connection to him and the North Pole, he could tell why Niko and Vork were so concerned with it.

"What *is* that Army?" Flea asked himself aloud, hoping the answer would come to him. The answer *did* come but from a source he hadn't quite expected.

"It is the North Pole's enemy," the slow-witted snowman said. "I am supposed to be watching the North Pole's enemy."

"I didn't know that the North Pole *had* an enemy," Flea said.

"Most normal elves do not know about it. Niko only trusted me with the information because he knows I can keep a secret," the snowman said. Flea wondered how this information could've remained such a secret when this snowman seemed so willing to talk about it. "Niko informed all of the elves about how dangerous it could be to wander too far south of the village but he didn't tell them about the approaching Army."

Although Flea didn't want to take his eyes away from the hologram, he periodically glanced over his shoulder to make sure that Niko didn't sneak up behind him. There was no doubt that Santa's son would be angry to find Flea in the security building, even more so to hear him questioning the snowman about classified information. But Niko wasn't around and Flea had plenty more questions.

"Who *is* the enemy? Where did the Army come from?"

"Isn't that obvious?" the snowman asked. "The enemy of the North Pole is *obviously* the South Pole."

"There's a South Pole, too?"

Flea continued to watch the hologram, noting the large white leader at the front of the Army. The animal paced back and forth on all fours, occasionally stopping to stand on its hind legs, towering over the rest of its snowy soldiers. Now that Flea had a chance to study the animal closer, he concluded that it look like some kind of monstrous polar bear.

"What else can you tell me about the South Pole?" Flea asked, hoping to extract as much information from the snowman as possible.

"Umm…" it said, clearly trying to think, a difficult task for the dim-witted snowman. When it finally came up with something, its snowy mouth curled into a smile. "I thought of something. One thing I know about the South Pole is that it's south of here."

Unfortunately, Flea could tell that the snowman wasn't joking. Flea knew that he'd better keep his questions specific.

"How long has the Army been there?"

"About twenty years now," the snowman answered. "During that time, it was able to move forward but slowly. Ever since the beginning of this Christmas building season, though, the Army has moved quicker than ever. Niko always thought it would be many years until the Army could reach the North Pole but now it seems like they could get here much sooner."

"But *why* has the Army suddenly been able to get closer? What has changed?" Flea asked.

The snowman didn't know the answer, nor did it have the mental ability to conjure a guess. Flea had never been to the North Pole before this year but as far as he knew, the only difference this Christmas season was his own arrival. His stomach turned at the thought that he could somehow be responsible, though he told himself that this was a ridiculous thought. After all, he was as low on the North Pole totem pole as he could possibly be and he saw no way that his presence alone could have such a major effect on the South Pole Army. Still, Vork's words about the elves disliking anything new replayed in his mind. Flea *needed* to ask Niko some questions and he didn't want to put this off another minute.

"I need to find Niko, do you know where he went?" he asked.

"No, but I may be able to help find him."

The snowman approached the hologram map and pushed several buttons. Flea had no idea how the dim-witted snowman could possibly work such a sophisticated machine, but its stick-arms moved so quickly that Flea couldn't keep up. Within seconds, the holographic image of the South Pole Army faded away and was replaced with an image of the North Pole village and its buildings. A few more button clicks illuminated hundreds of tiny elves on screen, though they looked more like tiny pictures than the actual elves.

"We have privacy laws here," the snowman explained. "Using this map, we can find *where* the elves are located but not *what* they're doing."

Several elves were scattered around the village grounds – including Artimus, who remained completely still just outside the ice bank – but the large majority of them were located inside the toy factory, many of them seemingly atop one another. Flea had not yet met most of the smiling elf images from inside the factory but he *did* recognize the only two elves in the dorm, though he was confused about the way Rome and Minko were moving. Even if Minko hadn't been walking gingerly from his brutal snowball hit, there was no way he could've possibly moved so fast. Rome's picture next to him traveled at the same fast speed. But when the two suddenly flipped upside down and then almost immediately turned rightside up – a pattern that repeated several times in a row – Flea figured out exactly what they were doing and couldn't help but laugh.

Minko really can't *pass up an opportunity to ride the roller coaster,* Flea thought.

He finally spotted Niko's picture at the edge of the village heading toward Santa's cabin. Inside the cabin, Flea spotted a generic picture of Santa Claus that could've come from any cartoon he had ever seen about the North Pole (most of which had gotten every detail about this place wrong). But the picture *next to* Santa was what Flea wondered about most, as the elf's face remained in shadows and was covered with a big question mark. Flea wanted to know who this was so he rushed out of the security building and hoped to catch Niko in time.

"Don't tell anyone I was here," Flea called out to the snowmen as he left.

He considered cutting through the center of the village to reach Santa's cabin quicker but didn't want to take the chance that Artimus had broken free. Instead, he circled around the village perimeter, avoiding contact with any other elves. He eventually spotted Niko – who was recognizable from afar by his big red hat – just as he reached the cabin's front door. Flea was about to call out to him when the cabin door opened and Flea saw a flash of red standing inside. He realized that the question-marked elf was Red-Robe. Flea stopped at the sight of the strange elf, suddenly forgetting why he wanted to find Niko in the first place. When the door to Santa's cabin closed, Flea headed back to the dorm. He wanted to find Minko and Rome and tell them everything he'd just seen but he thought better of it. Minko had a big mouth and the last thing Flea wanted was to make an enemy out of Niko, who'd sworn him to secrecy about North Pole security matters.

Flea headed straight for his room, which he found quicker this time. Although his body was physically drained and his bed felt as comfy as a soft cloud, his mind was on overdrive and kept him from falling asleep. Not only did the thought of the approaching South Pole Army worry him, but so did the fact that Niko and Red-Robe were meeting with Santa.

A meeting that Flea somehow knew was about him.

CHAPTER TWENTY-THREE
Christmas Tree Party

The three students continued to work very hard in the school's production center for what felt like weeks. Unfortunately, there seemed no end in sight for their orders. Flea continued to build fastest of the three, but Rome and Minko had both improved significantly. Hundreds and hundreds of birdhouses and toy chests and rocking horses and other wooden products flew out of their production room. During that time, Vork only stopped in once. The teacher seemed impressed by their improvements but still made a point to remind them that they would either pass or fail together, as they had to complete *all* of their orders by the end of the building season.

Multiple times throughout the course of building, Flea asked his friends if there was some way of finding out the exact number of orders they had left, but Rome and Minko were both adamant that they couldn't.

"And even if we *could* somehow find out, I wouldn't want to know," Minko said. "That goes against the elf code of conduct."

Although Flea didn't agree with his friends, he dropped the subject each time. After one particularly long building session, the three decided it was time to go outside for a quick break. By this time, Flea had grown accustomed to the beauty of the village, but new to this day was a sight as amazing as his first glance at Santa's sleigh.

Directly in the center of the village was a Christmas tree far taller than any that Flea had ever seen. It was several stories tall and nearly as wide. The full branches hung perfectly to create a proportionately circular base. Upon closer inspection of the tree, Flea noticed nearly a dozen tall ladders leaned against it. Several elves climbed those ladders while holding their Christmas balls.

"Oh, no," Rome said at the sight of the tree.

She sounded very worried so Flea quickly scanned the ladders for any sign of elves in danger, especially since many of them climbed near the top. But the elves appeared safe as they hung their ornaments from different sections of the tree.

"What's wrong?" Flea asked.

"Once the tree comes up, it's the beginning of the end," Rome explained. "As soon as an elf's Christmas ball stops giving orders, that elf is done for the holiday season and can rush out here to hang their ball on the tree. The higher up an elf is permitted to hang his or her ornament, the higher the class of builder."

One elf in particular stood on the very top rung on his ladder, balancing dangerously while placing his Christmas ball just below the very tip of the tree.

"It looks like Fuff is the big winner this year," Minko said pointing all the way up to the highest elf. "I wonder if Santa will choose him for the big prize or if Niko will get to go with him again next year."

"The big prize?"

Rome and Minko explained that becoming a top-of-the-tree level elf – which required years of high-quality building in the toy factory – instantly qualified an elf for Santa's big prize. That was the prize that all elves dreamed about but few got the chance to experience: riding in the sleigh with Santa while he delivered presents around the world.

"From what I've heard, it's an amazing journey," Rome said, "even *if* you don't get the chance to attend the post-building party."

"Well for Fuff's sake, I hope Santa chooses him to go on the delivery run next year," Minko said. "Fuff was the first to finish building last year but Santa decided to give this season's big prize to his son. Niko has gone on more delivery trips than anyone else, which doesn't seem fair to me at all. If I was the first to finish and didn't get picked, I would be *so* mad."

Flea continued to watch Fuff as he placed his Christmas ball near the top. Once he let go, his purple ball seemed to shine brighter than all of those around it. The upper section of the tree looked to be more decorated than the lower.

"I don't think I recognize him," Flea said about the North Pole's number-one builder.

"I doubt you would've seen *any* of the builders from the three or four highest tiers," Rome explained. "It's a fierce competition to reach the highest levels; the top elves are always sliding up and down those levels based upon their building performance. There are very few spots in each building-level so those elves *never* leave the factory during the holiday season until they're done. Do you see those other builders who've already finished and hung their decorations?" She pointed out nearly ten elves standing at the base of the Christmas tree, patting each other on the back and smiling proudly at their hanging decorations. "Their ornaments are already on the tree so they'll be moved to the highest building level next year to challenge Fuff."

"I want nothing more than to become a builder and win Santa's big prize one day but I doubt I'll *ever* have the determination needed to reach that level," Minko said with a hint of sadness. "Those elves don't spend *any* off time having fun. Instead, they use that time for extra hibernation so they're ready to build non-stop. Is it really worth being the best if you can't enjoy the only vacation we get?"

"Elves get to go on vacation?" Flea asked.

"Oh yeah, it's the best!" Minko said. "If it came down to being the card-elf forever or never going to the lake again, I'd gladly never step foot in the toy factory... well, maybe not *gladly*."

"What's so great about it?"

"Two words," Minko said. "Snow Wars."

Rome couldn't stop herself from chuckling. "But I've never seen you compete before. My friends... well, I guess I mean Artimus and his crew... they rule Snow Wars every year, at least until they have to face the penguins."

"I've competed before," Minko said defensively.

"When?" Rome asked.

"The twins were my partners about…" Minko's voice lowered to barely a whisper. "…twenty years ago."

"Russ and Guss?" Rome laughed. "Those two were *awful*, that's why they haven't competed since. Did you three even make it out of the qualification battle?"

"That doesn't matter now," Minko said, sidestepping the question. "With the three of *us* on a team together, *nobody* will be able to stop us, not even the penguins."

"Me on a team with *you*?" Rome asked. "I don't remember agreeing to that."

"And why *wouldn't* you want to be on my team?"

"Why *would* I?"

Rome and Minko continued to bicker back and forth. This Snow Wars competition was apparently a very serious matter to the two of them. Flea didn't know what was involved with it, but his two friends would certainly come in first place if the contest were based on the ability to argue. Sadly, Flea couldn't help but think that he might be long gone from the North Pole before he ever got the chance to compete.

"Isn't that one of Artimus's friends?" Flea asked, interrupting his friends before they exploded into an all-out war. He pointed to an attractive, well-dressed girl elf who didn't need a ladder to reach the low branch where she hung her yellow ball, which glowed much dimmer than the ornaments higher up.

"Yeah, that's Addy," Rome said. "Artimus isn't going to be happy if she moves to a higher level than the rest of the group.

They're all pretty good builders but Artimus keeps them so busy
with their clothes and hair that none of them finishes this early.
Addy will have a much larger assignment load next year but I'm sure
Artimus will harass her so much that she gets demoted back to the
lower level. I can't believe I let Artimus and the others hold me back
so much that I wasn't able to graduate elf school."

Rome's voice was full of shame and anger and it became
clear to Flea why she hadn't passed school the first time, despite her
obvious building skills.

"Don't worry, that will change for us *all* next year," Minko
said.

"How will we know when the rest of the elves are finished?"
Flea asked.

"Once the entire tree is filled with Christmas balls, the
factory whistle blows to mark the official end of the building
season," Rome said. "We *must* be done our work by then."

A few more elves trickled out of the factory, including a
familiar face. The last time Flea had seen this face, it was the only
part of the elf not covered in snow.

"I guess I see why Artimus hasn't been around to bother us,"
Minko said as the evil elf reached up to hang his Christmas ball on
one of the lowest branches.

"He probably wanted to finish his orders as soon as possible
so he can get back to his real job: harassing us," Rome said.

Artimus knocked Addy's yellow Christmas ornament to the ground and put his in its place. He didn't bother to pick hers up as he turned and waved to his three enemies.

"Let's get back to building and not give him that chance then," Flea said.

The Christmas tree was massive so the few ornaments hanging from its branches did not seem like much, but the three students knew that would change quickly, especially since more elves were emerging from the factory.

-    -   -   -   -   -   -   -   -   -   -

-    -   -   -

Flea needed sleep, but he built for days straight without leaving the school. His friends were relying on him and failure wasn't an option – nor was returning to his big, soft bed in the dorm. At one point, Flea pushed together two of Rome's toy chests and used that as a bed, though it was so uncomfortable that he barely got an hour of rest. The three of them pushed harder and built with more urgency than ever, but still had no idea if they were close to the end.

With every present that Flea completed, he grew increasingly disappointed – *and* worried – each time a new hologram appeared above his green Christmas ball. The only good part about the constant orders was that Flea's mind remained totally focused on one track; he had no time to worry about the South Pole Army or the ice bank incident or Red-Robe's meeting with Santa. Flea was a well-oiled building machine and though he was under constant pressure to build faster and faster, he actually enjoyed the work. The thought of his friends graduating school and becoming full-fledged elves spurred Flea on, although it wasn't the only source of motivation to keep him going. Flea thought of the hundreds of children who would be receiving the gifts he built, kids like him who might not have much and would be thrilled with any present on Christmas morning.

"I'll go check on the tree," Rome said. Though her building pace hadn't suffered, Rome's voice was low and sullen when she spoke, fatigued by the countless hours in the production room.

Ever since the students discovered the Christmas tree standing in the village center, they took turns checking on it every few hours to see how many more ornaments had been hung. Unfortunately – though not unexpectedly – they found more and more Christmas balls hanging on the tree every time they went outside. It was only natural that their confidence began to drain.

Before Rome made it out of the room, she stopped just long enough to say what all three of them had been thinking for a long time.

"There's no way we're going to finish in time."

"Don't say that, we have to stay positive," Minko said, though he seemed to believe his own words as much as Rome did. Still, she forced a smile and nodded her head before leaving.

For several minutes, Flea and Minko continued building in silence. But Rome's negativity was contagious and it wasn't long before Minko started to question the future, too.

"Do *you* think we'll finish?" he asked Flea.

Flea was too exhausted to pretend that he was totally confident.

"I really don't know," he answered. "But I *do* know that we'll all work as hard as possible, which is the most that we can do."

Minko went back to building but his loss of confidence quickly showed in his work, as he split a piece of wood with an errant nail.

"I just want to say I'm sorry in advance," Minko said. "Just in case we fail because of me."

"You have no reason to apologize," Flea said. "Obviously, there's nothing I want more than to graduate elf school and be able to stay at the North Pole. But if that doesn't happen for *any* reason, then I can leave here satisfied that I made two *real* friends and had the experience of a lifetime."

Flea truly meant those words. He glanced at Minko and saw that the big elf had tears in his eyes. Flea had the feeling that a big bear-hug was coming his way at any moment so he quickly changed the subject.

"What's taking Rome so long? She should've been back by now," Flea said.

Minko looked toward the production room door, which remained closed. Checking on the Christmas tree usually didn't take longer than a minute or two since it was so big and easy to spot. Flea had checked on it last and reported the tree just more than halfway covered with ornaments, as the village center was becoming more and more crowded with partying elves. Like usual, Artimus and his gang had been hanging around close to the elf school, watching for any sign of the students.

"Do you think Artimus could have done something to her?" Minko asked worriedly.

"I doubt he would do anything bad with so many elves outside the toy factory now, too many witnesses. Besides, I'm pretty sure Rome can take care of herself," Flea said, though his friend still looked concerned. So despite there being plenty of building left to do – at least as far as they could tell – Flea knew that Minko wouldn't be able to concentrate. "Let's go take a look, we could use a five-minute break anyway."

Normally, Minko would have balked at the idea of taking a break, as he never tired and constantly wanted to build. But for the first time since Flea had known him, Minko was first out the door. Outside, the party had grown even larger. Many more elves had finished building and hung their ornament on the tree, which was now closer to three-quarters full. Other decorations had also been set up all around and several groups of elves had banded together, singing well-known Christmas carols. There were even a few snowmen – Flea couldn't tell which variety – dressed up in costumes, entertaining the elves by acting out famous Christmas tales. Flea was too far away to hear the words being spoken by the snowman actors but he could still tell which play they were performing. The first snowman looked big and mean and wore a fancy top hat while the other was tiny and pathetic and leaned on a crutch. They were obviously supposed to be Mr. Scrooge and Tiny Tim from *A Christmas Carol*.

The elves that seemed to be having the best time were those stumbling around the village, singing the loudest – and the worst. All of these party-elves had one thing in common: each held large candy canes that they drank from.

"Oh great, it looks like they've busted out the candy-cane cider," Minko said as he spotted the obnoxious elves. "Now the party is going to get crazy."

"What's candy-cane cider?" Flea asked.

"It's what I like to call loopy juice," Minko said. "I've never actually tried it because I'm not old enough yet; the drinking age for cider is 100. But from what I've heard, the cider is strong and extra sugary and makes you go loopy with energy. Elves have to be careful how much they drink or funny things can happen. And the highest-level master builders are usually the craziest. I guess all that time working without a break makes them that way. One time after drinking a few too many canes, they covered one of their friends in snow but then forgot about him for an entire week. When they finally remembered to dig him out, his skin was completely blue and stayed that way for months."

Perfectly on cue, a cider-fueled elf approached Flea and threw an arm around his shoulder. Flea had never seen him before but this elf seemed to know him.

"Youdon'tseemas…dangerousas…everyonesays," the elf said, his words spoken so rapidly that they slurred together.

"And why do they think that?" Flea asked, humoring the friendly – yet extremely hyper – elf.

The loopy elf took a long drink from the candy cane and promptly burped. Flea couldn't turn his head in time and got a big whiff of the elf's breath, which reeked of a combination of strong peppermints and rocket fuel.

"Ican'twaitfor…Santatoleave, watchinghimtakeoff…isthe…*coolest*," the hyper elf said, ignoring Flea's question. He took another long sip from the candy cane, spilling a large amount of cider down the front of his shirt. "Youwant…a…sipofthis?" he asked, offering the cider. But before he gave Flea the chance to answer, the hyper elf scowled and pulled back the candy cane. "Areyouatleast…onehundredyearsold? Youbetternotbe…tryingtotrickme…togetmycider."

"No, I don't even want to – "

Flea was interrupted by another cider-fueled elf who rushed by, singing loudly and quickly. It took Flea a moment to recognize the song "Blue Christmas" but his new 'friend' quickly followed the other singer, joining in the horrible rendition of the song as they sprinted off into the party.

"Do you see Rome?" Minko asked as he scanned the growing crowd.

Flea didn't see her *or* Artimus's group, which normally should have concerned him. But somehow Flea knew that she wasn't in danger. Instead of worrying, he tried to absorb every detail of the celebration. It was such a festive atmosphere that Flea wanted to join

the crowd and just enjoy the party, make enough memories that he
could hold on to during a lifetime in the human world. Flea feared
that trying to complete his orders – which seemed an impossible task
– would risk him never taking part in this celebration.

"What is she doing with *him*?" Minko asked, snapping Flea
out of his momentary party trance.

Minko pointed through the crowd where Rome stood talking
to Artimus, her Christmas hat off her head and in her hands. Flea and
Minko had been expecting an attack from Artimus's group ever
since the snowball brawl and ice bank incident but nothing had
happened yet. They were worried that Artimus was planning
something *big* against them for revenge.

"Does it look like he's giving her a hard time?" Minko asked.
He picked up a huge handful of snow. Flea didn't bother to remind
Minko that his arm was too weak to hit Artimus from here.
Regardless, it didn't look like Artimus was threatening her.

"It looks like they're just talking," Flea said.

Minko frowned. Flea had to admit that he was also confused.
Artimus hadn't shown the slightest hint of remorse and Rome hadn't
said a single word to them about forgiving her friends, making this
sudden conversation between them all the more suspicious.

"I don't know what they could *possibly* be talking about,"
Minko said as he dropped the snowball to the ground.

Minko's statement wasn't totally true. While neither Flea nor
Minko said it aloud, both elves thought back to the moment when

Artimus told Rome that she would come back begging one day to rejoin their group of friends.

"Don't worry, I'm sure she'll let us know," Flea said hopefully. "Come on, we better get back to our orders."

Minko took one final glance toward Rome and Artimus before following Flea back into the elf school.

CHAPTER TWENTY-FOUR
Wrapping Time

Flea and Minko were in the middle of completing more orders when Rome strolled back into the production center several minutes later. Her hat was back on her head and she didn't appear quite as sad as when she left.

"What took you so long?" Minko asked.

The question threw Rome for a loop. She was usually such a smooth talker that her sudden stutter made Minko – and to a lesser extent, Flea – even more suspicious.

"I...uh...walked around the entire Christmas tree to see how much empty space was left," she said. "It really must've filled up since the last time Flea checked. There are only a handful of open spots left. I'm afraid that we might hear the factory whistle soon."

Rome rushed back to her workstation, where she started to build her next toy chest. Flea was more than happy to end the interrogation so they could all focus on building. But Minko had one final question.

"Why does your hat look so crooked? When you left, it was on perfectly straight."

Rome's hands shot up to her head and she straightened the hat.

"Oh, I... I took it off to... to scratch my head. This thing gets real itchy sometimes. Don't you think, Flea?"

"I guess so," Flea said, though he couldn't think of a single time when his head itched. In fact, Flea loved the hat; he wasn't sure why, but ever since he'd gotten to the North Pole and started wearing the hat at all times, he hadn't spotted a single speck of dandruff on his shoulders.

"Is that the *only* reason you took it off?" Minko pressed.

In an instant, Rome's expression changed from guilty to annoyed.

"Do you have some sort of problem with me?" she asked. "Because if you do, just come out and say it. We have too much work and too little time to waste asking stupid questions."

Minko looked mad but before he exploded with accusations toward Rome, he glanced at Flea, who slowly shook his head. Minko understood Flea's gesture not to push the subject any further and he actually gave in and continued building without saying another word.

With the threat of the factory whistle hanging over them, the three students continued to push ahead. Rome and Minko fought for validation, Flea for his mere existence at the North Pole. They all felt so much pressure about the impending whistle blow that any strange sound made their hearts sink. Flea felt like he was on the verge of cracking mentally and emotionally. His two friends shared the same feeling.

Rome was the first to break.

"That's it, I can't take this anymore," she said. Although she had bickered with Minko only an hour earlier, Rome suddenly turned to him for permission. "We need to find out how many orders we have left, don't you agree?"

Minko sighed.

"I thought you two said there wasn't a way to find that out," Flea said as he completed another birdhouse and hauled it toward the conveyor belt. When he glanced back at his Christmas ball, he saw the next tiny hologram already hovering above it.

"We said that *we* couldn't get that information, but I might be able to use my charm to see if *Niko* could find out for us," Rome said. "I know we're short of time but this suspense is making it impossible to focus. Minko?"

Minko had been so dead-set against the idea when Flea mentioned it before that Flea didn't think he would possibly agree to it now, especially since Rome brought it up. But Minko surprised Flea by giving her a one-word answer.

"Hurry."

For the second time in an hour, Rome rushed out of the room.

"Why didn't we do this sooner?" Flea asked. He'd gotten so skilled at building that his hands worked on their own while he talked to Minko.

"Like I said before, it goes against elf code to question your work. Even a *card-elf* understands that," Minko said. "But it doesn't seem to matter if we break that code since I doubt we'll finish anyway."

Flea completed yet another birdhouse. As he picked it up off his workstation, he continued talking to Minko.

"Well if asking Niko about our order lists is really that bad, maybe we should stop Rome before – "

Flea never completed his thought. From the corner of his eye, he spotted the tiniest change at his workstation: it appeared slightly dimmer than before. He didn't need to look at the overhead lights to know that they were all still shining brightly. Flea nearly dropped his birdhouse when he realized that there was no longer a hologram floating above his green Christmas ball. He rushed to the conveyor belt and dropped off the gift before running back to his table.

"What's wrong?" Minko asked.

Flea picked up his ornament and studied it closely. Nothing was broken. He shook the green ball expecting another hologram to appear, but nothing happened. Flea heard a loud bang behind him and turned to see that Minko had dropped his hammer to the floor. His friend's mouth hung open in shock.

"I think you're done," Minko whispered as he rushed toward Flea, nearly stumbling along the way because he couldn't take his eyes away from Flea's ornament. Minko's next words were shouted with joy. "I think you're *actually done!*"

Flea felt such a rush of adrenaline that he picked up his much bigger friend in a big bear-hug, surprising them both with his strength. Once the shock faded, Flea carried Minko back across the room.

"*You* have to hurry up and finish now, too," Flea said excitedly.

With his own burst of adrenaline, Minko wriggled free from Flea's grasp and rushed back to his workstation, where he felt totally re-energized and ready to finish his orders.

"I could help you finish, there can't be too much left on your order list," Flea suggested.

Minko didn't even look up when he answered.

"You can't build anything for me. Only the owner of a Christmas ball can complete the work assigned to him."

"There's *other* ways I can help," Flea said.

He rushed over to the pile of supplies and grabbed what Minko needed for his next assignment. He also provided Minko with words of encouragement as he built, though Flea's presence only made Minko more nervous. The two were disappointed after each finished order, as a new hologram appeared over Minko's ball every time.

"I think you should go and hang your ornament on the tree," Minko said after building several more rocking horses. "Maybe you won't be punished for Rome's and my failure, regardless of what Vork said."

Flea stared down at the green Christmas ball in his hand and wondered if Minko could be right, that it might be more difficult for Santa and Niko to kick him out of the North Pole if his ornament hung triumphantly on the Christmas tree. But as tempting as that idea sounded, Flea had his *own* code he planned to follow until the end, even if it led to his expulsion from the North Pole. Flea put his Christmas ball down on the table.

"The only time I'll hang my ornament is when all *three* of us do," he said. Flea could see his friend becoming teary-eyed again so he pointed to Minko's workstation. "Stay focused on what you're doing, it could be your last order."

"Rome is probably almost done, too," Minko said. "You need to hurry up and find her. She needs to know how close we are."

Flea rushed out of the production center, his insides doing flips with a mixture of excitement and worry. But when he reached the village, his heart sunk at the sight of the beautiful Christmas tree. It glowed even brighter now that it was almost completely covered. Flea had little time to waste. He ran straight into the middle of the party, which now consisted of hundreds of elves packed tightly together in the village center. Flea was reminded of watching the New Year's Eve ball drop in Times Square on his television. It didn't seem possible that so many bodies could squeeze into such a limited space. Though all the elves appeared to be having a great time, the scene couldn't possibly be worse for Flea; finding one particular elf in the sea of faces seemed impossible, especially with the threat of the whistle blowing at any second.

"Rome!" Flea called out at the top of his lungs, his voice barely audible over the noise of the crowd. He forced his way deeper and deeper into the crowd, frantically searching through dozens upon dozens of unfamiliar faces. "Rome!"

"Rome!" another voice called out, followed by a round of laughter. Flea looked up to see a large cluster of cider-drinking elves mocking him, including the elf who'd spoken to him earlier. Soon, nearly a dozen loud, obnoxious elves were screaming Rome's name. Normally, this would've annoyed Flea but the group was actually helping him, even if they were doing so inadvertently. In fact, Flea couldn't care less if *Santa himself* made fun of him just as long as he somehow found Rome sooner.

Even with the other elves calling out her name, it took Flea nearly fifteen minutes to spot her. Rome stood on the outskirts of the crowd, talking to a group of her former friends. Artimus and a few of the bigger guys weren't with them but Flea recognized Addy and a few other well-dressed girls. Flea wished he had time to observe Rome to see what she was up to, but he had much bigger issues right now.

"Rome!" he called out, surprising her and the other girls.

Rome quickly rushed over to him.

"What are you doing out here?" she asked.

"You're asking *me* what *I'm* doing?" Flea asked. "What are *you* doing talking to *them*?"

"I just found Niko a few minutes ago and begged him to look into our list of remaining orders. He promised to do that and I was on my way back to school when my friends stopped me and wanted to talk. Artimus wasn't around so I didn't want to be rude and blow them off, though it *does* seem strange that they kept talking even though I told them I had to go."

"So why didn't you just walk away?" Flea asked. Considering that Rome had already lied to him and Minko about talking to Artimus, Flea thought Rome's explanation sounded odd, and she was doing nothing to ease his suspicions. Flea hated that he had to doubt whether Rome had even spoken to Niko.

"Even though Artimus and a few of the guys are big jerks, a lot of my other friends aren't that bad. They might be followers and weak but I understand how hard it can be to stand up to Artimus," Rome said. "Actually, Addy and some of the girls seemed interested in how we were doing in school. I don't know, maybe they were only being nice because they've been drinking candy-cane cider that they swiped from the older elves. But after being around you and Minko for so long, it's kind of nice to talk to other girls again… no offense."

"And you think that *now* is the best time for a little chat with the girls?" Flea asked. He sounded eerily like Minko as he snapped at Rome, who quickly became angry herself.

"So now *you're* going to start lecturing me, too?" Rome snapped back, as the two were on the verge of having their first fight. Flea suddenly understood how Minko could get so frustrated with her. But once he remembered why he'd been searching for her in the first place, he dropped the argument.

"None of that matters. I came to let you know that my Christmas ball stopped giving me more holograms," Flea said. He smiled when he saw Rome's expression change from confusion to excited understanding.

"You're really done? Did you hang your ornament on the tree?" she asked.

"I won't do that without the two of you hanging yours with me," Flea said. He expected a similar level of gratitude from her that he received from Minko but didn't get it.

"Sometimes an elf has to do what's best for himself – or *herself* – without worrying about others," Rome said.

Flea wondered if Rome was talking about his situation or one of her own.

"I don't know about you but that's not the kind of elf I'd want to be," Flea said.

Rome frowned and the two glanced again at the tree. Flea spotted only a few tiny openings left and an elf was climbing the ladder toward one of them. The elf held his Christmas ball in one hand and a big candy cane in the other, as he tried to climb so quickly that he lost his grip and fell. Flea expected the crowd to be worried for the elf's safety but everyone just laughed as he hit the ground and kicked up a cloud of snow. A few other cider-fueled elves dragged their dazed friend to his feet and back toward the ladder. The crowd cheered on the elf during his second attempt to climb.

"Come on, you need to get back to building in school," Flea said as he and Rome forced their way through the crowd. "Hopefully, Minko will be done by the time we get back and you'll only have another order or two left."

Just as they emerged from the crowd, they spotted Artimus and his friends walking toward them from the direction of the school. Flea knew this was the worst possible time for the bullies to harass them so he prepared himself to quickly crush them in a snowball fight if it came to that. Oddly, Artimus simply laughed as he walked by without incident, which left Flea more worried than if there *had* been a fight.

"What was *that* about?" Flea asked Rome accusingly.

"I don't know," Rome said, though she noticed the look of doubt on Flea's face. "Seriously, I *don't* know."

Flea wasn't sure if he believed her but that didn't matter as they hurried to the production room at the end of the school's hallway. The moment they walked into the room, Flea knew something was wrong. Minko wasn't standing at his workstation, nor was he carrying a gift to the conveyor belt. It wasn't until Flea heard a loud *grunting* noise from the direction of the conveyor that he noticed the large wrapped gift stuck near the belt's exit chute. But the wrapping job on that large gift was terrible, obviously not done by the wrapping machine.

Plus it looks like there's a foot sticking out of it, Flea thought. *Wait, that* is *a foot!*

"Minko!" Flea yelled and the grunting became louder again as the 'gift' began to wiggle.

Flea and Rome ran across the room just as the 'gift' was about to be pulled into the chute. Although Flea had no idea of the dangers of the tunnel system, he didn't hesitate to dive into the chute. He grabbed hold of his friend just before the conveyor belt dipped down sharply. Rome in turn grabbed onto Flea's feet and proved that big strength could come from a tiny elf by pulling the two boys back into the light. Minko's entire body was wrapped so tightly in Christmas paper that it took both Rome and Flea to drag him off the conveyor belt. They tried to stand him up on his feet but he was so wobbly that he immediately tipped over and crashed to the floor. Minko continued to grunt angrily as Flea and Rome tore away the numerous layers of wrapping paper from his body. It took several minutes to get his head free, where Flea discovered that his friend's mouth had been gagged with tape. As he removed the tape, Flea saw Minko's eyes narrow at the sight of Rome. His angry grunting became lower-pitched and animal-like. Even though Rome helped remove the paper from his legs, Minko kicked wildly until she backed off.

"I don't want *her* touching me," Minko said once his mouth was free.

With the top two layers of wrapping paper finally yanked off, Minko used his angry energy to rip most of his body free.

"This is all *your* fault!" Minko yelled at her. "She helped set me up, I just *know* it."

"I had *nothing* to do with this," she argued back.

But before the two continued fighting, the three students heard the worst noise they could possibly imagine. Flea's heart instantly deflated.

CHAPTER TWENTY-FIVE
Smashed Hopes

The toy factory whistle blew for almost a minute straight. During that time, Flea, Minko and Rome stood completely still. When the noise ended, they heard a distant cheer from the elf crowd. Minko was the first to react, as he angrily ripped at the remaining paper that still bound his legs.

"Is there *any* possible way to get an extension after the whistle blows?" Flea asked quietly.

"No, no exceptions," Rome said.

"Big surprise that *you'd* say that," Minko said.

Although they'd *all* known that the whistle could blow at any moment, Rome seemed to be the elf most in shock. When she responded to Minko's angry accusation, she didn't snap back like usual. In fact, her words sounded just as hopeless as Flea's had.

"You know the rules, Minko. Once the last builder hangs his ornament, the whistle blows, the conveyor belts stop and the season is over," she said.

Flea glanced toward their conveyor belt, which had indeed come to a quiet stop.

"Since the belts stopped, I guess your little plan to get rid of me would've failed anyway," Minko said, his disappointment turning into an even greater sense of anger that he aimed at Rome. "If Flea hadn't saved me, I would've ended up stuck somewhere in the tunnels instead of the back of Santa's sleigh."

"Don't be a fool, Minko, I helped pull you off the conveyor belt, too," Rome said.

"What happened in here?" Flea asked.

"What do you think? Artimus and his two pals rushed in here and attacked me. They wrapped me up and put me on the conveyor belt. It's a good thing I'm not small or else I wouldn't have been able to stop from being pulled into the chute," Minko told Flea before he turned back to Rome. "But I guess you didn't think about that when you were helping your friends plan their attack."

Rome sighed, as anger was finally starting to overtake her shock.

"*I* didn't set you up, Minko. Artimus *isn't* my friend anymore, I gave up those friends for the two of you."

"Maybe at first, but once you realized we were going to fail, you rushed back to Artimus to find out what you had to do to squirm your way back into the group," Minko said.

Instead of simply getting an attitude, Rome became furious in a way that Flea had never seen from her. Her usually porcelain-skin turned bright red, tears streamed down her face and her hands shook.

"You *know* that's not true, not after everything I've done for you guys," Rome said. "You two are my only *real* friends, at least before you started believing lies about me."

"You expect us to buy that? And don't act like you've done a *single* thing for me and Flea. Everything you've done was for your own good, like *always*," Minko said. "Who knows? Maybe you never even *wanted* us to succeed. Maybe you were sabotaging us all along to make sure we never finished our orders."

"That's ridiculous! How could I be sabotaging us when *I* did more work than *you*?" Rome yelled back.

"The only thing I can't figure out," Minko started, ignoring her question, "is why you'd want to stay a *gift wrapper* forever?"

Rome looked like she'd been punched in the gut. But instead of fighting back with Minko, she turned her anger on Flea, who'd been a bystander up to this point.

"You *promised* not to tell him!" she yelled at Flea.

"I didn't say anything to him."

"Flea didn't *have* to tell me," Minko said. "Do you really think that everyone would know only about the *pathetic* card elf and not the *pathetic* gift wrapper, too? I know how much something like that hurts and I was too nice to throw it in your face. And in return, you stab me and Flea in the back."

"Flea, you don't really believe any of this, do you?" she asked.

"I don't know *what* to think anymore," Flea said.

Rome shook her head as tears continued to flow from her eyes. Flea thought she looked genuinely upset but it was hard to trust her since she'd obviously been keeping secrets from them recently.

"It's just that Minko and I *did* see you talking to Artimus the last time you went to check on the tree," Flea said, finally admitting what they'd seen. "You didn't tell us about it and you lied about what took you so long."

"Artimus tried apologizing to me. None of his friends were around so he figured he didn't have to be mean to me," Rome explained without hesitation. "But I didn't accept because of everything he's put us through. The only reason I kept it a secret from you guys was because I didn't want to distract you from your orders."

"Yeah, sounds *real* convenient if you ask me," Minko said.

Rome seemed resigned to the fact that *nothing* she could say would convince Minko. Instead, she turned to Flea for any sign that he believed her. Flea wanted to trust Rome but he had even more condemning information about her than even Minko knew about.

"I'm sorry, Rome, but it seems strange to me that you were just outside talking to the rest of your 'friends' as Minko was in here being attacked by Artimus," Flea said.

"Ha!" Minko said. "So you went out there to tell your friends to come and get us."

"How many times do I have to say this? I went *out there* to find Niko and ask how much work *we* have left," Rome said, growing more frustrated by the moment. "I did that *for us*."

Minko continued to shake his head.

"It's a lucky thing that you went after her, Flea. I'm sure she planned for her friends to come after *both* of us," Minko said.

Rome finally reached her emotional breaking point. She unleashed all of her frustrations by shoving Minko as hard as she could. Minko's ankles were still bound together with wrapping paper so he stumbled to the floor. He grunted in pain, but the last of the

paper ripped free from his body. Flea quickly jumped between the
two but Minko remained sitting on the ground, angrily staring up at
her. Flea was shocked that Rome had resorted to such violence. He
looked at her with disappointment.

"Did you honestly have anything to do with setting him up?"
Flea asked her sadly. "Did you even go to talk to Niko?"

"What else do you want me to say? I *didn't do anything!*"
Rome yelled. "But maybe I *shouldn't* have given up my friends for
you two!"

Minko jumped to his feet but did not approach Rome. In fact,
he rushed in the opposite direction, heading toward their
workstations at the back of the large production center.

"You're a *liar* and a *traitor* and because of that, we all
failed," Minko said. "You never deserved your second chance to
become a real elf."

Minko walked right past his own table and stopped in front
of Rome's, where he picked up her red Christmas ball.

"Hey, don't touch my – "

Minko spiked the ornament on the floor. A bright red light
ignited around him and was followed by a piercingly loud *screech*,
which sounded like the angry wail of a thousand sad children. Once
the awful sound and bright light disappeared, Flea stared in disbelief
at his friend, shocked by Minko's harshness. For a moment, even
Minko looked like he felt awful.

"What does it matter? None of us need our ornaments
anyway," Minko said.

Quiet tears continued to stream down Rome's cheeks. The sight of her smashed Christmas ball had taken away the last of her fighting spirit.

"I don't have *any* friends left," she said.

Rome turned and bolted from the room. Minko took several steps toward the door but stopped next to Flea. The two stared at the open door, as if Rome was going to come back at any second.

"You saw her talking to her friends. *We* saw her talking to Artimus," Minko said quietly. "That couldn't have been a coincidence, right?"

"I don't know what to believe anymore," Flea said. "If she really doesn't want to be friends with us, then why would she keep lying?"

"Hmm," Minko said, as they kept waiting for Rome to return. "I guess I didn't think about that."

"So what happens now?" Flea asked.

Flea and Minko heard the distant sound of the singing elves, a stark reminder that they would not be having such fun any time soon.

"The party will get a bit crazier since everyone is so excited to be finished. Santa will stay in his cabin for about another hour or two so he can make his final flight plans. Then, the reindeer are brought out of the stables and the sleigh is unveiled," Minko said. "I wonder what the big sleigh change will be this year. What do you think?"

"I don't really care about that right now," Flea said bluntly. "Can we stay focused?"

"Oh, sorry. Once the reindeer are hooked to the sleigh, Santa says a few words to the crowd and then he and his chosen helper elf take off to make the deliveries," Minko explained. "The party continues while they're gone and all the elves have fun until Santa gets back at 12:01 and Christmas ends. After that, time goes back to normal across the world and everyone at the North Pole sleeps for a *long* time."

"How long will it take for Santa to deliver the presents?" Flea asked.

"Maybe about a month."

"What do you think is going to happen to me?"

When the two looked at the door again, they weren't waiting for only Rome to arrive this time.

"Now we hope to avoid seeing Niko or Vork…or Santa," Minko said. "They haven't shown up *yet,* so maybe they're reconsidering kicking you out."

"Or maybe they're just waiting until Santa takes off to expel me," Flea said somberly.

While Flea was upset at the thought of leaving the North Pole forever, his friend appeared even more distraught. Still, Minko tried to force a smile.

"There's no sense of waiting around *here*," Minko said. "May as well try to enjoy the party and the spectacle of Santa's takeoff. At least you'll have fun during the long party."

Flea took one final glance at the room – where he'd spent so much time and almost gained his builder-elf status– before he and Minko left the production center. The thought of spending another month at the North Pole made him feel a *little* better but his mind wasn't focused on his own misfortunes at the moment. Instead, Flea couldn't stop thinking about Rome, about the disappointed expression on her face as she rushed away. Flea was suddenly unsure about her guilt, though there *was* one thing he was sure about: if getting Rome to graduate elf school had been the only way to 'save her', then he had failed.

CHAPTER TWENTY-SIX
The Invisible Barrier

The Christmas tree in the village center glowed so brightly that Flea had to cover his eyes until they adjusted to the light. With the snow falling even heavier, the North Pole looked more brilliant and alive than ever, causing a great feeling of hopelessness in the pit of Flea's stomach.

He knew that he would never be a part of this amazing society.

"Something doesn't feel right," he said.

"I know," Minko agreed. "*We* should be out there having a good time with everyone else. *We* should be celebrating the end of the building season. It's really not fair that you are being punished even though you didn't fail."

"That's not what I'm talking about," Flea said as he continued to scan the crowd. "It's something *else*."

The tall ladders had been removed from the tree, which was probably a good thing since the crowd had grown even rowdier. There was still plenty of singing and dancing going on but the wild cider-drinkers were more out of control, as they ran amongst the crowd, throwing huge armfuls of snow up in the air. Many of the others finally had enough of the crazy elves and started to pelt them with snowballs. Soon, snow was flying everywhere, though it appeared to be good-spirited as the singing grew louder.

"It always ends up in a snowball fight, *always*," Minko said with a smile. "Do you want to join in? It might be fun."

Flea had to admit that some fun might be just what the doctor ordered, but he couldn't shake the ominous feeling that gnawed at his mind. Before he could answer Minko, a familiar face emerged from the crowd and ran in their direction.

"Minko and Funny Flea!" Wrench called out. His bright red hair was still spiked but there was a snowy white splotch on the side of his head where he'd been hit with a snowball.

"Where's Grinder?" Minko asked. "Making last minute repairs on the big sleigh change?"

The mechanic looked offended.

"Do you really think I'd let him work on the sleigh by himself?" Wrench asked. "I love my brother but I would *never* leave him alone with it. You should have heard some of his *boring* suggestions for the change we should have made. Let's face it, *I'm* the brains in our operation."

"Can you give me any hint about what you did?" Minko asked.

"Let's just say that this year's change might be the biggest and best ever. You sure picked a good year to come to the North Pole, Funny Flea," Wrench said. "But don't worry, it's not much longer until Santa comes out of his cabin."

"Good, we're really excited to see what you did," Minko said.

Wrench suddenly glanced around.

"Where's your girlfriend?" he asked Minko. "Is she excited, too?"

"Rome is *not* my girlfriend," Minko said firmly.

For a moment, Wrench looked confused until something dawned on him. He smiled and slowly nodded his head.

"They broke up, huh?" the mechanic asked Flea. "That explains *a lot*."

"We *didn't* break up because we were never together," Minko said angrily. "Rome, mistletoe and I would *never* go together."

"What did you mean before?" Flea asked Wrench. "When you said 'that explains *a lot*', what did you mean?"

"I just saw her a few minutes ago. She looked pretty upset, she was crying I think," Wrench explained.

Wrench excused himself and headed off toward his garage for the eventual unveiling. For the second time in the last hour, Flea scanned the crowd for any sign of Rome. But his chances of spotting her this time were even more distant, as the huge snowfight made it impossible to spot anyone.

"We should find Rome," Flea said.

"She's *not* my girlfriend!" Minko snapped.

"You think I don't know that?" Flea chuckled before turning serious again. "Still, I think we need to find her and make sure she's okay."

"Why? She's probably just hanging out with Artimus and her friends, laughing about what they did to me," Minko said. "Do you really want to look stupid in front of them?"

"That's a chance I'm willing to take," Flea said, though it was obvious that Minko wasn't quite as certain. "Besides, what if she *wasn't* lying to us? How would *you* have felt if she smashed your Christmas ball for no reason?"

"What does it matter? The ornament was worthless," Minko answered right away. But after a second, he sighed. "Fine, let's go look for her."

Flea and Minko braved the crowd, searching through all the smiling faces, getting hit in the head with several mounds of snow for their efforts. Flea resisted the urge to fight back but Minko couldn't stop himself from retaliating a few times. By the time they reached the Christmas tree, Flea and Minko were half-covered in snow. Still, they saw no sign of Rome. Just when Flea thought they would have to make a second trip through the chaos, Minko tapped him on the shoulder and called out a single word over the noise of the crowd.

"Artimus!"

He pointed to a much smaller group beyond the tree. Artimus and his friends stood apart from the rest of the crowd, undoubtedly concerned about what flying snow might do to their clothes and hair. Minko bent over and picked up two snowballs, handing one to Flea. The two marched toward the gang, ready for a fight if it came to that. When Artimus saw them approaching, he snapped his fingers and his bigger friends took a defensive position in front of him. Once the gang leader felt safe, he pointed to Minko and started to laugh.

"You forgot to take the bow off your head," the bully called out.

Minko's hand instinctively reached for his head, though there was no bow stuck to him. Still, Artimus and his gang had a good laugh at Minko's expense, especially when the pudgy elf turned red.

"You and Rome think you're *so* clever setting me up like that," Minko said. He was so angry that he failed to notice that there was one elf missing from the group. "Too bad you had to bring your friends with you to get the job done. If you'd come alone, I guarantee that *you'd* be in a box in the back of Santa's sleigh."

Flea watched his friend's throwing arm tense so he immediately grabbed it to stop a fight from breaking out.

"Did you say that *Rome* was clever?" Artimus asked. He was clearly confused at first but soon forced a chuckle. "The idea of Rome having *any* sort of intelligence is downright laughable."

Flea's heart sunk as he whispered to Minko that Rome was nowhere to be found.

"Where is Rome?" Flea asked Artimus, afraid that he already knew the answer.

"She could be kissing a reindeer's backside for all I care," Artimus said, causing another round of laughter from his friends. "I figured she would be with you two freaks."

Minko tried to throw his snowball but Flea caught his friend's hand, causing the snow to melt to slushy water.

"Come on, she's not here," Flea said, pulling his friend away.

Artimus and his gang threw several snowballs but Flea stopped each of them. Flea finally launched one of his own, though it smashed to the ground just inches in front of Artimus's feet.

"If you try to throw another one or follow us, I won't purposely miss my next throw," Flea said. This made the well-dressed gang pause just long enough for Minko and Flea to escape.

"We'll settle this at *Snow Wars*!" Artimus called out. "*If* you two losers can convince a *third* loser to join you."

Minko was in a shocked state as they rushed away from Artimus. He muttered the same sentence over and over, as he finally realized the damage he'd caused.

"I can't believe I smashed her ornament."

Flea grew more and more nervous when Rome was nowhere to be found. Red-robe's warning screamed inside of his head. All of the happiness and fun occurring around him made Flea feel overwhelmed and anxious. Despite the fact that he wanted to avoid Niko at all costs, Flea decided to head to the security building. However, he spotted another familiar face – or at least another familiar *hair-do*.

"Is everything okay?" Grinder asked, a look of concern on his face. "I just saw your friend rushing away. I tried to ask her what was wrong but all she said was how much she hates being at the North Pole."

"Where did she go?" Flea asked hurriedly.

The green-haired mechanic turned and pointed toward the southern part of the village. The elf dorm was the only building located in that area. Flea prayed to the snow gods that Rome was simply going to her room to sleep off her misery but he had a bad feeling that this wasn't the case. Flea thanked Grinder and dragged Minko even farther away from the party. Since the snow was falling harder and the North Pole's entire elf population was located in the village center, a fresh blanket of snow covered the ground leading toward the elf dorm. Only one set of footprints led away from the party and Flea was certain that Rome had made them.

"Maybe she's just really mad and is tying pieces of white cloth on all the door handles," Flea said hopefully.

But before they reached the building, Flea's worst fears were confirmed: Rome's footprints turned away from the dorm and headed due south. He desperately tried to spot her through the falling snow but had no such luck.

Rome was gone and headed straight toward the South Pole Army.

-      -   -   -   -   -   -   -   -   -

-      -   -   -

"What is she thinking going that way?" Flea asked nervously, continuing to follow Rome's tracks. "Didn't Niko tell everyone to stay away from the area south of the North Pole village?"

"I guess, but I doubt anyone took that warning seriously," Minko said. "After all, he never told us what – *or if* – anything was even out there."

"It's the South Pole, *they* are waiting out there," Flea said.

"What are you talking about?" Minko asked.

Flea's first instinct was to keep Niko's secret from his big-mouthed friend. But since he was going to be kicked out of the North Pole anyway, Flea decided that it was only fair for Minko to know the danger he was about to get himself into. Flea told him everything – from the advancing snowman army to the fierce animal leader to Flea's assumption that his presence at the North Pole had increased the danger from the South Pole. By the time Flea was finished explaining, Minko could hardly believe what he'd heard.

"I thought all those stories about the North Pole having an enemy were just make-believe," Minko said.

"I assure you, it's all true," Flea said. "I've been in the security building on two different occasions and saw all of this with my own two eyes."

When Minko realized what this could mean, he trudged through the snow even faster as they followed Rome's footsteps. Flea struggled to keep up with his bigger friend, especially since the snow was deeper this far away from the village.

"Do you think Rome could've wandered outside the safety zone?" Minko asked. "Niko always told us to stay within the North Pole village, he never explained how close we should stay before it became dangerous."

Flea tried to recall specifics from the hologram map but couldn't remember if there was any hint of how far away the village was from the Army. Only one elf would be able to give them that information.

"Maybe we should stop and find Niko," Flea said as he glanced back toward the village, which was becoming harder to see through the snowfall. "He could figure out how far we have to go if Rome is in trouble."

"There's no time for that," Minko said, continuing to rush forward. "If you want to turn around for any reason, I would understand. But I can't go back, not if there's a chance that Rome is in trouble."

Flea knew that heading back to tell Niko was probably the smarter, more responsible choice. But there was no way he was going to abandon his two best friends in their greatest time of need, regardless of the possible danger.

"Of course I'm not going to leave you now," Flea said. "If there's going to be a fight, you'll need me."

Within minutes, the joyous sounds of the elf celebration faded away and the bright glow of the Christmas tree was no larger than a tiny dot on the horizon behind them. The snow fell heavier and the temperature felt cooler the farther they walked. The *howling* wind seemed to warn them of bad things to come. Flea and Minko started to call out Rome's name but their voices were severely muffled by the wind. Eventually, the two even had trouble following Rome's tracks, which began to fade beneath the blowing snow.

"How far do we go?" Flea called out over the *howling* wind.

"As far as we *have to*," Minko yelled back. "Like I said, I've only traveled *north* of the village, never *south*. But Rome couldn't have gone much farther, the wind would've blown her away."

Flea worried that the end of the safety zone was not far. He watched closely not just for any sign of Rome, but also the first line of Army snowmen and the biggest cause for concern.

"Make sure you keep an eye out for an animal that looks like a giant polar bear!" Flea yelled.

"I thought you said the Army was made up of snowmen!"

"It *is*," Flea answered. "But the polar bear is in charge of the Army, like some sort of general. The bear is no regular animal, either. It walks upright on its hind legs and looks like it can communicate like a regular person… or a regular elf. I think the bear might be in charge of the entire South Pole."

Since they'd started tracking Rome's footprints, Minko hadn't slowed at all, at least not until Flea's last comment. He stopped in his tracks and turned to face Flea.

"Until today, I never thought the elf tales about the South Pole were true," he started. "But from the stories I've heard, the leader of the South Pole is *far worse* than some animal that walks on two legs."

"Not just *some* animal, a *polar bear*," Flea said. "A monstrous, mean-looking *polar bear!*"

Flea tried to stress the importance of the potential danger from the polar bear general but Minko clearly didn't understand.

"I don't care if this polar bear is meaner than an *ice shark*. It can't be worse than the South Pole leader from the legends passed down by the much older elves."

"Who *is* the leader then?" Flea asked.

Minko shivered, but not because of the cold wind. He opened his mouth to answer but closed it just as quickly, shaking his head. He turned and continued walking along Rome's path. Flea hurried to catch up again, curious about what Minko wasn't telling him.

"I don't even want to consider that it could be true," Minko said. "I can only hope that the legends are wrong... or that we find Rome *soon*."

Before Flea had the chance to pester him further, he noticed something strange about the falling snow and immediately grabbed his friend's arm. Minko tried to drag Flea along but the pudgy elf then noticed something as well.

"Her tracks are gone! It's like she disappeared!" Minko called out. He glanced all around but there was no sign of Rome. Flea thought he might know why.

"Look at the snow blowing away from us," Flea said.

The two watched as the strong wind kept blowing the snow south, though none of the falling snowflakes ever touched the ground. Instead, they seemed to disappear in midair whenever they reached a certain point.

"It must be the end of the safety zone," Flea said, pointing in the direction of the invisible barrier. "We can't even see what's out there. What should we do?"

"We go after her!"

Without hesitation, Minko stepped through the invisible barrier and disappeared from view. Flea took a deep breath and followed his friend.

\-   \-   \-   \-   \-   \-   \-   \-   \-   \-   \-

\-   \-   \-   \-

Right away, Flea knew this was going to be bad. While the interior of the North Pole borders had remained in a constant state of dusk, Flea and Minko stepped into a world of night. It was just as dark as 11:59 *should* appear. Through the heavy cloud cover, the moon shined dimly. Just enough light reflected off the white snowy ground to keep the two elves from bumping into each other. Even worse than the difference in light was the change in weather.

Flea barely took two steps out of the North Pole before a gust of wind lifted his tiny body off the ground and blew him over. He had difficulty pulling himself up as the wind continued to knock him down. The wind threatened to rip Flea's hat off his head so he pulled it nearly below his eyes. Luckily, Minko was big enough to hold himself steady and yank Flea to his feet.

"We have to k…k…keep going…g…,g…" Minko yelled over the sound of even louder wind.

Minko's voice quivered in the freezing cold. The snow fell in such heavy white sheets that they wouldn't have been able to see the South Pole Army if it was ten feet in front of them. Still, Minko was somehow able to spot something even smaller on the snowy ground.

"Footsteps! Rome must've gone this way!" Minko called out and waved Flea ahead.

The snow was so deep that with every step Flea took, his leg became buried up to his thigh. Moving was slow-going but by staying close behind Minko, Flea used his bigger friend's size to cut back on the wind that threatened to blow him away.

"What part of the world is this?" Flea asked.

"Northern Canada!" Minko answered. "Isn't this weather b...b...beautiful?"

Flea barely heard his friend over the sound of his own chattering teeth. For several minutes, he kept his head down as he followed in Minko's bigger footsteps. But Flea eventually bumped into his back when Minko finally came to a stop.

"Do you see that?" Minko called out.

As Flea slowly stepped around him to get a better view, his mind raced at the thought of what might be out there. He didn't want to see the polar bear general and the huge Army – or *anything* from the holographic map for that matter. But as he squinted through the extreme weather, he saw nothing.

"Where?" Flea yelled.

Minko pointed just ahead and to the right. It took a few moments for Flea's eyes to adjust before he spotted a tiny form through the snow. But as far as Flea could tell, the form was nothing more than an unusually-shaped mound of snow. Minko was convinced that he saw something and rushed toward it. When they got closer, Flea was relieved to see the outline of an elf.

"Rome!" Minko called out. But she was too far away to hear him over the wind.

Her back was turned to them as they quickly rushed toward her, Flea and Minko both calling out her name. When the two got close enough, Rome slowly turned around to face them. What Flea and Minko saw caused them both to stop dead in their tracks. Rome had a look of utter fear on her face and her wrists were bound together by a big block of ice, which threatened to topple her over at any moment. Minko and Flea rushed toward her again, but when Rome yelled to them, her voice cut through the wind loud and clear.

"Go back now! It's a *trap!*"

CHAPTER TWENTY-SEVEN
The General

Flea's heart sunk at the mention of the word 'trap' but the warning didn't slow Minko. Flea still followed knowing that the danger grew greater with every step he took.

"Stop!" Rome kept yelling at them. "You have to go back!"

Her screams became more frantic with every passing second but she was in trouble and they weren't about to abandon her now, regardless of the danger. Because the landscape was barren, Flea started to think that she might be overreacting. But just then, the snowy ground surrounding them seemed to explode up. In seconds, hundreds of Army snowmen – the same ones Flea had seen on the security maps – encircled the three elves. Their eyes bright red and their spears icy sharp, these snowmen looked every bit as dangerous – if not *more* – than the security force protecting the ice bank.

And Flea had a bad feeling that these snowmen would punish him in a much harsher manner than just turning him into a block of snow.

"What are you two doing?" Rome yelled. "Run!"

But Minko ignored the threat around them. Nothing was going to stop him from reaching Rome. Unfortunately, this meant that he didn't see the first spear thrown toward his back. Flea was too shocked to react but Rome somehow pushed Minko aside with the big ice block before he was hit. Seeing his friends in mortal danger triggered Flea's instinct to fight and he had an unlimited supply of ammo on the ground around him. He began to throw snowball after snowball, his aim perfect as he hit and destroyed the snowman closest to his friends. But the snowmen were quick learners and some started to use their spears to deflect the snowballs.

While Flea and his friends were outnumbered, very few in the Army attacked. It wasn't long before a pair of snowmen threw their spears in Flea's direction. The first icy spear melted when Flea lifted his hand. But his ring suddenly glowed and created a quick blast of wind that pushed the second spear off its course. Flea expected more spears but instead felt a deep rumbling under his feet. As Minko continued attempting to free Rome from the ice block, Flea heard a loud roar and saw a flash of white movement from amongst the Army. Someone – or some*thing* – very large ran and jumped over several rows of snowmen.

When it landed, the ground shook so violently that Flea was nearly knocked off his feet.

"I said do *not* attack!" a deep voice growled loudly.

Flea realized he was watching the polar bear general, who landed next to the pair of spear-tossing snowmen. With one quick swipe from his massive paw, the polar bear completely disintegrated the snowmen before he turned to Flea, who fired a snowball at the animal without thinking. The polar bear easily swatted it away with his free hand before standing on his hind legs.

Flea had never witnessed a more frightening sight in his entire life. Although he'd seen a holographic version of the animal on the security map, that image had not done the polar bear justice.

Standing well over ten feet tall, the animal wasn't just three times Flea's height but nearly twice that of any Army snowman. As if the bear's height and monstrously-muscled body wasn't intimidating enough, he wore a suit of body armor made of thick ice blocks that made the one on Rome's wrist look like an ice cube. While the polar bear had destroyed two snowmen and stopped Flea's snowball with his free paw, his *other* paw held a weapon that was bigger than Flea. The double-sided weapon had a three-foot ice blade on one end while the other side consisted of an icy chain with a huge snowy block attached. Upon closer inspection, Flea saw dozens of tiny ice daggers sticking out of that snow block.

Though General Polar Bear had easily swatted away the first attack, Flea grabbed another handful of snow to defend himself.

"If you throw another snowball, I promise your friends will pay," the polar bear snarled deeply. When the animal spoke, Flea saw his razor-sharp teeth and blood-red mouth and knew the general could destroy him and his friends in any number of painful ways.

Flea turned to see that Minko had also been taken into custody, his hands fastened together with an ice block several times larger than Rome's. Nearly a dozen ice spears were held threateningly against his two friends so Flea dropped the snowball. General Polar Bear approached Flea and roughly grabbed him by the arm, his muscular paw nearly snapping Flea's bone like a twig. The general easily tossed Flea several feet through the air and he crashed down in front of his friends.

"Put him in ice restraints, too," General Polar Bear ordered. "And be careful, he's a feisty one."

A pair of snowmen approached Flea, who relented to them forcing his wrists together and fusing two halves of an icy block over his hands. Once the snowmen were satisfied that Flea was properly restrained, they stepped away and rejoined their place in the Army ranks. Luckily, neither the snowmen nor the polar bear knew of the effect that Flea's hands had on ice and snow. Within seconds of being shackled, Flea already felt the icy block beginning to melt.

"Who are you?" the general asked.

"I already told you, we're – "

"Not you, girl!" the general growled angrily, bearing his teeth at Rome. "I want one of *them* to answer, we'll learn if you're telling the truth. Now *who are the three of you?*"

Minko tensed in anger as the animal threatened Rome, so Flea quickly answered before his best friend got himself – or them *all* – into even more trouble.

"We're only elf students," Flea answered.

The polar bear looked at Rome and nodded.

"I see that you have your cover story straight but I still don't believe you," the general said. "Who will be coming to save you?"

"Nobody, sir," Flea answered.

"Don't *lie* to me," the polar bear warned.

"I promise you, I am telling you the truth," Flea said. "*Nobody* knows that we're out here."

"Then why have you left your precious North Pole?" General Polar Bear demanded.

"We didn't know it was dangerous," Rome said.

"That is a lesson I'm certain to teach you," the polar bear said. He growled deeply again in what Flea assumed was the bear's form of laughter.

"What are you and your Army doing outside the North Pole?" Flea asked, hopeful that the polar bear wouldn't punish him for asking a question.

One of the snowmen slid forward to answer proudly.

"We are here to serve our master, J – "

The general growled again and jumped to action. For an animal so tall and muscular, General Polar Bear moved like lightning. He swung the snow-block end of his weapon in a wide arc. Flea watched in horror as the dozens of tiny daggers swung directly toward his head. He was so shocked by the sudden movement that he didn't budge, though he heard his two friends gasp in horror behind him. Flea instinctively shut his eyes before impact, but no pain ever came. Instead, he felt a stiff breeze that nearly ripped the hat off his head. When he opened his eyes and turned around, Flea saw the polar bear had hit the talking snowman and turned it into a snowy puff of nothingness. Another Army snowman immediately moved forward and took its new place in line.

"Nobody else is to speak to these prisoners except me," the polar bear growled at his troops. "Front line, slide forward!"

The first line of snowmen simultaneously moved several feet ahead. The general ordered the squad to proceed to the edge of the North Pole zone to wait for any potential rescuers. The squad quickly disappeared into the heavy snow.

"Hopefully Santa Claus himself comes looking for you," the polar bear growled, licking his lips at the thought. "If I can destroy him and the North Pole, then I can destroy Christmas once and for all."

"No, you can't do that," Rome pleaded. She was clearly distraught and for good reason; *she* had been the one to stumble into danger and felt at fault for anything bad that would happen.

In one quick step, the polar bear crossed the distance to Rome and raised his weapon. Minko tried to move between Rome and the general but his ice-block handcuffs were so heavy that he lost his balance and crashed to the ground, the sight of which caused the bear to growl in laughter again. He lowered his weapon but remained inches in front of Rome's face.

"I can do *what* I want *when* I want," he growled. "And why shouldn't I? Once the North Pole is wiped off the face of the planet, I will become the second-most powerful being this world has ever known. I've waited years for this opportunity, for anyone to wander out of the North Pole, and I have *you* to thank for that."

The general returned to his upright position and paced in front of them. Rome looked sick about what the general had just said but she wasn't alone.

"This is finally the chance I need to accomplish my goal," the polar bear continued, "as long as I can either destroy Santa or capture the elf with a split ear."

Flea suddenly felt like he'd been whacked in the stomach with the general's ice block. He had no idea how *anyone* – especially the polar bear – could know about his ear or why the South Pole could want him captured. As the wind continued to whip around them, Flea was suddenly more aware that the top of his hat flapped in the wind and threatened to blow off at any moment. Instinctively, he reached his hands toward his head to make sure his hat stayed secure. But he felt the ice-block crumbling around his wrists and knew that any sudden movement might cause it to break free. Since Flea didn't want the polar bear to know that he could free himself, he remained still and hoped his hat would hold tight.

"Do any of you know of such a split-eared elf?" the polar bear asked.

"No!" Rome and Minko said at the same time, answering a bit too quickly. Flea knew his two friends well enough to know when they were lying, though he couldn't remember them ever having seen his deformed ear.

General Polar Bear also must've sensed their dishonesty because he approached Rome and ripped the big red hat off her head. As the bear closely examined Rome's ear, Flea watched her hat blow away, headed in the direction of the North Pole. The polar bear then moved on to Minko, who he handled roughly while checking the side of the pudgy elf's head. Flea tried not to panic but a part of his mind screamed for him to take this last opportunity to attempt escape. But Flea knew that it would be impossible to get his friends out of here with so many snowmen around and the general so close.

"Why are you suddenly so quiet?" the polar bear growled as he rumbled toward Flea.

Flea could do nothing but shrug his shoulders as the general ripped the hat off his head. Flea's hair blew in the wind and he could feel the frigid air on his split ear, which had always been a bit more sensitive than any of his other facial features. The general casually looked him over but Flea saw the powerful animal tense when he looked at his ear. The polar bear's powerful paw yanked Flea clear off his feet and pulled him so close for an examination that he could smell the sour stench of death on the animal's breath.

"I can't believe it," General Polar Bear growled excitedly as he continued to hold Flea. "It's him, I've found *the* elf!"

CHAPTER TWENTY-EIGHT
Split Ears

When General Polar Bear gently placed Flea back on the ground, the entire snowman Army simultaneously backed up. Flea wasn't sure how he expected the enemy to react but he *definitely* hadn't expected the bear to be *nicer* to him. Flea saw expressions of shock on his friends' faces but he merely shrugged at them, as he had no idea what was happening.

"I'm *what* elf?" Flea asked.

"I must bring you to *him* right away," the polar bear said. The general suddenly became nervous and paced back and forth. "Now we'll finally be able to stop Christmas."

"*Who* are you bringing me to? I don't understand what's going on," Flea said.

The general stopped pacing and returned to all fours, coming face to face with Flea.

"Don't play dumb with me," he growled. "You *know* what the split ear means. If you weren't so important to my master's cause, I would destroy you right now for lying to me."

The general slammed the blade-end of his weapon into the snowy ground before reaching into his icy armor and producing a small pouch. He dumped the contents of this pouch – some sort of silvery, sparkly dust – into his huge paw and studied it closely. He glanced toward Rome and Minko before grabbing Flea with his free paw.

"I only have enough for you and me. But that's plenty since I *never* want to come back here again," the general growled to Flea. The animal turned toward Rome and Minko as he addressed his snowy troops. "There's a chance they're telling the truth and nobody else at the North Pole knows they're here. And that's exactly how I want it to stay. Once I'm gone, finish these two off and make sure their bodies are never found."

"*No,* just let them go, *please*," Flea begged. "You've got me, you've got what you want. You don't have to hurt them."

But the general obviously disagreed. He snarled in the direction of Flea's friends. Flea started to break free from the icy cuffs just as the general lifted the dust above both of their heads. However, both the elf and animal stopped when they heard a commotion in the distance. Flea recognized the sound of *clashing* ice and within seconds, pieces of destroyed snowmen flew toward them and landed at their feet. The polar bear growled as he looked through the falling snow. With the general's attention turned away, Flea took the opportunity to act. His ringed-hand glowed golden within the icy block and a gust of wind shot directly toward the general's paw. Nearly half the dust blew away before the polar bear noticed and shielded his paw from the wind.

General Polar Bear *roared* with rage and shoved Flea to the ground before carefully placing the remaining dust back into the pouch. He yanked his weapon from the ground and prepared himself for a fight as more snowman fragments soared toward them. Through the heavy snowfall, they all watched a figure approach.

"That's not the elf you want!" a familiar voice called out.

Niko was the last elf Flea expected to come after them – *well, maybe Artimus is the very last one I'd expect,* he thought.

"Get him!" General Polar Bear ordered.

An entire row of snowmen slid forward and attacked Niko. Flea thought that there was no way a single elf could survive such an assault, but Niko surprised them all by going on the offensive. With only a simple ice spear – far smaller and less dangerous-looking than the weapons wielded by the Army – Niko sliced and diced his way through dozens of snowmen. Santa's son didn't waste a single movement as he ducked and dodged, bobbed and weaved, flipped and rolled, all the while striking down the squad sent after him. Needless to say, Flea and his friends were amazed by his fighting abilities, especially since Niko still looked so insubstantial wearing his familiar red Christmas hat.

Once the last snowman was obliterated, the next row began to slide forward until the general held up a paw to stop them. Instead, he raised his weapon and stepped in front of Niko.

"How do you know which elf I want?" General Polar Bear asked.

"Because you probably want the one with a split ear, right?" Niko asked matter-of-factly.

The general roughly grabbed Flea and turned him, showing Niko the split ear. Flea tried to break free from the bear's grip but that was impossible for a mere mortal.

"My master has been waiting *years* for the chance to find the elf boy with a split ear," the general growled. "And he stumbled right into my waiting paws."

"Too bad that's *not* the elf you want," Niko said.

Niko spiked his spear into the ground and for the first time since Flea had known him, Niko carefully removed his hat. Niko turned his head and the moonlight shined perfectly onto his ear, which was split exactly like Flea's.

\-   \-   \-   \-   \-   \-   \-   \-   \-   \-   \-

\-   \-   \-   \-

Although the wind still *howled* loudly, Flea heard the gasp from his two friends behind him.

"Does that mean that Flea and Niko are…" Minko started. Even though Flea lost the last word in the wind, he figured it was the same thing he'd been thinking.

Brothers.

General Polar Bear was clearly confused as he looked from Niko to Flea, seeing the same exact ear.

"It can't be you," the general finally growled at Niko. "You look too old, my master said the elf with the split ear would be very young."

"He *is* young for an elf, one of the youngest at the North Pole," Rome said.

"I did not *ask* for your opinion," the general growled at Rome. He was clearly frustrated by this new problem.

"You'd better not send the wrong elf to your master," Niko warned the polar bear. "I know that *I* wouldn't want to anger him."

General Polar Bear growled as he continued to look at Niko's ear. But when the general turned away from him to study Flea again, Niko reacted. In one swift motion, Niko grabbed his spear and launched himself toward the general. The animal might have been quick but not enough to move out of the way. Unfortunately for Niko, the bear's strength *was* enough to keep him safe.

Niko plunged the spear into an exposed part of the general's shoulder but the weapon merely snapped in half against thick muscle. Niko landed perfectly on his feet but could not avoid the back of the general's paw, which struck him in the face and sent him flying through the air. By the time Niko crashed to the ground in front of Minko and Rome, he was already unconscious.

"He should *not* have done that," the general growled.

General Polar Bear shoved Flea to the ground next to Niko's unmoving body. When Flea tried to stand up, the polar bear growled at him.

"Stay still and turn your ear so I can see."

Flea did as he was told and lay face down in the snow. A pair of snowmen approached Niko and placed his limp hands in a big ice block. Finally, the general made his decision.

"Get up and drag your friend over with the others," he ordered, before turning to the next line of snowmen. "I only have enough dust for *one* to travel to the South Pole but I can't take the risk of choosing wrong. That's why *I'll* go back and let my master know what has happened. *He* can come back with me and determine which elf is the correct one. It should only take me a few minutes to get him so you better watch the prisoners closely. If anything happens to them – especially the two with split ears – I assure you that you'll *all* pay severely."

"What will we do with the *wrong* split-eared elf?" one of the snowmen asked.

"The same thing as the other two. *I'll* personally make sure they never return to the North Pole – at least not in one piece," the polar bear said. He turned to the four elves – only three of whom were conscious – and warned, "You better not try any funny business or I *will* find you."

Flea and his friends nodded. The general proceeded to take out the pouch again, but this time he didn't hesitate to sprinkle the dust over himself. Flea was amazed as he watched the monstrous animal disappear before his eyes. Now that the general was gone and they were out of immediate danger, Flea had the chance to look closer at Niko and his ear. He didn't think it could be coincidence that they both had the same split ear. Flea wondered if his connection to the North Pole might possibly run deeper than just an ability to build…

Could I actually have a real family here? Flea wondered as he thought about Niko and Santa Claus and whether he was related to the world's most famous holiday icon.

"I'm so sorry for getting you two into this mess," Rome said as the tears flowing down her face turned to ice before sliding off her cheek. "I was so stupid to ignore Niko's warning and I can't believe you two came after me despite the danger. What have I done?"

"*I* should be the one apologizing for making you so upset. I never should've smashed your Christmas ball. This is all *my* fault," Minko said. He also appeared on the verge of tears, as the two surely realized the hopelessness of their predicament. "I hope Santa doesn't curse our names forever for putting his son in such danger. How do you think Niko knew to come out here after us?"

"I was trying to find Rome," Niko croaked as he slowly returned to consciousness. When he looked up and saw Flea staring at him, Flea instantly turned away. "I had some information to give her about your building lists. Not that it matters now, but all of you were really close to finishing."

Flea and Minko looked at each other. Neither had to say a word, however, as both felt terrible for having questioned Rome. She *had* been telling the truth all along despite their doubts. Niko got stronger with every passing second and pulled himself into a sitting position.

"Anyway, I checked the security maps to find her and saw *you two* wandering away from the North Pole," Niko told Flea and Minko. Santa's son was clearly annoyed with them, especially Flea. "This was the last thing that *you* should've done. You've jeopardized everything and everyone at the North Pole by coming after Rome."

Niko became angrier and angrier as he scolded the three elves, though most of his fury was aimed directly at Flea. Santa's son struggled to his feet and while Flea wanted to help him, he couldn't let the watching snowmen know that his hands were no longer secured in ice. Flea tried to focus on Niko's words but he couldn't stop looking at his split ear, nor could he stop himself from asking the question he knew Niko didn't want to answer.

"Does this mean that you and I are – "

"We don't have time for this," Niko snapped. "The general should be back from the South Pole with *him* any minute and then we're *all* in serious trouble."

"*Who* is the polar bear coming back with?" Flea wondered.

Niko sighed with annoyance, a sign that he had fully recovered from being struck so hard.

"The one who's trying to rid the world of the North Pole, Santa Claus and Christmas," Niko said. "*Jack Frost*."

CHAPTER TWENTY-NINE
Jack Frost & Santa Claus

Flea shivered at the mention of the name, as a freezing blast of wind nipped him squarely in the nose. But before he had the chance to ask anything else about Jack Frost, Niko stressed the importance of getting back to the North Pole right away. One of the front row snowmen slid toward Niko, its weapon raised.

"You are not allowed to leave here, the general wants you to remain in our custody," the red-eyed snowman said. "If you try to leave, you will force us into action."

Niko ignored the warning and started to kick at his ice block, slowly chipping away at it.

"This is your final warning," the snowman said.

"Do you really expect me to be afraid of *you* when I know that the general and Jack Frost will be back at any moment?" Niko asked, as he continued to slam his foot into the heavy ice block. "Why don't you do me a favor and go somewhere that's *really* hot!"

The snowman turned to two others in the front row and ordered them to bring over another ice block. They approached Niko and told him to lay down on the ground and put his feet together so they could place his ankles into the block. Niko refused and kept kicking away, although he wasn't making much progress to free himself. The Army snowmen weren't happy about being disobeyed and Flea knew the situation was about to turn ugly. Flea realized that the time to act had come. With all the attention focused on Niko,

Flea ripped his hands out of the ice block, which finally cracked in half. He hurled the two big ice chunks at the snowmen near Niko, destroying them both before anyone realized what had happened. Flea then turned toward the snowmen closest to Rome and Niko.

"Duck!" he called out as he hurled several snowballs.

His friends crouched low just as the snowballs soared over their heads and connected with the guards right behind them. Although Flea had *plenty* of other targets to choose from, he knew it would take more than just his throwing ability to rescue his friends. So instead of trying to destroy more of the Army, he kneeled next to Niko and placed his hands on the ice block.

"What are you *doing*?" Niko yelled as the rest of the Army began to converge around them.

"Just *trust* me!" Flea yelled back. His ringed-hand glowed beneath his glove as his hands melted through the thick ice.

"Well whatever you're doing, *hurry up!*"

Flea glanced up to see the first row of snowmen – their sharp ice spears drawn and ready for use – only a few feet away. Just before the first snowman could plunge its weapon into Flea's back, Minko heaved his heavy ice block off the ground and smashed it through the snowman, which instantly disintegrated. Unfortunately for Minko, the momentum of swinging the massive block sent him crashing to the ground. But the distraction provided Flea just enough time to break through the rest of Niko's ice and free his hands. Flea expected some sort of thanks or appreciation but the moment Niko was free, he grabbed the ice spear from the recently-destroyed snowman and swung it just inches above Flea's head. At first, Flea wondered if Niko was attacking him but he turned around to see Santa's son slice apart a nearby snowman.

"Help!" Rome called out.

In one fluid motion, Flea grabbed a handful of snow, spun around and launched a snowball, which crashed into an Army snowman that was swinging its spear toward Rome. Other snowmen also tried rushing toward her but the entire scene seemed to move in slow motion to Flea, who had an instinctual ability to spot the most immediate danger and eliminate it with a well-placed throw.

"Run!" Niko called out to Rome and Minko, who struggled to move with the heavy ice blocks still weighing them down. Flea wanted to free his friends as well but he no longer had the element of surprise on his side as he had with Niko. In fact, his friends stood little chance of surviving if Flea stopped firing snowballs for even the briefest moment.

Fueled by adrenaline, Rome and Minko found the strength needed to lift the ice blocks and rush back toward the North Pole. The weather was so bad and the snow so deep that their escape was slowed to a crawl, but Flea's *whizzing* snowballs and Niko's acrobatic fighting skills held off the Army, at least for a few minutes.

"Flea, you have to go ahead!" Niko yelled as the Army started getting closer. Dozens of flying spears crashed to the ground by their feet and it seemed only a matter of time before one of the weapons hit them. "Hurry, before the Army gets you or Jack Frost shows up!"

Flea looked toward the North Pole but couldn't tell how much farther they had to go to reach safety. Rome and Minko struggled through the snow and were only a few feet ahead, not yet far enough from the Army to guarantee that they'd reach safety.

"I'm not leaving my friends *or* you!" Flea said. He stood his ground and continued to pick off the snowmen, which were easier targets to hit now that they'd gotten closer.

"None of *us* matter!" Niko yelled. "It's most important that *you* survive!"

Now was not the time for thinking, which was a mistake that nearly cost Flea his life. He stopped to ponder Niko's words just long enough to miss spotting a snowman throw an ice spear at him. Flea created a gust of wind that blew the spear enough to the left that it ripped a hole in the side of his white puffy shirt. Upon seeing Flea's close call, Niko again yelled for him to run and proceeded to take his own advice – but in the opposite direction. Niko rushed straight into the first group of snowmen, swinging his spear like a possessed elf. Flea watched in horror as Niko was all but swallowed by the swarm of snowmen, although he still saw a hurricane of motion followed by an explosion of snowmen fragments. Flea threw snowball after snowball at the Army surrounding Niko but he couldn't see Santa's son within the chaos.

"Flea!" Minko yelled behind him. "We reached the safety zone!"

Flea turned just in time to see his two friends disappear through the invisible barrier to the North Pole.

"Niko! They reached it!" Flea yelled. For several long, anxious moments, Flea watched the group of violent snowmen, which he continued to pick off one by one. But before he gave up hope, he saw Niko soar over the crowd, smashing several snowmen as he made his escape.

"Go!" Niko yelled as he sprinted toward Flea.

This time, Flea listened. After throwing his last snowball, he turned and rushed toward the barrier. Somehow Niko had mastered the art of running in the deep snow, but Flea had no such skill. His retreat was slow and Niko caught up with him in a matter of seconds.

"You have to go quicker!" Niko yelled, still annoyed even in the middle of a life-or-death situation.

"I'm *trying!*" Flea yelled back. He wanted to run faster but his buried feet couldn't keep up with the rest of his body and he fell. Niko sighed as he dragged him to his feet. When Flea glanced back to see the Army getting closer, he saw a bright silvery light that blinded him. Accompanying the bright light was a deep sonic boom that once again knocked Flea off his feet.

"Don't look back," Niko warned. For the first time since he showed up to rescue Flea and his friends, Niko actually sounded frightened. "Just run!"

But telling Flea not to look at the light was like telling a small child not to look at a Christmas tree full of presents. Through the light, he saw the polar bear reappear but he was not alone. Standing beside the general was the most amazing-looking being that Flea had ever seen. Not nearly as tall or muscular as the bear, this being was still a far more commanding sight to behold. He appeared to be the size of a regular human man but was made totally of a sparkling ice. His entire body shimmered in the night. Flowing in the breeze behind him was a long cape made of an icy – yet steamy – vapor. When the icy being looked at Flea, he had the most piercing set of ice-blue eyes imaginable, which seemed to bore a hole into Flea's mind. His eyes were the only part of the ice-man that appeared human.

The Army had stopped its approach when the ice-man arrived but General Polar Bear didn't hesitate to act. He sprinted toward Flea and Niko, swiping through any snowmen that got in his way.

"*You* must not hurt the split-eared ones," the ice-man yelled at the general. His voice sounded similar to the noise made when he'd suddenly appeared, more of a deep sonic boom than a human – *or elf* – voice. The snowmen backed away to give him a clear path, as the icy being quickly glided over the snow. Flea was momentarily frozen in place as he watched the incredible being but the sound of Niko's yelling voice snapped him from his trance.

"Run! It's Jack Frost!"

Jack Frost almost looked too majestic to be dangerous. Flea considered throwing a snowball at him but doubted that would accomplish anything. Instead, he turned and ran behind Niko, who no longer seemed willing to stand still and fight so Flea could escape. Flea tried to run in his friends' footsteps and saw that they disappeared just ahead. When he glanced back, he saw that Jack

Frost and his general had both slowed as they got closer to the border and Flea knew he couldn't be caught now. But when his eyes met Jack Frost's, those icy-blue eyes skewed in such a look of anger that Flea understood Niko's fear of the ice demon.

"Stop or I'll destroy you!" Jack Frost boomed, the vibrations from his voice nearly knocking Flea down. But Flea managed to stay on his feet when Niko grabbed his hand and pulled him forward.

"Jump!" Niko yelled.

Flea jumped but his feet were so deep in the snow already that he didn't get as high at Niko. Knowing that he would cross into the North Pole at any moment, Flea couldn't resist taking one more look back. Jack Frost pointed his hand toward Flea and shot something; there was no doubt that his target was Flea and not Niko. Flea heard a high-pitched *squeal* becoming louder and just as he saw Niko disappear through the barrier, Flea felt a sharp jolt from behind as he crossed into the North Pole.

He crashed to his stomach on the snowy ground. Instantly, Flea felt the change in weather, as the wind no longer blew so hard and the cold wasn't so biting. He also noticed the increase of light inside the North Pole, which always appeared to be at dusk. Flea lifted his head just enough to see the large ice-blocks already melting off his friends' hands. He knew that the three others were safe.

At that moment, he felt an explosion of pain in his back and saw his friends rush toward him. Flea no longer had the strength to hold up his head so he collapsed facedown into the snow. He heard

Minko and Rome both cry out his name just before his world went black...

-     -   -   -   -   -   -   -   -   -   -

-     -   -   -

    Not surprisingly, Flea felt very groggy when he next woke up. But instead of laying in the cold snow, he felt warm and comfortable. He slowly opened his eyes and expected to see the bright red and green walls of his dorm room but immediately realized he was wrong. This room was much darker, with the only light glowing orange from the nearby fireplace. Flea knew that he was inside Santa's cabin, a thought that might've excited him had his mind not been in such a haze. His eyes begged for him to close them, but he fought off unconsciousness and soon regained his sense of hearing, too.

    At first, the voices sounded distant and he couldn't understand any of the words being spoken. He did, however, recognize at least two of the voices that seemed to be speaking the most: Niko and Vork.

    "He should've known better than to risk his life for his friends," Niko said. "And when I rescued them from the Army, he refused to follow my orders because he didn't want to take the chance of Rome and Minko being left behind. That's exactly why I've never gotten close with anyone here."

    "Only he can save her."

    Flea was surprised to hear red-robe's eerie voice.

"I *know,* you've *already* said that," Niko said.

"We must all understand that Flea is very young and impressionable, especially for a human. He seemed to have bonded at school with those two rejects," Vork added.

"No elf should be called a reject, Vork," a fourth voice said. It was strangely familiar to Flea, though maybe this was how he'd always expected Santa's voice to sound. "You even admitted that Flea and his friends made significant progress during the building season."

"But not nearly enough to be trusted inside the toy factory. They're *all* too reckless," Vork said. "That's why I must agree with Niko: the boy has to leave for the safety of the North Pole."

"Jack Frost will push his troops as far as they can go now that he knows Flea is here," Niko said. "And since the North Pole border has shrunk much faster since Flea has gotten here, it won't be long until Frost can reach us. And that's saying *nothing* about the effect Frost will have on worldwide weather."

"It *is* a dangerous situation, I must admit," Santa said sadly.

From the sound of this conversation, Flea didn't like his chances of being allowed to stay. But he was even more concerned about the future of his two best friends. Despite the pain in his back, Flea pulled himself up on the couch and battled the dizziness that threatened to plunge him back into blackness.

With the dim light from the fire, Flea looked across the small room and clearly saw Niko and Vork, while red-robe and Santa – who was by far the tallest of the bunch – remained in the shadows.

"Rome and Minko deserve the chance to become *real* builders," Flea croaked, many of the words barely escaping his lips. The four quickly quieted and turned to him. Flea knew this might be his only chance to ask Santa a question so he tried to think of the best one possible. "Why does Jack Frost want to hurt me?"

But Santa Claus didn't react. Instead, red-robe slowly floated toward the couch and gently guided Flea back to a laying position. In this dim light, the ancient elf looked much younger than Flea remembered, though he figured that his eyes were playing tricks on him. Flea grunted in pain as his shoulder burned cold. But when red-robe sprinkled dust on him, the pain went away and Flea instantly drifted back to sleep...

CHAPTER THIRTY
The Big Change

The next time Flea opened his eyes, he looked into the faces of two much friendlier elves. Minko and Rome sighed in relief and smiled when they saw their friend awake. The bright walls beyond his friends meant that he had been brought back to his room in the elf dorm. In the distance, he could hear the partying at the North Pole, though the heavy curtains were drawn over his window.

"How do you feel?" Rome asked.

"Comfortable, but I'm not sure beyond that," Flea croaked. He felt embarrassed to be lying down in front of his friends so he pulled himself to an upright position. Moving gave Flea a better indication of how he *truly* felt. "Actually, my shoulder kind of hurts but it's nowhere near as bad as before. What happened to me? Nobody told me yet."

Rome frowned, clearly hesitant to relive the awful ordeal. Minko, however, excitedly jumped in with the details.

"You got shot in the shoulder by one of Jack Frost's ice crystals," Minko explained. "We were all really worried because the crystal barely missed your heart. You were really lucky to survive, I doubt Jack Frost misses very often. It's a good thing it was so windy."

"I'm sorry I almost..." Rome started to say through quivering lips. Eventually, the tears started to flow down her face again. "...I almost got you killed."

"No, Minko and I are sorry for doubting you in the first place. I think we're *all* to blame for what happened," Flea said.

Flea meant to calm her down but this only made Rome cry harder, as she threw her arms around Flea and hugged him. She squeezed so hard that Flea's shoulder burned, but he didn't make a sound and endured the pain. Flea thought he saw a hint of jealousy on Minko's face while Rome embraced him.

"Stop crying already," Minko told her. "I didn't know you were such a *girl*."

Rome wiped the tears from her face and then slugged Minko in the arm, causing him to wince in pain.

"There's no need to keep thinking about what happened. It's over and we're all safe," Flea said. "I even got to see the inside of Santa's cabin, though it was pretty dark in there. I just wish I'd been able to see him better and ask if he's my… to ask him some questions. Did Niko admit anything to you guys about why Jack Frost was after me?"

"We were too focused on rushing you back to the village to talk much," Rome said. "And once we reached Santa's cabin, the snow guards popped up and stopped me and Minko from entering."

Flea sighed. He felt more confused now than he had on the first day he arrived at the North Pole. But the sound of singing elves in the village center took Flea's mind off his many questions. Minko – who kept glancing toward Flea's closed curtains – obviously thought of the party as well.

"Did they unveil the sleigh yet?" Flea asked.

"No, probably any minute now," Minko said longingly.

Although Flea still felt very weak, he forced himself up on two wobbly legs, much to Rome's dismay.

"They said you're supposed to rest," Rome said.

"Maybe, but I don't have much time left here and I don't want to miss seeing the big change to the sleigh," Flea said, winking at Minko. "I think we should hurry up and get outside before we miss it."

"There's *no way* I'm letting *that* happen, especially for the *big change*," Rome snickered, as she apparently wasn't as excited as the boys. "Your wound needs to stay out of the colder weather for a while."

On cue, Flea felt the cold burning sensation in his shoulder again, a pain that made him weak in the knees. Flea told them that he was more than willing to brave the cold, but even Minko agreed that going outside was a bad idea.

"I hate to say it but Rome is right... *this* time, at least," Minko said, earning himself a second punch to the arm in a matter of minutes. "Oww, you hit pretty hard for a crybaby."

Rome readied herself to punch again but Minko flinched so much that he tripped over the corner of Flea's bed and crashed to the floor. The three friends shared a good laugh but a sudden excited cheer from outside told them that something big was happening.

"We should at least watch from the window," Flea said as he hobbled across the room and threw back the curtains. Outside, the snow fell heavier and they didn't have a good angle to see much of anything except the huge glowing Christmas tree.

"We won't be able to see much from here," Minko said.

"You two can go if you want," Flea said. "I understand how big a deal this moment is and I don't want you to miss it because of me."

"Don't be silly," Minko said right away. "We can watch from the dorm but we need something to help us see better. Let's hurry up and get to my room, I think I have a few pair of binoculars laying around."

Flea struggled to keep up with his friends as they rushed out of his room. He barely reached his own doorway when he had to stop and take a deep breath. Flea doubted whether he could make it all the way to Minko's room, especially since he didn't know how far away that room was.

"Are you going to be okay?" Rome asked. She and Minko stopped at the next door over and waited for Flea to catch up.

"I'm not sure," Flea answered honestly.

"Come on, Flea, I know you can do it," Minko said.

"Don't push him too hard, he's been through a lot," Rome snapped.

The last thing Flea wanted to do was start his friends fighting – not that *that* took much – so he rushed to reach them at the next door. He figured the two could help him if they had to go much farther – or even worse, up the 'hopwell' or down the 'slidewell.'

"See, I knew you could make it," Minko said. But instead of rushing off down the hallway again, Minko turned to the nearby door and grabbed the handle. "Welcome to Casa de Minko."

Minko and Rome walked into the room littered with broken and old-fashioned toys, a room that Flea had stumbled into several times while looking for his own.

"Well, are you coming in?" Minko asked.

"You live next door to me?" he asked.

Minko stuck his head into the hallway and looked toward Flea's room, the next one over.

"Yeah, I guess I do."

"Why didn't you ever tell me?"

"I don't know, you never asked," Minko said.

Flea could do nothing more than smile and shake his head. He followed Minko into his room. Minko's closet door was wide open and blinked with hundreds of tiny lights from his wardrobe.

"I know what you two are thinking," Minko said as he rummaged through several layers of junk on the floor. "'How does he get all of these cool, new toys even though he's never worked in the factory?'"

Flea raised an eyebrow and looked at Rome, who just smiled and shook her head.

"I have connections with a few elves from the toy factory. I still get a lot of the best stuff available," Minko said. "Ah, here we go, I found them."

Minko dug out three pairs of binoculars and handed one to Rome and Flea. The three took position in front of the room's large window and looked down at the village center.

"Looks like we're just in time," Minko said.

Unfortunately for Flea, he had a difficult time focusing the binoculars. No matter which way he turned the lens, he couldn't get a perfectly clear view of the party, not to mention the fact that his binoculars were already cracked. Flea focused them as best he could and watched the slightly blurry scene below.

"Here comes Santa Claus," Minko said. Flea watched as the big man in red –the extent of the details he could make out – stepped in front of a large covered object. "That's the sleigh, here comes Wrench and Grinder, too."

Indeed, Flea saw two blurry elves make their way to the front of the crowd, the twins recognizable by their red and green hair. The crowd went crazy as the mechanics waved to them and approached the covered sleigh. Flea, Minko and Rome could hear the crowd chanting, "Big Change! Big Change!"

"I can't wait for this part," Minko whispered.

"*Big* change, ha!" Rome said.

The twins ripped away the cover and presented the sleigh to the crowd, which instantly went quiet. Although Flea couldn't see specific details, the sleigh appeared exactly the same as it had the first – and only – time he'd ever seen it. Flea was just as confused as the crowd, especially since he'd walked by the garage dozens of times and always heard the twins hard at work. He'd expected the sleigh to look totally different, which couldn't have been further from reality.

"Wow, isn't that incredible?" Minko asked.

This confused Flea even more, as he studied the sleigh again but still couldn't spot a single difference.

"What did they do?" Flea finally asked.

"*I* can't tell the difference," Rome said, which made Flea feel better. "And I don't really think Minko can, either."

"Sure I do," Minko said quickly.

"Then what is it?" Rome asked.

"Umm…well…maybe you need to look closer," Minko said.

Flea also had the feeling that his friend didn't really know. The twins proceeded to turn the sleigh around for the confused crowd. As soon as they did, the crowd erupted in cheerful laughter and applause. At the bottom part of the sleigh's cargo hold, a left arrow blinked red and a right arrow blinked green.

"I *told* you those two are geniuses," Minko said.

"Turn signals?" Rome asked, clearly annoyed. "Why would Santa possibly need turn signals on a sleigh?"

"You never know. I'm sure you probably thought the same thing about the sleigh's headlights, too," Minko shot back at her. "And look what happened the last time the sleigh needed headlights, look who they had to turn to for help."

"Are you talking about Rudolph the Red-Nosed Reindeer?" Flea asked, recalling the well-known Christmas song.

He turned and looked at his friends, both of whom wore expressions of disgust.

"Don't get me started on that song, he plays it *over and over* at the stable," Rome said.

"And he *refuses* to answer to any name but *Dolpho*," Minko added.

Flea felt another sharp pain in his shoulder, causing him to drop the binoculars. He reached back and touched the sensitive part of his shoulder, which felt icy to the touch. His friends continued to look out the window through the binoculars but when Flea attempted his again, the small crack had grown even larger, making his view worse. Santa emerged from the stables with several huge reindeer following. The reindeer were hooked into the sleigh's harness and seemed to glimmer in the light. Flea was certain that the animals must be even more impressive specimens up close. While many of the reindeer looked similar from so far away, Flea noticed that one of them was clearly absent.

"There's no Rudolph... err, I mean Dolpho," he said.

"Luckily for Santa and the other reindeer, the flying weather looks clear so Dolpho isn't needed," Minko said.

With the reindeer fastened to the sleigh, Santa stepped to the front of the crowd, which instantly hushed.

"This is where Santa introduces the helper he's chosen to accompany him on the delivery trip," Minko explained. "But I don't see Niko anywhere. Before the building season this year, he was chosen to go again."

It wasn't long before the elf crowd exploded in applause.

"Wow, I don't know who Santa introduced but I doubt Niko would get *that big* of a cheer," Rome said.

Flea watched as a path cleared amongst the crowd and a single elf made his way to the front. Flea's broken binoculars stopped him from identifying the elf but his friends had no such problem.

"Fuff!" Rome and Minko said simultaneously.

"I guess Niko *isn't* going with Santa this year. I wonder why," Minko added.

Santa Claus and Fuff climbed into the sleigh and the crowd parted down the middle. The elves all cheered when the reindeer began to move. Flea was astounded by how quickly the huge animals accelerated. It only took a few seconds for the reindeer to cross the distance between the village center and the dorm building, which they seemed headed straight for.

"Are they going to hit – "

As an entire unit, the reindeer suddenly took off the ground. It didn't look to Flea like the reindeer were flying – more like running on air, as their legs continued to churn as they lifted higher and higher. The reindeer and sleigh still looked like they were headed for the dorm but at the last second, the pair of lead reindeer banked to the left and turned them completely around. The sleigh barely cleared the top of the Christmas tree but once they soared higher into the sky, Flea saw the shimmering once again underneath the animals. Within seconds, the reindeer and Santa's sleigh disappeared into the distance and a great cheer exploded from the crowd.

"Wow," Flea said. "Now I understand why the sleigh launch is such a big deal. I just wish I could've seen it from the ground."

"Maybe next..." Minko started but then became very sad. "Oh yeah, sorry about that."

"I wonder what happens to me now," Flea said. "I hope I get to stay for at least a *little* while longer."

But a knock on the door confirmed that Flea had just jinxed himself.

\-   -   -   -   -   -   -   -   -   -   -

\-   -   -   -

The three elves turned away from the window to see Niko and Vork standing in the open doorway, a sight that filled them all with dread.

"I'm here to make this official," Vork said without so much as a hello. "Even though the three of you were close to finishing your orders – which frankly, I didn't expect to happen – I can't pass you through elf school and into the toy factory."

"And that means Flea must leave the North Pole now," Niko said. Santa's son didn't look nearly as thrilled to give this news as Flea expected.

"That's not fair," Rome said angrily. "Flea finished, we didn't. He shouldn't be punished for that."

"The decision has already been made by Santa Claus," Niko said.

"Can he at least stay a little while longer?" Minko asked. "At least let him enjoy the celebration, even just a few hours."

Niko slowly shook his head. "I can't allow that. Jack Frost is a much bigger threat to us when Flea is here. Flea can't stay because we need to halt – and hopefully push *back* – the advancing South Pole Army."

"Will you at least tell me what I have to do with that?" Flea asked.

"All I can say is that you are a *very* important elf," Niko said.

"What about my *real* family? Can't you tell me about them?"

Niko looked at Minko and Rome. It was obvious that he didn't want to say too much in front of them.

"This isn't the right moment to discuss that," Niko said.

Flea sighed. He had tried to remain patient and polite to Niko but Santa's son was starting to annoy – and anger – him.

"If I'm about to be expelled from the North Pole forever, then when *will* be the right moment?"

For a split second, Flea thought he saw the hint of a smile on Niko's face, which angered him even more. But Niko turned to Vork for this answer.

"The elf school will open again next Christmas season," the teacher said. "There will definitely be a third student joining Minko and Rome in class."

"And there is a chanc*e* – a *small* chance – that Flea will be allowed back to be the fourth," Niko added. "By only *if* the danger subsides from the South Pole. I have a feeling it will take *months* to determine that, though."

Flea turned to his friends and smiled, genuinely happy that they would get another chance to become real builder elves. But Rome and Minko didn't appear nearly as happy about their brighter futures if Flea wouldn't be there to experience it with them.

"Good luck, the two of you deserve it," Flea told them.

When he saw tears in both of his friends' eyes, Flea couldn't help but get choked up himself. Minko stepped forward and Flea knew this would be one bear-hug he couldn't avoid.

"Watch the shoulder!" Flea grunted in pain.

"Sorry," Minko said and gently placed him down. "And don't worry, I *know* you'll be back next year, even if I have to go fight back the South Pole Army all by myself."

Niko glared angrily at Minko, who said he was only joking as he winked at Flea.

"We'll see you soon, I hope," Rome said as she kissed Flea on the cheek (much to Minko's dismay).

"Okay, Flea, you come with me," Niko said. "Hurry up, I promised Santa to get you out of here as soon as possible."

As Flea walked from the room, he glanced one more time at his best friends, trying to remember every possible detail in case he was never allowed to see them again. The three of them had come a long way since he first arrived and it broke his heart to think that this could be the end of the only true friendships he'd ever made.

When Flea was alone in the hallway with Niko, he just *had* to ask about how the two of them were related.

"We have the same exact split ear, that has to mean something," Flea said. "And why would Jack Frost want me?"

Niko stopped and faced Flea.

"I see you haven't taken my advice about keeping your questions to yourself," Niko said. "But you need to listen to me carefully and trust that I know what I'm talking about. Santa thinks you are very important to the North Pole's future and shouldn't take serious risks. Going after Rome was a very *stupid* move."

"But Rome is my friend," Flea said. "I knew she was walking into danger and I *had* to try and help."

Niko sighed, though he didn't look nearly as mad as Flea expected.

"I hate to admit it, but your bravery and loyalty are two admirable qualities," Niko said. "I'm still very suspicious of you being here but I suppose I can understand why Santa hopes you are able to come back one day."

"Santa really thinks that?" Flea asked, swelling with pride.

Niko nodded and continued down the hallway, stopping in front of Flea's open door. Niko gestured Flea into the open doorway. As Flea walked into his room, he finally had the confidence to ask the one question that was most on his mind.

"Is Santa Claus my real fa – "

CHAPTER THIRTY-ONE

A Tiny Box

Flea's eyes snapped open and he felt fully awake. Still, he was confused by the darkness surrounding him, especially when he sat up in bed and didn't see the bright red and green walls. It took him a long moment to recognize his old room inside Miss Mabel's apartment. The only light came from the digital clock next to his bed, which displayed a time of 12:01.

Flea quickly sat up and looked down at himself. He no longer wore his crazy elf outfit and when he put his hands on his head, he found the big red Christmas hat gone, too. Even the ring on his finger seemed to lack the golden glow, though it still felt stuck when he tried to pull it off. He had the sinking feeling that he'd only been dreaming, a thought that made him feel sick. But when he jumped out of bed, Flea was actually relieved when he felt a sharp pain in his shoulder. He flipped on his bedroom light and rushed over to a mirror, where he lowered the back of his shirt to reveal a long silver scar that felt like ice when he touched it.

It wasn't *a dream,* he thought, breathing a deep sigh of relief. Since the time was now 12:01, Flea knew that Santa must've finished with his deliveries. He quietly sneaked into his living room – where he found most of his belongings still piled in moving boxes by the front door – and was glad that Miss Mabel wasn't around, at least for the moment. It had been so long since he'd last seen her that Flea strangely missed her yelling at him.

He fully intended to press her for more information about his past.

But that could wait until later, as Flea had more pressing matters at this moment. Having just learned from Niko that he had gained Santa's respect, Flea expected to finally receive a lot of good presents under his Christmas tree. But his heart sank with disappointment when he looked at the tilting plastic tree on his coffee table without anything beneath it. Before he became too upset, though, he spotted a tiny box just behind the tree. He tiptoed across the room for a closer look and found a small card attached to the box.

Flea was so excited to read the card that he rushed over to the window and opened the heavy curtains, allowing the moonlight to filter into the otherwise dark apartment. Flea ripped open the envelope and read:

"To: *Flea,*

Thanks for all of your hard work this year.

Don't lose this gift.

From: *Santa*"

Flea's heart pounded with excitement as he started to lift the lid off the tiny box. Suddenly, a light flipped on in the living room. Flea shoved the box and card into his pocket and turned to face Miss Mabel.

"Flea, what are you doing out of bed this late?" she yelled. "I got nervous when I heard all this shuffling out here."

"I'm sorry, Miss Mabel, I didn't mean to scare you," Flea said. "I'll go back to bed now."

"I *know* you will," Miss Mabel said.

Much to Miss Mabel's surprise, Flea stopped and gave her a big hug on his way back to his room. Even more surprising to Flea was the fact that she hugged him back, tightly.

"Now go to bed," she ordered once they let go of each other.

Flea rushed to his room, excited to discover the Christmas present that Santa had wrapped for him in this box…

MY PLEA TO READERS – As an independent author, it is difficult to convince readers to try my books; for that, I thank you. But to help spread the word, please leave me feedback on the web-site where you purchased this book. I've found that reviews are the most important determination in whether many readers will try a new author.

U.S. version http://www.amazon.com/dp/B0050211UQ

U.K. version https://www.amazon.co.uk/dp/B0050211UQ

Thanks for your support!

- Kevin

TO LEAVE COMMENTS FOR THE AUTHOR OR FIND OUT ABOUT FLEA'S FIVE CHRISTMASES, BECOME A FAN OF "KEVIN GEORGE – AUTHOR" FAN PAGE ON FACEBOOK!

OTHER WORKS BY AUTHOR
FLEA'S FIVE CHRISTMASES
THE NORTH POLE CHALLENGE – BOOK ONE
THE RUDOLPH CHALLENGE – BOOK TWO
THE JACK FROST CHALLENGE – BOOK THREE
THE FROSTIE CHALLENGE – BOOK FOUR
THE SOUTH POLE CHALLENGE – BOOK FIVE

EDDIE AND JEREMY ADVENTURES
BOOK ONE – EDDIE AND JEREMY GO TO THE AQUARIUM

BOOK TWO – EDDIE AND JEREMY GO TO THE NORTH POLE

THE GREAT BLUE ABOVE SERIES
BOOK ONE – THE CITY BELOW
BOOK TWO – THE DOME OF LIFE
More books coming soon...

KEEPER OF THE WATER SERIES
DRINKING LIFE – BOOK ONE
RECRUITS – BOOK TWO
THE WATER QUEENS – BOOK THREE

CRYO-MAN SERIES
CRYO-MAN – BOOK ONE
ROBOTROPOLIS – BOOK TWO
DEARBORN – BOOK THREE
BEYOND RIVER CITY – BOOK FOUR

LIFE, INC. – a novel

COMET CLEMENT SERIES
THE INNER CIRCLE – BOOK ONE
INTERCEPTION – BOOK TWO
THE NEW SPACE RACE – BOOK THREE
THE THREE ARKS – BOOK FOUR

EVACUATION EARTH – BOOK FIVE

FINAL DAYS – BOOK SIX

IMPACT – BOOK SEVEN

UNINVITED – BOOK EIGHT

TAKEOVER – BOOK NINE

MISSION: SURVIVAL – BOOK TEN

RELOCATION – BOOK ELEVEN

A SECOND CHANCE – BOOK TWELVE

Made in the USA
Middletown, DE
23 November 2018